THAT WAS BEFORE

A NOVEL BY **DAN LAWTON**

Black Rose Writing | Texas

This is a work of fiction. Names, characters, businesses, places, events, and incidents are either the products of the author's imagination or used in a fictitious manner. Any resemblance to actual persons, living or dead, or actual events is purely coincidental.

ISBN: 978-1-68433-692-0
PUBLISHED BY BLACK ROSE WRITING
www.blackrosewriting.com

Printed in the United States of America
Suggested Retail Price (SRP) $19.95

That Was Before is printed in Palatino Linotype

*As a planet-friendly publisher, Black Rose Writing does its best to eliminate unnecessary waste to reduce paper usage and energy costs, while never compromising the reading experience. As a result, the final word count vs. page count may not meet common expectations.

DEDICATION

Thank you to my usual beta readers—this is for you. And to the new one, Avree Clark—thanks for your attention to detail.

THAT WAS BEFORE

CHAPTER ONE

No more than thirty seconds after he slid into his truck and celebrated his remarkable yet unfathomable achievement, the supermarket brilliantly exploded behind him.

It was the same supermarket he was inside just minutes before. The same supermarket where he had just gotten the jubilant cashier's phone number.

Sheila.

That was before.

Before, he found his reflection in the window and straightened the strands of hair the wind swept out of place, pushed them to the right and smoothed the part; he inspected his teeth for remnants of breakfast, found none; he adjusted his collar, pressed it flat. He felt good. Confident. Surprisingly edgy in a way he had not since he was a teenager. The sliding glass doors welcomed him like outstretched arms as he walked through and into the wonderfully chilled, always reliable refrigerated air.

There was a woman who worked at the supermarket he had a particular regard for. Shelby or Sheila, her name he failed to remember at the time. He had been to the supermarket thrice this week, if only to catch a glimpse of her. There were now more than a dozen green bananas at the house because of it—and he did not much care for bananas. A stockwoman smiled at him as he weaved through the basket displays of brightly colored berries and lush greens, past the stacked towers of red and green and yellow apples, but his attention was elsewhere. Another woman with a young child in the carriage buried her face into a notepad and blocked his view from the registers, so he moved to a new angle. The spice of the bell peppers tickled his throat as he stood and watched, waiting for his opportunity.

Then he spotted her. A crimson apron covered her from chest to knees with the strings in the back knotted in what used to be a bow. She smiled at the customers in her line, laughed with them, spoke sweetly to them. Her optimism for life, he could tell, infected him like a sickness. But it was more a drug than a sickness because he craved it as much as an addict would their venom of choice.

He scooped up a hand of bananas from a nearby display and tucked them under his arm.

The beep from the register scanner grew louder as he approached, as if a pacemaker he did not have struggled to keep up with what he asked it to do. He felt jitters he had not in many years. Decades. The line at the register—her register—thinned out, so he stepped closer and dropped the bananas on the conveyor belt. His throat burned with dryness. The woman looked up at him.

"Hello," she said.

He smiled, felt his cheeks redden.

She dropped her hand on the bunch and pulled it toward her, then turned and hit some keys on her computer.

Randolph's tongue stuck to the roof of his mouth as if it were permanently cemented there, and he thought he might suffocate. Fear rushed over him, left droplets of nervous sweat on his collar. His eyes shifted down and found a magnetic badge that hung near the woman's clavicle, which offered temporary relief. A distraction.

Sheila.

"You must love bananas," Sheila said. Indents formed in her cheeks as her lips parted.

He struggled for air. The strain of the tension of the muscles in his tongue was too much. It cramped and he winced, but he managed to stave off the pain and say, "Pardon me?"

"The bananas. You've been in everyday this week."

Randolph winced again as the tension threatened to morph into a spasm. Part of him wanted to run away, to escape what was about to happen—his body had clearly rejected his efforts—but he knew he would regret it if he did. "You remember?"

"Course I do! I wouldn't ever forget a handsome fella like yourself." She smiled at him again.

Magically, the stress in his mouth dissipated and he felt instant relief as if a switch had been flipped. A sharp inhale cleansed him, offered rejuvenation. He felt better, acutely aware of the moment and the beautiful woman who stood in front of him. Within him, there was a sense of justification that told him he was doing the right thing.

"If I didn't know any better, I'd half be wondering if you keep coming in here to see me."

There was no one else in line behind him. He stepped closer to the register, careful not to crowd, straightened his shoulders and puffed out his chest to improve his posture. His stomach rolled. "I'd like to take you out some time."

The smile fell from Sheila's face as if it were thieved. "That's very sweet of you," she said, "but I can't."

Randolph's chest flurried. That was not the answer he expected, or hoped for. "Can't, or won't?"

Sheila fell back on her heels and sunk a quarter of an inch. Randolph towered over her. "Well," she said, then she faked a cough into her fist. "What I meant is right now. I can't right now. I'm working."

"I see that." Randolph smiled at her, and she smiled back. He watched her muscles relax as her torso dipped. "When are you free?"

"I could do lunch tomorrow."

A weight lifted. "That sounds perfect."—Randolph pressed his hands against his chest, then his hips, then his rear—"If I can get your number, I could—"

"Let me." Sheila pressed a button on the cash register and ashen register tape poked out from the top of the dispenser. She tore off a piece and pushed it in front of him.

Randolph patted himself some more.

"Use mine." She pulled a pen from her breast pocket and handed it over.

Randolph took it and thanked her.

She gave him her number.

"No, keep it," she said when he tried to hand the pen back.

He put it down next to the credit card terminal and retrieved his wallet. "How much do I owe you?"

Sheila looked at her computer then told him the amount. He handed her two singles. The machine dinged when she pushed the drawer closed. He left the change in the donation cup.

"So, do I get to know your name?" she said.

He laughed because he did not know what else to do. How could he have forgotten that part? "I'm sorry, of course. It's Randolph."

"Sheila." She outstretched her arm.

He took her hand and shook it. Her skin was clammy against his, the grip solid. Moxie burst through him as his fingertips grazed hers, and he felt the testosterone pump through his veins like fire. He offered his best not too eager yet not too modest smile. "It's been a real pleasure, Sheila. I'll reach out, set something up for tomorrow."

"Tomorrow it is then."

"Tomorrow."

Outside, he pulled the truck door closed and tossed the bananas on the seat next to him. He found his reflection in the rearview and approved of the smile he still maintained, then laughed, then smacked his hands together so loud his ears rang.

And they rang even louder during and after the explosion that followed.

Now was after.

CHAPTER TWO

The truck's floor rocked as if there were an earthquake under his feet. His hands went to the steering wheel and gripped it so hard his fingers hurt. A kaleidoscope of colors reflected against the rearview in front of him. He was unable to make sense of what was happening.

He spun to watch.

On the other side of the glass, patrons screamed. A woman hurried with her two children in tow under her arms, the plastic bags she carried left strewn across the pavement as if discarded garbage; a man with a cane lumbered with a pace he surely had not in years; a trio of young men sprinted as if competing in Olympic trials against each other. Gray smoke billowed from the shattered supermarket window—the same window Randolph had inspected his reflection in just minutes before. Emergency sirens rang out in the distance.

He trembled as he opened the door and slid out of the truck and slammed his heels hard against the earth.

He knew he was defenseless to the universe's catastrophes, but he still wondered what he could do to help. While people ran away from the smoke, toward where he was, to safety, he considered the opposite. Stuck inside were innocent civilians with shopping carts full of food for their families, and children and vacationers and helpless elderly. He remembered the fire extinguisher mounted on the wall near the entrance. But what would he do with it? From where he stood, there were no flames, only smoke. He was flustered, frozen with confusion.

More people rushed out of the supermarket. Alarms rang out all around him—piercingly loud alarms, so loud they rattled his skull. Voices screamed; children wailed. A dog barked. His ears buzzed as if he were stuck in a twilight zone, unable to escape life's treachery. Police and fire and rescue sirens got louder, closer. He stood motionless, trapped in the labyrinth of his mind, unsure whether he had control over his fight-or-flight sensors.

"Run!" a man yelled as he passed by, the expression on his face that of sheer panic.

Randolph was stuck, conflicted about what he should do and what he wanted to do, yet without a plan. His feet were glued to the pavement, his muscles stiff. Time froze.

Then it hit him, and the decision was no longer one.

Sheila!

It was ridiculous considering they had just officially met, but he felt like he knew her. Perhaps it was the lust talking—the flicker of hope he felt when she smiled at him, the way he felt fifty pounds lighter when he strolled out of the store with a swagger he thought he lost and the sense of invincibility men half his age felt—but he had to do something. She was still inside. Trapped.

He cracked the glue that caked his feet and stepped toward the smoke and the crowd of onlookers who formed nearby. Just then, the first fire engine roared into the parking lot—its sirens deafening, tires screeching, the Cedar Rapids script prominent on the underside of the ladder. Another engine quickly followed.

Chaos ensued. Mobile phones rang; lights strobed; men and women in uniforms barked orders at the bystanders to back away. Soon, a line of wooden A-frames barricaded the onlookers far from the supermarket while the professionals carried out their civic duties. Police vehicles and ambulances joined and strengthened the barricade. Brown and neon suits leaped from the trucks, unraveled the hoses faster than Randolph had ever seen, and just as quickly disappeared behind a cloud of smoke. It all happened so fast, in what felt like an instant.

By now, the back of Randolph's neck was soaked, his collar drenched. The surrounding shops in the plaza emptied, which formed additional groups of curious and anxious bystanders. Worry blanketed the faces of many of the lanyard-wearing tenants and those who had chosen to wait until now to run their errands. A pale man near Randolph spoke animatedly to someone on the telephone and mentioned something about a terrorist attack. Others reacted to it in a frenzy. One lady shrieked and nearly collapsed, but was caught by a fellow onlooker who looked young enough to be her son.

All the while, amid the chaos and the impossible to know information others thought they knew and insisted on sharing with others who would inaccurately disseminate it further, Randolph kept his focus on the entrance of the supermarket.

Sheila never came out.

A couple of hours passed. The smoke was mostly gone, having floated to the heavens in the blue above the supermarket, though remnants of the odor lingered. Randolph overheard a quartet of rescue workers chat about what they saw—a pair of firefighters and a pair of policemen. They said there was a contained fire at one of the registers that was suffocated before it spread, and though no patrons were injured, a small group of employees could have inhaled too much smoke and were being transported to the hospital to be monitored.

"What the hell happened?" one of the police officers said—a young guy with jet black hair who wore a gold band around his finger. He fingered the butt of the pistol on his hip.

"We found remnants of what might be a mini pipe bomb, though it'll need to be analyzed further before we know for sure," a fireman said. His helmet dangled in his hand near his knee. Black soot drew lines across his face.

"We're not talking about—"

"Not here," the other police officer said, an older one. The veteran of the group. The four men walked out of earshot.

Sheila.

It sounded like she was okay, which was a relief. Randolph must have missed her when she came out, though he did not know how that was possible—he had not taken his eyes off the entrance.

He retreated to his truck. His heart raced to where he felt exhausted and weak, even once he sat. The steering wheel was hot to the touch, as if the fire had been inside the cabin of the truck instead of the supermarket, but he kept his grip; he needed something to do with his hands. Brown and black dots painted the skin of the bananas in the seat next to him. He leaned back and dug his shoulder blades into the cloth against his back and tried to relax, though it felt too soon. He was rattled. Tension knots twisted inside him. He felt nauseous.

Sheila.

Though he did not know how or when, he was determined to see her again. He would find a way. Some things were too important to let pass by the wayside without a fight. For matters of the heart, this especially rang true. He had loved and unloved and loved again, so he knew what he wanted. The addiction of that feeling, the euphoria of it, had been absent from his life for too long. And now, the potential of it felt so close he could wrap his arms around it and cradle it and never let it go—the loss of it hurt just as much as not having it to begin with. It could not, would not, end this way.

With that thought, he cranked the engine and shifted the truck into gear, then used his mirrors to reverse his way out of the grid of painted white lines. And with Sheila on his mind—how he would finagle a way to see her again, whatever it took—he drove the long way around the parking lot, away from the lights and the crowd of uniforms that remained, and headed home.

CHAPTER THREE

Patricia was home when he arrived.

Patricia was his wife.

Their relationship was complicated. Though in some ways, it was not. Patricia no longer wanted to be married to him, and he knew that. For him, while the only feelings that remained were resentment and something that mirrored animosity but was not quite as vindictive, he was not ready for it yet—the split. It was not as easy as drawing a line down the middle and taking his half to start a new life. There was a history involved. Baggage. Other people to consider.

Luckily for him—though not luck, rather responsible planning— he held the cards. And Patricia knew it too. She was not going anywhere unless he wanted her to.

Her voice echoed through the foyer of their grand entryway as Randolph sliced through it. The excitement in her tone, the unreasonably high volume of her laughter, was how she acted these days. It felt like a performance, one that could easily fool those who did not know her as well as Randolph did. Though he had not kept track, it had gone on like this for multiple months. She had never been happier.

Did it hurt?

It did, at first. But then it got easier, then an afterthought. It had become Randolph's life—living with the woman he once loved so deeply he would have done anything for her, to simply being strangers in their own house. Even still, he did not wish ill will upon her. Not happiness though, either. Somewhere in between those two extremes.

Her back was to him when he entered the kitchen. She switched the phone from hand to hand, moved it from ear to ear. A glass bowl filled with chunks of bright red licorice—one of her favorite snacks since forever—sat on the edge of the countertop. The countertop was a high-end quartz, and it was the most unnecessary expenditure Randolph had ever made. He agreed because she wanted it, and at the time, he wanted nothing more than to aid in her happiness any way he could. So quartz it was. If only he had a crystal ball.

He dropped the bananas on the counter next to the others and said, "Patricia."

She shrieked as if she were being attacked by a piranha that lurked under the counter. The phone she held slipped from her grip and smashed against the tile under her feet. As she spun, her belt latched onto the bowl and tossed it across the kitchen. Glass scattered everywhere in thousands of tiny glittering shards, and all Randolph could think was how long it would take him to clean it. He would, undoubtedly, find glass for weeks, even in the smallest, most seemingly impossible to penetrate crevices of the floor.

He stepped back and surveyed the damage. That was when he saw the butcher knife in Patricia's hand. Though he did not know why, he froze at the sight.

What had been a startle quickly morphed to something else. Patricia's face turned white and her shoulders shrunk. It was as if she had seen a burglar or a ghost, and the knife slipped out of her hand.

"Jesus Christ, Patricia," Randolph said. He was not afraid of her—she had never, nor would ever, inflict physical harm; she had caused enough emotional destruction to surpass any amount of damage she could impose physically. But the knife still alarmed him. "What are you doing?"

On the floor, a muffled voice hollered something inaudible.

"What am I doing?" she said. "What are you doing?"

"There was an incident at the supermarket earlier."

"I mean, what are you doing here?"

Before Randolph could answer, she squatted and disappeared behind the quartz. She told whoever it was on the other end of the phone that she had to go. Just some glass, she said. Then she said again she had to go.

Randolph stood where he was and waited.

After Patricia reappeared and brushed herself off as if nothing happened, she grabbed the butcher's handle and pulled it toward her, then slid it into the knife block. She did not look as happy as she had sounded on the phone just moments before.

"What are you doing home?" she said.

"Like I said, there was an incident at the supermarket."

"Why were you at the supermarket?"

"What kind of question is that?"

"It's the middle of the day on a Tuesday. Why aren't you at work?"

"I quit," he said, which he did. An hour before he went to the supermarket for the third time this week, he called his boss at the firm and resigned, effective immediately. He no longer had the desire to work, nor did he need the money, so he would no longer pretend he did.

Patricia did not react at first. She eventually folded her arms and disapprovingly eyed him as if he were a failure of a man. Though he saw right through her and her act—he knew this was her worst nightmare. And worse, for her, she did not have a countermove. It was their version of chess. Marriage roulette. A power move. Though for Randolph, it was not about that; he had truly had enough of the daily grind of a career he no longer loved. He was sure Patricia would see it differently, regardless of what he told her.

Her phone rang. She looked at it quickly, then pressed the screen to silence the ringer. She glared at Randolph. Her nose wriggled. "What's that smell?" she said. "Is that smoke?"

"There was a fire at the supermarket."

She nodded. "Tell me again why you were at the supermarket in the middle of the day."

He did not.

"Why were you just holding a knife?" he said.

"I just finished cleaning up. Is that okay?"

The phone on the countertop rang again. Patricia looked down at the screen, sighed, and picked it up. "Now's a bad time," she said into it. Then: "Just glass...Everything's fine...I know. I heard." Then she hung up.

The perfume she wore struck Randolph's nose when she walked past and left the room without another word. He did not recognize it, though why would he? Her walking past him was as close as they had been in months. Seconds later, the front door opened then closed, and she was gone. Again.

He sighed.

Patricia's phone reminded him of his own, which he powered down after he resigned to avoid the barrage that would follow. He pulled the phone from his pocket and held his finger against the power button, waited. When it came to life, the photo of their son and grandson in the background forced a smile. Bruce was Randolph and Patricia's only child, and Bruce now had a son of his own—Maxwell, though everyone called him Max. They lived in Utah. Randolph would occasionally receive updated photos in his email, and they would chat on the phone a few times a year—holidays and birthdays or if someone in the family was getting married or was pregnant or died. They were not as close as Randolph would have liked, but that was life; the distance made it difficult to maintain the bond.

Nine missed calls popped up on the screen, along with six voicemails. The firm would miss him dearly, more than they would know. His designs were incomplete, and though he kept detailed notes and diagrams, many of the other engineers on staff were juniors. Randolph had designed engines for heavy machinery for a quarter of a century, primarily for airplanes most recently. While he lost the passion for it long ago, it was what he was trained to do and it was what he was good at, so he was without regret. While it led to a predictable and secure lifestyle, it had been a solid and respectable career. It paid for the massive house he did not care much about, and the truck he did. The disposable income was plentiful, which kept Patricia happy for many years. But he was finished with the monotony of it, was ready for a new adventure. The profession had changed with the times, and he felt left behind in a world that used to exist—all his work was digitized and templated now. The freedom to design and explore new ideas was a thing of the past. It was time to move on.

Of the missed calls with corresponding voicemails, six were from the firm. To be expected. The others, though, were unexpected. They were spaced out ten minutes apart, the first of which registered shortly after the explosion.

All three, strangely, were from Patricia.

The missed calls themselves were not unusual. She did occasionally call when she needed something—reluctantly, they were still wed and shared certain responsibilities. And with an excuse to not return home immediately after work, Randolph usually obliged. Not to do something nice for her, though, but rather for himself—to limit the time he spent in the same house with her. The timing of the calls Randolph credited to coincidence. Though why she did not mention them just now was a mystery. But she was shrouded in mystery these days—the secretive phone calls at all hours of the day, the late nights, the weekends she spent out of town—so that was not out of character for her either. Randolph was not blind to her behavior; he just did not care to fight for it anymore, for her. His energy was depleted beyond repair. Plus, he was recently distracted by something else. Someone.

Sheila.

And he had to follow his heart and see where that led. After all, what did he have to lose?

CHAPTER FOUR

"I'm coming over," she said, "and you better not be wearing pants." Then she hung up.

She was Cheyenne, and she said things like that a lot. And she meant them. She was fierce.

Benji was a barista who lacked motivation for anything more and lived on the west side of town in a shoddy studio apartment. He used drugs recreationally and was not an addict. He had not considered himself to be a sexual deviant until he met Cheyenne, who turned his world—and his perspective—upside down. That was two months ago. She had introduced him to some taboo tricks since then, some things he would not have ever thought he would enjoy but did. Some of them he had never heard of. His highlight reel far exceeded any expectations he had for himself.

To him, Cheyenne was a sexual goddess.

She was at least twice his age and still had the energy of a firecracker. And with a tighter body than he expected from someone her age, she was a good lay. Phenomenal, even. The best. She left him raw on more than one occasion, yet she rarely seemed satisfied. It was a mid-twenties man's dream.

Benji was home—a day off from the coffee shop—and Cheyenne would not be long. He stripped to his boxers and got ready for her. He lit a joint and took a hit to free his mind, then went to the sink and brushed his teeth afterward. He turned off the TV; he combed his hair; he left a couple of rubbers on the sofa side table.

No more than fifteen minutes passed before the intercom shouted and Benji buzzed her in. Two minutes after that, she straddled him on the sofa and tore off her blouse. A button burst and skidded across the floor, disappeared somewhere to be found and questioned by a future tenant. She bit down on Benji's lower lip so hard it seemed she wanted to tear it off. But he loved it. She grabbed his head and pressed his face to her chest and forced him in between her. Her groans and moans and filthy mouth made him hard. It was as if she had been starved, though it had only been two days since the last time—in the back alley of the coffee shop while Benji was on his lunch break. But Cheyenne was a machine, and she was down for anything at any time. It was Benji who sometimes needed to be coaxed.

The thing was, Benji felt no emotional connection with Cheyenne—the age gap between them meant they had very little in common. She was old enough to be his mother, he her son, and while their bodies fit together perfectly, there would never be anything more between them.

But Cheyenne did not know that was how he felt.

The first time he slept with her was thirty minutes after they met. And half of that was spent in the car. That told him a lot about the type of person she was. She walked into the coffee shop with a tightly cropped blouse with one too many buttons undone, high waisted jeans, and brown boots with short heels. Her hair was straightened and swept to the side, and she wore too much makeup for an innocent trip to satisfy her caffeine craving. But she smelled like a queen, and she was on the prowl.

Benji was her prey.

She leaned over the counter and sweet-talked Benji while he made her a chilled macchiato with extra drizzle—not an accident, he was sure. And after a tip larger than his daily wages and a napkin with her name and number on it, Benji knew. He took an early lunch and drove them to his studio. He held her hand as they ascended the metal staircase in a hurry, and they got it on when they made it to the top—

he stripped her, she him. First against the outside the door, then inside. Then the bed, the sofa, the floor. Everywhere.

For Benji, that was the game. He met women, sometimes slept with them, and they went home. Nothing further. It was a common practice among those in his generation. It was just sex, only physical. Nothing intimate. There was a woman who had his heart and his emotional devotion, and she was not Cheyenne. Shay was her name. Though he was not stupid—he kept the information about his sexual polygamy to himself out of fear Shay would not agree with the mentality; it was not something they had discussed, certainly, in case they had differing opinions.

Cheyenne slid off him and rested against the arm of the sofa. Heavy breaths slipped through her lips and she held a lengthy groan as if she were having another orgasm. Benji's glutes convulsed as his body tried to recover from the madness that rocked his world. The indisputable smell of used latex overpowered the tiny apartment.

Still undressed, Cheyenne stood up and cracked a window, then grabbed the rolled joint from the end table and lit it. Benji cleaned himself up and pulled on a pair of jeans.

"Can you not, please?" he said as he zipped the front of his denim.

"Can I not what?" She blew a mouthful of smoke into the open air above the sexed-up sofa.

"Out the window, come on."

She took another hit and blew the smoke out the open window this time.

"Listen, I have stuff to do this afternoon," Benji said.

"Are you kicking me out?" One hand held the joint while the other fingered one of her hard nipples.

"I've got something going on."

"I see what's going on here."—she stood and walked toward him—"You just want a fuck buddy, is that it?" Her hand launched at his crotch and found his manhood, and she squeezed.

Benji recoiled as the pain shot through him and stole his breath. He leaned forward and tried to squirm away, but the agony intensified as Cheyenne squeezed tighter.

"Fine," she said, then she let go. "I'll go. But don't expect me to come running when you're feeling frisky."

Despite the sharpness of the pain that wreaked havoc on the inner workings of his midsection, Benji reached forward and plucked the joint from her lips.

"Though I might." Cheyenne smiled promiscuously over her shoulder as she bent down to fetch her clothes. Her back was to him.

Benji had a clear view of everything. Worth repeating: Everything, as in more than he cared to see. If he could count the rings of a tree and learn the age of said tree . . .

He looked away after he saw the twinkle in her eye that told him she was ready for round two if he was. She was never satisfied, and he only had so much to give—his batteries required a recharge. After she piled her clothes in her arms and walked past him and went into the bathroom and closed the door, Benji stumbled toward the sofa and plopped himself down. He stubbed out the joint and tried to nurse his manhood, which pulsated with pain that still stretched deep inside his gut. A wet spot on the cushion next to him served as a reminder to keep a towel nearby for next time—that part was something they failed to show in pornography, the aftermath.

His phone was nearby, which he grabbed. He had not heard from Shay since the morning, and he was concerned about her. Shay was the one person he had ever let himself go with, and he cared for her. A lot. Their relationship was still new, but he saw potential with her. A future. There was something special about her that he could not put his finger on—he just knew. He sent her a text.

"How are the marbles?"

Benji looked up and found Cheyenne there in front of him, fully clothed.

"Why do you have to do shit like that?"

"What, you can't handle it? I thought you liked it rough?"

"That's not rough. That's cruel."

Cheyenne took a step toward him with wide eyes. She bent her knees and leaned forward. "Want me to kiss them?"

Benji covered himself. "You've done enough for one day, I think."

Cheyenne stopped, stood up straight, and shrugged. "Suit yourself." Then she turned and clacked toward the door in her heels. Before she left, she looked over her shoulder and said, "Goodbye, lover."

The door closed.

Benji exhaled, let himself relax. The pain in his groin lingered. Worsened, even. The pressure was remarkable. Deep. The smoke from the stubbed out joint wafted and remained prominent around him, which he was annoyed by—that was what the window was for. He leaned toward the window and tried to open it further, but it was out of his reach.

Below, on the sidewalk outside, an argument ensued. A woman was in tears and inconsolable, while a man berated her with a verbal rampage. Benji figured it was the downstairs neighbors, who often screamed at one another until early in the morning, only to reconcile shortly after with a loud, usually brief sexual encounter—made clear by the street-facing bedroom window that remained open. The pattern repeated itself regularly, so much so where nobody in the building called the police anymore. The old bag down the hall did once, but after the police came and went without an arrest, all it did was cause tensions to rise in the building. Her cat went missing the next day and never returned, and no one had bothered the downstairs neighbors since, as far as Benji knew. Some things in life were better left unsaid, or ignored—it was often an easier existence that way.

Next to him, his phone sat idly, awkwardly close to the damp ring on the cushion. He picked it up and tapped the screen and waited for the new message alert to pop up.

But it never came. Shay did not respond. And Benji was now officially worried.

CHAPTER FIVE

The next day, the morning news led with the explosion at the supermarket—there was no threat to the public, the anchor said, nothing to worry about. An isolated incident. Otherwise, there were few details made public. It was an ongoing investigation.

Randolph called around. There were multiple hospitals in Cedar Rapids. The receptionists he spoke to at each failed to offer insight to specific patient names, and without Sheila's last name anyhow, Randolph could do nothing to convince them otherwise. What he did find out, though, was where she was: Mercy Medical Center. All the victims were brought there yesterday. So that was where he would go.

He was without a firm plan, though he had some ideas about how to approach it. He could call the supermarket and ask for her by name, see if he could find out information that way. But they would be closed because of yesterday's events, so it was not an option. He could go to the hospital and impersonate a news reporter, though without media credentials, he would not get far. He could profess to be a concerned long-lost relative or friend who heard about what happened on the news, but without Sheila's last name, how close to her could he really be? No one would buy it. He had a better, more practical idea.

He went outside. The chill in the air licked his skin and soothed his worry, and he felt confident. The sun was bright with clouds nowhere in sight. The trees squawked above him. It was a glorious day for a fresh start.

Patricia's car was gone from the driveway, as it had been all night—a common occurrence these days; she slept elsewhere a few nights each week, sometimes more. While Randolph enjoyed the space and time to himself, and the quiet, her behavior still irked him. He struggled to understand who she had become and why, and where things went wrong between them. All that remained were memories of what used to be a happy life.

The truck came to life in an instant when he cranked the ignition. Its engine roared through his wrists and into his fingertips and up to his chest. There was nothing quite like the power behind a Hemi V8 that made Randolph feel alive. It dominated the road, demanded respect, hemorrhaged masculinity. While Patricia routinely poked holes in his virility through the years, she could not compete with a man and his truck. For Randolph, it was less about the truck and more about what was under the hood. Which made sense when he considered his life's work. It was what could not be seen that oftentimes did the heavy lifting, that kept everything in check, that was depended on—that was the mindset that drove him through a sometimes stagnant and repetitive line of work. Or at least it used to.

That was before.

Now was after.

Before he went to Mercy Medical Center, he had two stops to make. First, he stood in line at the florist longer than he typically would, paid with a fifty-dollar bill, and left with an assortment of mismatched flowers—all different colors to give him as many chances of success as possible. After, a bakery was next door. Onions hit his nose and played tricks on his mind when he walked in. A familiar taste lingered on his tongue and drove an intense craving—one that reminded him of a better time when he and Patricia enjoyed French onion soup on the coast of Lake Winnipeg. They were young and carefree and crazy about one another then—before raising Bruce and the daily challenges that came with it, before they entered the twilight of their relationship and whatever treachery followed.

That was before

Now was after.

Those were just memories. Now he wanted the soup—and it was just soup, regardless of who he shared it with. But that would have to wait. Despite his original intentions, he left with a brown paper bag with two onion bagels and house-made cream cheese inside. The aromatic onions tormented him on the drive to the hospital, moistened his palate. The soup remained sharply on his mind.

With his hands full, Randolph walked into the lobby of the hospital and took in his surroundings. Colorful flowerpots and cushioned armchairs and wooden side tables with stacks of magazines on top lined the walls, while moderately sized televisions hung mounted near the ceiling so the programming was viewable from nearly every angle. A massive sign with a giant arrow pointed him in the direction of the reception area, which he approached. Glass separated him from the three women on the other side, who all wore purple nursing scrubs. The woman closest to him smiled.

"May I help you?" she said.

"I hope so."

His plan?

Honesty.

"Here's the thing," Randolph said, getting to it, "for the first time in a long time, I'm supposed to have a date today. I met a woman in the supermarket, got her number, and left. And then, well, it's going to sound ridiculous—"

"The explosion," the woman said.

A weight fell from Randolph's chest. He had been more anxious about this than he realized. "Right."

"Sir, I—"

"I'm going to be straightforward with you. I don't know her last name. First dates, you know? But her first name is Sheila. It's my understanding all the victims from the explosion were brought here."

"Sir, I really can't."

"I'm not asking you to do anything that will get you in trouble."

The woman leaned back in her chair and folded her arms, studied him. She squinted and pressed her lips together, though did not speak. Randolph sensed the wheels turning in her mind and knew he had a chance, though he had to tread lightly so to not be overeager and overstep.

"What I'm asking is that you call her room. Tell her I'm here. My name is Randolph. If she wants to see me, great. If she doesn't, I'll leave."

The woman craned her neck and nodded in the direction of the bouquet Randolph held. "Those for her?"

Randolph held up the bag from the bakery. "This too. Chivalry isn't dead, am I right?" He smirked, forced out a laugh.

The woman did not reciprocate. "If she says no, you'll leave?"

"I'll leave, no questions asked."

She unfolded her arms and leaned forward and rested her elbows on the desk in front of her. She flicked her eyebrows toward the waiting area. "Wait there. I'll call her."

"Thank you," he said. "Very much."

Randolph went and waited. He sat in the middle of the row and balanced the bouquet on his knee, unsure where to look or what to do. Desperate for a distraction, he clutched onto the paper bag as if it were the final meal he would ever eat. An older woman sat in the waiting area too, and she looked at him. Her eyes switched between the bouquet and Randolph's face, and by the third time through, she smiled. Randolph smiled back but looked away to avoid a conversation. The onions made his stomach growl.

Minutes passed. Before long, the woman behind the glass dropped the phone on the receiver and spun in her chair to chat with the other ladies in her cube. One of them laughed. Randolph felt their eyes on him, felt them size him up. He felt judged. It was then he realized he still wore his wedding band, and he felt immediately uncomfortable. Embarrassed. Worse than that, he was humiliated to where he considered leaving the hospital, getting in his truck, and driving home and never thinking about Sheila again. Maybe he was out of his league. Maybe he did not belong here. He spun the ring, wiggled it around his knuckle, and yanked it off, then slid it into his pocket.

Just then, the same woman called out his name from behind the glass. He stood too fast. The bouquet slipped from his lap and landed hard on the tile, but the plastic that surrounded the flowers took all the impact. Randolph leaned forward and grabbed the bouquet, refused to make eye contact with the older woman who now stared, and made his way toward the reception desk. He almost did not look up but had no choice not to.

The woman behind the glass smiled at him. All three of them did. One of them had the tip of her thumb in her mouth and groaned as she looked on.

"Room B6," the woman said. "Second floor."

He took the stairs, in part to walk out the nerves. He felt like a boy full of jitters and was unsure what he would say when he saw her.

Sheila.

To feel an intense emotional longing for a woman he hardly knew—if he was honest with himself, he would acknowledge it was even less than that; he did not know her at all—was something out of character for him. Admittedly, he had been predictable throughout his adult life, and while some may have viewed it as a flaw in his personality—Patricia, for one—he rather enjoyed that about himself. It meant stability and longevity and consistency. Contrary, he had begun to enjoy the new feelings too—the spontaneity and impulsiveness and excitement—and he wondered if Patricia had been onto something. Perhaps if he had done something differently...

Nonsense.

B6 was halfway down the corridor which was empty. Ghostly. The door to B6 was closed. Randolph stood outside and listened, pressed his ear against the door. His pulse drummed in his temples and his breathing sped up. Nervous was an understatement. With a knuckle, he tapped twice on the door, softly and cautiously so not to spook anyone—himself included. The plastic sleeve around the bouquet shook as he trembled.

Nothing.

He tried again, harder this time. Then two more knocks. By the third set without response, he lost hope and began to question if it was inappropriate for him to be there. He thought it was—or it teetered on the line at the very least—but he reminded himself he had been given permission.

He reached for the handle and twisted.

"Hello?" he said, quietly but not too quietly. "Sheila?"

A toilet flushed.

Randolph froze.

On the opposite wall, a door creaked. The light disappeared as soon as Randolph saw it, and when Sheila appeared and looked up, she did not seem startled. Her hands—fronts and backs—slid back and forth on the front of her red and white checkered gown. She looked at him as if they were old friends.

"Hi," she said.

He was unsure what to say or what not to. He awkwardly pointed behind his back, toward the door. "Sorry, I don't mean to intrude. There was no answer. The woman at the desk, she said she called."

"She did."

Again, he was at a loss. "Oh, great. I, uh—"

"What are you doing here?"

He felt out of place, an outcast. Unwelcomed.

"You smell that?" Sheila said. She wriggled her nose and flared her nostrils. "What is that? Is that onion?"

Randolph did not smell anything. He was numb. But then he remembered and held up the paper bag. "Bagels."

Sheila held strong, said nothing.

"It's not too early for lunch, is it?"

It was not. They ate. The cream cheese was seeded and had a tangerine aftertaste that lingered like bitters. Spread on the onion bagel, the arrangement gave him all the right feels, and pushed the memory of the French onion soup to the side for now. The bagels were gone quickly. Devoured. Silence overpowered the room.

"What's up with the flowers?" Sheila said.

"They're for you."

"I know, but why?"

"We had a date, right?"

She looked away, fingered the crumbs her bagel left behind.

"Is everything all right?" he said.

"Thank you. I don't understand it, but thank you."

"What, you're not used to nice guys?"

She looked at him and smiled. She blinked quickly, repeatedly, as if to keep the tears at bay.

Silence returned. Despite the quiet, the moment felt critical, as if it were a make it or break it moment in time. One wrong move would ruin whatever it was they had, and one right one would change everything. Randolph went with his gut, which screamed at him to say what was on his mind.

"We should go somewhere, you and me," he said.

"Like where?"

"Away from here. Out of town. Just go."

Sheila stared at him hard. He gave it back, flashed her a smile. He swore he saw a twinkle appear in her irises, which were as green as emeralds.

"We hardly know each other," she said. "How do I know you're not a serial killer?"

"I'm not."

"How do you know I'm not?"

"Are you?"

No answer, only a slight crank of the neck and a smirk.

"I'll take my chances."

She got up from the end of the bed and left her crumpled bagel wrapper where it was. She moved toward the window and appeared to look out. She kept silent.

Randolph sensed it was another crucial moment. Should he press her further and risk pushing her away? Or not, but what if he was too casual and she thought his intentions were duplicitous? He had forgotten how the game was supposed to be played.

Do nothing, he decided. Let her make the next move.

Eventually, Sheila backed away from the window, returned to the bed, and sat. There was not a manufactured scent that hit his nose, but rather something natural; something precious and beautiful. Sheila gave off a callused, hardened energy, which was unlike how Randolph had ever seen her. He was curious as to the reason behind it, but he did not know her well enough to call her on it. Instead, he concentrated to keep his expression neutral—calm, cool, in control—though he was anything but.

"Randolph, you're a wonderful man, a true gentleman. I can tell."

But?

"But I don't think we should do this. You're too kind, really. I think it's better if we pretend like we never met."

Randolph deflated.

Sheila dropped her hand on his and kept it there. Her skin was like velvet, so smooth, not at all clammy like the day before. A shiver ran through his spine and forced his eyes shut.

"I'm sorry," she said.

Randolph held his position for a second longer and took in what would be the last time he would ever see Sheila—those emerald eyes, the laugh he longed to hear more of, the smile that created indents in her cheeks. Maybe his instincts were off and he misread the situation, or maybe he should have come on stronger. It had been so long since he had been in the game, he was resigned to the idea he just did not have it anymore like he used to. Maybe it was better this way.

"Okay," he said. Then he pulled his hand away and stood up. "If that's what you want."

On the counter by the sink on the other side of the room, a nurse's notepad sat. Randolph walked toward it and scooped it up, as did he the pen he found in one of the drawers underneath it.

"While I respect your decision," he said while he walked back toward the bed, his face buried in the notepad, "I'd like you to know that I hope you change your mind. So this is what I'm going to do."—he jotted his phone number on the notepad, tore off the top sheet, and handed it to Sheila, who took it—"I'm going to leave my number in case you do. Change your mind, that is. If you decide to give me a call, great. If not, that's fine too." He met her eyes and smiled at her, but it felt disingenuous. He hoped she could not tell.

Sheila looked down at the sheet in her hand and stared at it, though said nothing. She neither looked back up nor said anything, so Randolph left.

He closed the door behind him and pressed his back against the bricks. Deep, lonely breaths. He felt sad, though not devastated. Disappointed was most accurate. It was difficult to pinpoint where the emotion stemmed from. What about what just happened made him feel that way? He would not dwell on it, not here. It was not the first time a woman rejected him.

He waited outside the door for a minute. He half-wondered if Sheila would change her mind and run after him, though the detachment that blanketed her face before told him that was unrealistic. She was not interested, for whatever reason. Defeated, it seemed. So he would move on like he always did. He would continue to find his own happiness as he had trained himself to do having been married to Patricia.

When he made it back to the reception area, the old woman from before was gone, though a handful of others occupied the waiting room chairs. He wondered what the old woman was there for, who she was there to see. An ailing husband or a recovering child? Or was she the patient with an invisible sickness there for her biweekly examination? Would she recover? Now, where the old woman once was, an exhausted mother tended to her visibly unwell child. She stroked his hair in a way only a mother could, and the boy leaned into her clavicle while tears streamed down his swollen cheeks. The boy would be all right—they always were in Randolph's experience—and the bond between child and parent would grow stronger.

Randolph thought of Bruce—his son—and remembered when he was a boy. While it seemed like just yesterday, it could not have been further from reality. Time flew at an unfair pace, so many yesterdays gone, so many moments passed that would never be recouped. Bruce was a man now, and he had Max, so he must have understood what it was like to love someone unconditionally. Randolph wished Bruce would work harder to allow Randolph to be a part of his life—they were not estranged, but they were not close either. Their relationship consisted of quarterly telephone calls, the occasional text message, and gifts for the major holidays and birthdays. Randolph was unfulfilled with the arrangement. He wondered if a surprise visit to Utah was out of the question, now that he had nothing to hold him back.

A man walked in—but not just any man; a man who looked important. His button-down shirt was nicely pressed and without wrinkles, and was tucked neatly into his pleated khakis; the brown of the leather of his shoes matched his belt to perfection, and his hair shined with slick; his face was clean-shaven; a mobile phone hung on his belt. Randolph watched him.

The man took large, confident steps toward the reception desk, keeping his posture tight. His chest filled the button-down as if it had been designed with him in mind. He leaned in and spoke to the same woman Randolph had spoken to earlier. Randolph was close, closer than he realized, because he heard every word of the conversation with perfect clarity.

"Hello, Miss, my name is Gary O'Reilly," the man said. "I'm here to see Sheila Backe."

Sheila?

"Are you family?" the woman said.

"Not family. I'm here on official business. I'd like to ask her a few questions about a case I'm investigating."

"Are you a police officer?"

"No, ma'am."—he pulled a sheet of folded paper from his back pocket and passed it through the glass—"But I have this."

The woman took it and looked it over. Then she slipped it back under the glass and slammed her keyboard without looking down. "Room B6," she said. "Second floor."

CHAPTER SIX

Backe was her last name. Sheila Backe. Who was she?

Through the windshield, the sky radiated and warmed Randolph's skin. Blue clouds slowly lingered through the shade band, then crawled by as if they were leashed pups. A stillness crept into the truck through the open window. The medical center's main entrance was clear in his view, its large silver typography simple yet impactful. A cross made all feel welcome, even those who either chose not to or those who were not wired to believe in its significance.

And that man, O'Reilly. Who was he?

The scene replayed in Randolph's head. Sheila's unorthodox behavior, her lack of engagement, the coldness she emitted was unlike anything he had seen from her. He had to remind himself he hardly knew her, that her persona at the supermarket could have been for appearances, simply a character she played to attract customers to the business. Everyone did it—played a part they sometimes felt uncomfortable with; acted a certain way around strangers. It was an emotional complex every person had, a wall someone could put up to protect themselves. Armor. Even still, it felt off. The energy was different.

But Randolph knew nothing about any of that—he was a trained engineer, not a doctor of emotional well-being. As a human man who had experienced life and its many emotions over his long journey—

which was still, he hoped, only roughly halfway through—he had acquired a sense about people—who was genuine, who was not. Randolph sensed Sheila was more than a character, but rather an honest woman with a sincere heart.

But he had been wrong before.

The woman he married came to mind.

The curiosity about it all had him on edge. In a matter of twenty-four short hours, his emotions had been teased and twisted and duped. First, it was the bliss about the acceptance, then the shock about the explosion, then the utter confusion about Sheila's unorthodox and unexpected reaction to his arrival. For all he knew, Sheila was merely cranky about what happened to her, about why she was in the hospital. Which would have been fair—she just survived an explosion the day before. Maybe he had been insensitive about the whole situation and needed to give her more time. Or perhaps having a near-death experience changed her perspective about her life and if she wanted him in it. The events of today could influence the events of tomorrow—that could have been what was happening here.

But still, he could not reign in his thoughts.

What about Gary O'Reilly? Who was he and who did he work for? And most importantly, what did he want with Sheila? Randolph could not begin to fathom the possibilities. Beyond that, something else occupied his mind. Aside from the need to satisfy his curiosity, what did he hope to accomplish? It was not clear to even him what he envisioned for his future. While his lust for Sheila was strong, it was an emotion he could take a stranglehold of and suppress. He could forget about her and move on and wake up tomorrow the same way he did yesterday. Either way, his problems would not disappear. They were still with him if he pursued whatever it was to be pursued. He did not even know what it was. But something was happening to him, and he could not get enough.

He decided to wait for O'Reilly. He had nowhere to be and nobody to bother him or ask probing questions—aside from Patricia, whose opinion hardly mattered. So he would at least satisfy his desire to feed his curiosity. From there, he would see where it took him.

Just then, the well-dressed man appeared in the mouth of the sliding doors. O'Reilly. He pressed a phone against his ear with one hand and smoothed the part on his head with the other. A lump formed like a fast-growing tumor in Randolph's throat, made worse by the repetitive thumps in his chest. He felt uneasy and anxious about what he would say, but he knew he may change his mind if he waited too long.

So he went for it.

He yanked on the door handle, slipped out of the truck, and approached the man on foot.

O'Reilly's back was to him. The man's stride was fierce, so Randolph had to hurry. The phone call O'Reilly had been on ended and the phone was back in its holster on his hip, and the man fumbled with something in his pocket.

Randolph picked up his pace further. The brisk power walk turned into a light jog, and the gap tightened. When he thought O'Reilly may be in earshot, he called out, "Excuse me."

They both kept moving.

"Excuse me, Gary."

O'Reilly stopped with a jolt as if zapped by a shock of electricity. He spun quickly and faced Randolph. Sweat illuminated on his brow. "Who's asking?"

Randolph did not know what to say. Or do. Should he offer the man his hand and shake it like they were old friends?

"Do I know you?" O'Reilly said.

"No, I don't think so."

"How do you know my name?"

"My name is—"

"I don't care who you are. How do you know my name?" O'Reilly stepped closer. The aftershave on his neck punched Randolph in the nose. It was so masculine it made him uncomfortable.

"I saw you inside," Randolph said.

"Saw me? What the hell is that supposed to mean? Are you following me? Who sent you?"

"Hold on, now. I'm not following you. Nobody sent me. Take it easy."

O'Reilly's hand fell to his waist, and Randolph got the feeling things were about to go from bad to worse very quickly if he was not careful.

"How do you know Sheila Backe?" Randolph said, desperate to change the subject.

That made O'Reilly pause. He fell back on his heels. "How do you?"

"She's a friend."

"A friend, huh? Sheila doesn't have any friends."

Huh?

"I met her at the supermarket."

O'Reilly's eyes widened. The wrinkles around them unraveled as if they were ancient scrolls. "Is that so? What do you know about what happened there?"

The explosion. "Nothing."

O'Reilly stepped back and scanned him all over.

"Is that why you're here?" Randolph said. "To try and find out what happened? Are you an investigator?"

"Something like that."

"That document you showed to the receptionist inside—what was it?"

"That's confidential information."

"Are you a cop?"

"I feel like you already know the answer to that question. Sounds like you know an awful lot about me already. More than you should, frankly."

"Sorry, I don't mean to intrude."

"Yet here we are."

"I heard you say Sheila's name and it piqued my interest."

"So, you're friends, you say. How much do you know about her?"

Randolph thought about that for a moment. "Not much."

"My advice? Keep it that way."

Randolph's pocket began to vibrate. "Why's that?"

"Just trust me, okay? You don't want to get involved."

"Involved in what?" The pulse against his thigh sped up.

"What did you say your name was again?"

"I didn't."

"Well?"

"Randolph."

"Randolph, huh? Just Randolph?"

"Spiers."

"Randolph Spiers. Sounds like a pro ballplayer's name."

"I'm anything but." The vibration stopped.

"I'd introduce myself, but you already know."

Randolph's leg vibrated again. This time, he retrieved the phone from his pocket and glanced at the screen. "Excuse me one second," he said. "I should get this."

"I'm going anyway." O'Reilly turned and took a step in the opposite direction.

"Hold up."

O'Reilly stopped, turned back. "What?"

"What about Sheila?"

"What about her?"

"How do you know her?"

O'Reilly inhaled sharply, then pushed it out. "Pretend we never met. You don't want to get involved."

"But what if I do?"

"You don't." —he motioned to the phone in Randolph's hand— "You should get that. Never let a ringing phone go unanswered. You never know who will be on the other end and what it is they want."

Randolph watched him walk away.

In his hand, the phone still vibrated. His fingers shook under the constant motion and distracted him from where O'Reilly was headed. The number was not in his contact list, and he did not recognize the area code. When he looked back up, O'Reilly was gone.

He answered: "Hello?"

"Randolph?"

It was a woman.

"Yeah."

"It's Sheila."

Sheila.

"Sheila?"

"The number you gave me worked."

"Of course it does. Why wouldn't it?"

No response.

"Sheila?"

"What you said earlier, did you mean it?"

"Which part?"

"About going somewhere, leaving here."

"Yes."

Another pause.

"If the offer still stands," she said, "I've changed my mind."

Knots of intensity thumped through Randolph's chest like a stampede. The adrenaline boiled so hotly in his veins he thought he might explode. He yanked the phone away from his ear and caught his breath. He thought about the proposition, considered the logistics. Could he actually go through with it?

Sheila's muffled voice crept through the speaker, but he ignored it. When he was ready, his decision clear, he steadied the phone near his jawline and spoke into the microphone, "Sheila?"

"Yes?"

"When should I pick you up?"

CHAPTER SEVEN

Not a peep from Shay overnight. Benji hardly slept. It was obvious there was trouble.

The word made him uncomfortable, so he had not told her how he felt, but he was in love with Shay. With her, it was not about sex or the physical connection, but rather something stronger than that. Something deeper, more meaningful; something personal. They bonded. They shared stories of their childhoods—about how his father abandoned him and how his drug-addicted mother raised him and his three brothers on government checks and sexual favors for the neighbors; about how Shay's family migrated from the Nordics when she was young, about how she illegally worked under the table and washed dishes and scrubbed floors to help her parents with the rent. Shay was nearly a decade his senior, but their lives had been similar—difficult and unfair and lacked purpose—and their connection was real. The lack of commonalities in pop culture references and tastes in music and film aside, they connected on a human level. About the things that actually mattered.

Benji really loved her.

Then why sleep with Cheyenne, right? He knew that was the next logical question to ask. And his answer was this: Emotions aside, there was an unquenchable need etched in his DNA to be desired in all variants of the word. The lust for the physical release he and Cheyenne shared was special. He had slept with a lot of women, and none of them showed the level of experience or interest or commitment to the craft as Cheyenne. He wondered if that was something that came with age or if Cheyenne was a unicorn. How could anyone pass up the intense releases he had with her? Physically, the way she made his body feel was unmatched.

That is where it got complicated. Shay had more of a traditional mindset. She was not a virgin, but she had not had many positive experiences either. That was something she would not talk about much with Benji, at least not yet, but he understood the gist. Benji wondered if that had something to do with why she no longer had contact with her father—but it was purely speculation. She had not declared they wait until marriage, only until she felt stable and secure. Which Benji agreed was fair. But the desire within him still attacked his cells like an amoeba, and he craved the release. Needed it. So when Cheyenne entered his life, it felt like the perfect arrangement—Benji would feed his need to be desired and for physical release; Cheyenne would get to experiment on a younger man who would have the stamina to keep up; and Shay would not be pressured to do something she was not ready for. That was how he saw it.

Justifiable, was it not?

Benji missed her—Shay, that was. She was not one to go dark without explanation or not return his calls. He felt ridiculous in a way. He had never been in love, and the way it made him feel surprised him—borderline obsessive and possessive and jealous. He thought about her constantly. Was that what love was about? He was still in the process of figuring it out, albeit being his first time. Admittedly, he struggled with what to do with the powerful emotions trapped within him at times, with how to tame them. He would do anything to not mess up what he had with Shay.

There were ninety minutes before his shift started at the coffee shop. That would be more than enough time to drive over to Shay's apartment—not to spy on her or stalk her, but to check on her because he was worried. Surely there was an explanation about what happened. He was not angry with her; he just needed to know the truth so they could fix it and move on.

A black leather jacket dangled over the back of the chair—Benji grabbed it and tossed it over his shoulder. The pressure on his clavicle was like that from a lead vest, but he looked good in it. Felt good. So it was worth it, even when it left him overheated. He crossed the room, slipped into his shoes, and reached for the door handle. As he did, a knock came from the other side of it, which gave him pause.

"Who's there?" he said to the door.

"It's me, lover."

Cheyenne.

Benji twisted the knob and pulled the door toward him. A gust of wind smacked him in the chest, pushed him back. There she stood, her hair tied back, a peacoat buttoned up the front. Makeup was heavy around her eyes and the crimson lipstick overpowered her face. That perfume, though. It hit him like a ton of bricks.

"What are you doing here?" he asked.

"Nice to see you, too."

"How'd you get up?"

"That's not a very nice way to greet a guest."

He said nothing.

"A fine-looking young stud like yourself so graciously held the door for me when he was walking out, if you must know. Don't worry about that. I'm here, and that's all that matters."—a pause—"Aren't you going to invite me in?"

"Actually, I was just about to—"

Cheyenne quickly unbuttoned her peacoat and pulled it open. Her eyes shone with delight. A seductive grin formed on her lips.

Benji got hard.

A corset the same color as his jacket flashed provocatively back at him. Straps connected the bust to the hips, which clipped on the tops of Cheyenne's transparent stockings. Underneath was bare. The waist was pulled tight, and the top was cupless and lifted Cheyenne's bosom upward. Her areolas bulged and made a pink mantle for her stimulated nipples. Benji tried not to but could not help but stare.

"Well?" she said. The smile on her face told Benji she was pleased with herself. She had him shook. "You like?"

Benji smiled. Widely. "Would you like to come in?"

"I thought you'd never ask."

She jumped him in the doorway.

. . . . .

Sweat drenched his back. The sex sofa licked up their juices and trapped their scents. Benji still had not left a towel nearby, just in case, which he regretted. He was short of breath.

"My God," he said. "You're insane."

Cheyenne rolled off him. She leaned over the edge of the sofa and lit a joint, then blew smoke out the open window. "You really know how to flatter a woman."

"I meant it as a compliment."

She took another hit.

Benji scanned the studio and squinted to read the clock on the microwave. "Ah, shit."

"What?"

"I have to go."

Cheyenne nodded, took another hit. "You said that."

"No, like I really have to go."

"What's the rush?"

"Work."

"Skip it."

"I can't just skip it. The rent's not going to pay itself."

Cheyenne stood. She faced the open window and blew a puff of smoke out it. She lingered longer than was necessary as if to give a free show to an onlooker in the building across the street, then turned back. Benji scrambled to find his clothes.

"Aren't you the responsible one?" she said.

"Here." Benji gave her a pile of her clothes. There was not much.

"Want to go for round two?"

Benji stopped, looked at her. "Did you not hear what I said? I should have left ten minutes ago."

"I'm not finished yet." She meant the joint.

"Take it."

Cheyenne paused, nodded, and dressed. Kind of. She kept her clothes off and chose instead to remain nude under the peacoat. Benji pulled a T-shirt over his head and rushed to the door. He hopped on one foot as he struggled to slip his shoe back on. Once composed, he yanked on the knob and held the door open, and waited for Cheyenne to follow.

"You realize we need to talk, right?" she said as she approached. The joint hung from her lips like a cigarette in one of those retro Camel commercials.

"Not right now we don't."

"Soon."

Cheyenne transferred the joint to her hand and leaned in, the perfume still luscious on her nape, and pressed her lips against Benji's. He kept his tight against hers, sealed until her tongue parted them and massaged him. His entire body tingled.

Cheyenne pulled away and said, "Goodbye, lover." Then she left.

Benji waited until she descended fully and the exterior door closed behind her. Echoes from her stilettos clanked in the stairwell. Benji gave it a minute more, then he left too. All the while, he thought of Shay and hoped she was okay.

CHAPTER EIGHT

Did O'Reilly's warning mean anything? Should it? Randolph knew nothing about the man—his relationship with Sheila, or his intentions—so he had to make his own judgment. A skeptic could wonder the same thing about Sheila since Randolph hardly knew her either, and they would not be wrong. But life was nothing more than a compilation of split-second decisions made at the moments they arose—Randolph made his, and he was comfortable with it.

He had a few hours to kill. Sheila would be released before dinner. So he drove home. When he arrived, he was alone. Again. Patricia's car was nowhere in sight, having hauled its driver to somewhere beyond Randolph's wildest imagination. Patricia had morphed into someone he hardly knew, someone he disliked. Irresponsibility crept into her life in a flash, and it turned her into someone Randolph hardly recognized.

The love was gone, but that was normal. A marriage the length of theirs was bound to experience romantic lulls—and they had other times too. But with devotion and commitment and effort and a realignment of priorities and needs, it came back. It always had. But this time was different. Beyond the lost love, there was a genuine dislike and discontentment between them. Randolph felt it, and he was sure Patricia felt it too, though he had not asked. He no longer cared to hear her opinion, or to listen to her personally attack him and blame him for her unhappiness. It was time to move on.

But it was more difficult than that, there was more at stake. There was his life's wealth—both the sizable fortune he inherited from his parents' passing and the abundance he amassed through his work as an engineer—and all the physical assets they shared. And there was Bruce and Max and that already delicate situation. More personally, there were Randolph's insecurities about what he had to offer and what type of women he might attract if they knew his net worth. Simply, Randolph was not ready for all that would be involved to completely sever the relationship. Not yet. He needed more time to figure everything out.

He packed. Or he tried. The effort was daunting. Without a plan on where he and Sheila would go or what they would do or how long they would be gone, Randolph was out of his element. Tens of hangers draped button-downs and polos and well-pressed sweaters over the rows of shoes on the closet floor. Multicolored chinos and khakis and a handful of pairs of high-quality denim were folded in perfect squares on the shelves on the back wall. Brown and orange and black belts hugged the tie rack. None of it felt appropriate.

Was it a vacation, or a permanent move? Randolph could not say. When he thought about it, he felt foolish. Who would pay the mortgage? Who would cut the grass? Who would attend next week's town meeting about the inevitable property tax hike being discussed? It would not be Patricia. Those were all his jobs, along with being the sole provider and plumber and electrician and handyman. His home was his castle, regardless if he wanted it to be, and part of him did not want to leave.

But he wanted something more. Needed it. He could not rationalize leaving on a whim without explanation or his affairs in order, but he could not justify staying either. So where did that leave him? Sheila told him yes, and it had been a while since he heard that word from a woman. He owed it to himself to explore that feeling more, to chase that high. Where it would go was the beauty of the mystery of the universe. The house and all the responsibilities that came with it would not go anywhere.

He tossed the bag on the bed. In the bureau was his casual attire—the old T-shirts and cargo shorts stained with paint, the torn pair of denim he refused to part with—and underwear and socks. He emptied it. The clothes he wore were neutral colors and age-appropriate and comfortable enough, and the flat front pants were versatile for lots of situations. He tossed a pair of sneakers on top of the pile and slipped it all into the bag. Then he did the same with the necessary toiletries from the master bathroom and zipped the bag. It was enough.

Downstairs, he killed all the lights, locked the front door, draped a light jacket over his shoulder, and left.

. . . . . .

A before dinner release was about as unspecific as it could get. Randolph did not want to be late. He brought a paperback from the house and tried to read in the parking lot, but he struggled to concentrate. The words failed to register, even after he read then reread the sections that did not process the first time. Sentences became a jumbled mess, entire paragraphs an impossibility to get through. He could not focus. He closed the book and tossed it on the seat next to him.

A half-hour became a full one. One became two. Randolph dozed in and out of wakefulness. The phone in the cupholder failed to ring or chime with a new message—the firm had apparently moved on, and the women were without need. He debated going inside and asking for an update, or to see her again, but he thought that might delay the process. So he waited. Comfortability came and went and his temperature fluctuated—jacket on, jacket off; windows up, windows down—but he was calm. Anxiousness was suppressed and replaced with the anticipation of seeing her again, of what was to come. His decision seemed validated.

When he became restless, he slid out of the truck to stretch his legs. A crack shuttered through his spine when he leaned too far to one side. But life was good. He felt good, great even. Excited. For wherever the forthcoming adventure would bring him, his mind was open. More so, his heart was open too. And he was ready to let someone in.

Sheila.

Then just like that, as if the universe had listened to his thoughts and sent a messenger to answer them, there she was. In the mouth of the sliding glass, underneath the cross that blessed the patients inside, Sheila stood. Street clothes and all. A nurse stood by her side. Randolph straightened, instinctively reached to ensure his shirt was properly tucked but stopped himself. His heart leaped.

He moved out of the shadow of the track and into the open. The nurse nodded at Sheila and turned back inside, then disappeared. Sheila looked both ways, her head on a swivel. A phone was in her hand, though she failed to look down at it.

Then she looked right at him, or what appeared to be. But she did not react, nor did she appear to recognize it was him from a distance. Randolph raised his shoulder blade and sliced his fingers through the air above him to try to capture her attention. And it worked. Sheila saw him and raised her arm too, and waved back. She stepped off the sidewalk and started toward him.

It was a long walk, and Randolph felt awkward. What should he do? Should he walk toward her and meet her in the middle? Or should he wait where he was? Should he watch her as she approached, or did that make him seem like a creep? Should he smile or play it cool when she approached? What about his hands—what should he do with them? So much internal debate, yet no right answers. No answers, period. The best part? While he pondered the questions and flipped back and forth on the answers, Sheila got closer. Then she got really close, then she was at an arm's length. Then she stopped in front of him.

"Hi," she said.

"Hi."

"You came?"

It was phrased as a question.

"Why wouldn't I?"

No answer.

"I'm glad you called. Are you feeling better?"

"I'm fine. Just hungry."

"Oh, I'm sorry. I would have—"

"It's okay, that's not what I meant."

Randolph nodded. Then silence fell. Heavy, hollow silence. What now?

Sheila flashed him a smile. It was awfully close to the smile she wore at the supermarket, and Randolph felt his face flush and the tension lessen.

Sheila.

"So," she said, "where to?"

CHAPTER NINE

The lady was hungry, so they stopped to eat. It seemed like a good place to start. Randolph had a few favorite places in Cedar Rapids, but he thought better of showing up at any of them with another woman. Soon it would be normal—he and Patricia living separate lives, introducing new lovers into the mix—but for now, it felt taboo. Instead, they wound up at a highway diner in a tiny town called Center Point, which was barely more than a dozen miles from the city and still within Linn County. Even better, he knew nobody who lived there.

Far from the bustle of the restaurants in Cedar Rapids, the diner was half-empty. It had a throwback vibe—bright red booth benches and counter-high padded bar stools without backs; vintage photography of muscle cars and train stations and auto mechanic shops hung on the walls; country-western classics rang out from the twenty-five-cent jukebox on the far wall; the chefs rang the call bell on the counter when a meal was ready; and the waitresses wore dresses and a pink apron.

Randolph scanned the diner for anyone he knew, found none. No surprise. A plate of greasy bacon and scrambled eggs and pancakes stacked three high left the kitchen, followed by a mound of meatloaf with an absurd amount of thick, oozing gravy. Some patrons sipped room temperature coffee while others gulped down carbonated beverages in all shades of colors—it was the full twenty-four-hour diner experience. The number of conflicting aromas was a shock to Randolph's system to where he failed to recognize any of them. His stomach either churned or growled—it was hard to tell the difference.

He watched Sheila. Her eyes scoped out their surroundings, though her neck remained still. Her lips were pressed against each other and did not move. She traced the edges of the coffee-stained menu with a subtlety and gentleness that made it seem as if it provided her comfort. She had not looked at it once.

"What are you thinking?" Randolph said.

She stopped, looked at him. "Huh?"

"What are you going to eat?"

"Oh."—she looked relieved—"I haven't decided yet."

Randolph nodded. What else was he to do? He leaned in. "Can I ask you something?"

"You just did."

He leaned back.

"Kidding," she said. Then she flashed him that smile.

Randolph returned the smile and felt a wave of joy rush over him. "You never answered my question from earlier."

"Which was what?"

"Are you a serial killer?"

Shelia exploded with laughter. It began with a smile, then a chuckle, then full-blown belly laughter. Sheila howled with a joy typically reserved for a child, and as much as Randolph tried to contain himself, he could not. Quickly, it became infectious. Before long, tears streamed down his face and moistened his cheeks. Once he regained control, he used the napkins from the metallic tray to dab his eyes. His stomach still hurt, but it was for a different reason now. Other patrons looked their way—some unhappily, others with smiling faces.

"I haven't laughed like that in a long time," Sheila said. She mimicked Randolph's tear drying tactic.

"Me either. I hate to spoil the fun, but I feel I must warn you. I'm not usually that funny."

Sheila balled a napkin and dropped it on the corner of the table. "Well, that's disappointing. But to answer your question, no, I'm not a serial killer. Never killed anyone, actually."

Randolph laughed. "That's good to hear. Neither have I."

After they settled and a silence that bordered awkward took over, Sheila said, "Okay, my turn."

"To what?"

"Ask you a question."

Randolph leaned forward. "It's only fair."

"You're married, aren't you?"

Ouch.

Randolph slid back. He felt deflated, like a balloon that had been pricked. The ring that was in his pocket suddenly reminded him of its presence—it felt like a led bullet against his thigh. He would not lie to her.

"Yes, I'm married," he said. "Legally."

Sheila nodded, though her expression was unchanged.

"It's a long story."

"I'm sure it is."

"Maybe I'll tell you about it sometime."

"Maybe."

Randolph could not gauge her reaction. Was she angry? It was hard to judge. "Let me put it this way: Have you ever been married?"

"No."

"I'm sure you've ended a relationship with a boyfriend or two, though?"

She hesitated but said, "Of course."

"It works the same way. Two people fall out of love and decide to break it off, but the logistics can be complicated. It's not like you can cut off all communication and move on with your life. When you're married, there are steps that need to be taken. Assets and debts to split. Paperwork to file. Lawyers to debrief. It can take time."

Sheila remained still.

"Does that make sense?"

"Sure. It makes perfect sense. For the record, I'm not judging you. I was just curious."

"Oh." Randolph felt relieved.

"I noticed you wore a ring earlier, at the supermarket, but you're not now."

"You caught that, did you? Old habit I guess. Totally forgot it was there."

Sheila smiled at him. He was tempted to lean over the table and kiss her but did not. Too soon.

"What else are you hiding?" she said.

"Nothing. Look, I'm sorry if—"

She leaned across the table and dropped a hand on his. "I'm kidding."—that smile again—"You're too uptight. Just relax."

Randolph looked down. Sheila's palm was as smooth as silk to the touch, yet the top of her hand was worn and slightly callused. Amazingly white cuticles led to short and unpainted nails. Randolph tingled as her longest finger stroked the top of his knuckle.

A waitress came and they ordered—Sheila, apparently, had come to a decision. Before long, most patrons vacated and a few new ones came, and the diner quieted. Then the jukebox stopped and the only sounds were of clanking silverware and sizzled bacon and the occasional bell chime. Randolph felt as if every time he spoke he was the loudest voice in the room, and he disliked it. But he also knew he would have to get past it and care less about the opinions of the people around him if he were to make himself happy, which was what he was trying to do.

"What made you change your mind?" he asked between bites. Honey mustard oozed off his club sandwich and dripped onto his napkin. His earlier craving had passed.

"Honestly, I don't know. You seemed nice and all, but it's hard to tell someone's intentions sometimes. You know?"

"And now?"

"You still seem nice."

Randolph took another bite of the club.

"Why are you so nice to me?" she said.

Randolph chewed, thought about the answer. "I'm nice to everyone."—he swallowed—"And I like you."

Sheila stopped mid-bite, left the brisket floating in her hands above the plate. "You don't know me."

"Not yet."

Sheila smiled again, this time with a blush. "I'm starting to like you too."

CHAPTER TEN

They went to a bar. Randolph had not been to one since he was in college, and it was far noisier than he remembered. People were packed like sardines. Young men and women crowded him, brushed their backs and fronts against his, invaded his space in a way that made him feel uncomfortable. After a Scotch and a few handfuls of germy bar nuts and some ice chips, his head pounded. The music that blasted from the speakers was nothing he was familiar with and frankly, he disliked it. Everyone around him looked barely old enough to drive.

Sheila quietly but boldly threw back a clear spirit. It was her third. Even still, she seemed to be in control of herself. Relaxed. The vodka was heavy on her breath.

"After this," she said, "where are we going? What's the big grand plan?"

That was the question, was it not? Randolph did not exactly know the answer. "You ever been to Wyoming?" he said. He had to yell over the intrusively loud bass that rattled his everything and contributed to the worsening of the pain in his head.

"Wyoming? Has anyone ever been to Wyoming?"

Randolph laughed.

"Seriously, what's in Wyoming?"

"Nothing," he said. "Absolutely nothing."

"I don't understand. If there's nothing in Wyoming, why go?"

"There's nothing there—no responsibilities, no commitments, nobody. It's a fresh start."

"Are you having a midlife crisis or something?"

"What makes you say that?"

"Look at you. An old guy in trousers at a bar with a bunch of drunken twenty-something idiots."—she laughed—"No offense, I'm just saying."

He reached for his glass and fingered the rim. It was almost empty. The bartender walked past and Randolph raised the glass, which was quickly replaced with an identical one. Brown liquor filled it a third of the way, maybe less.

"I'm not that old," he said.

"I'm just teasing you."

"How old do you think I am?"

"I don't know."

"Come on, guess."

"Fine. Fifty."

"Close. Fifty-two."

"How old do you think I am?"

"Honestly? No idea. Thirty? Thirty-one?"

Sheila smiled. "Good answer. Close, but wrong. Thirty-four."

Randolph lifted his glass and took a swig. It burned all the way down, but it felt so good. It warmed his belly when it settled. "The good news is, I'm not quite old enough to be your father."

Now Sheila laughed. "Doesn't bother me. I like older men."

"Do you?" He took another swig, this one large. His head swam.

"All types, really."

He smirked and shook his head. "You're something else, aren't you?"

She leaned in. Her breath was hot. "You want to kiss me right now, don't you?"

"What if I do?"

"Why don't you?"

Randolph's first instinct was to lean back, to give her space. But he fought that instinct. Instead, he leaned in closer and slowed his breaths, locked eyes with Sheila. His chest pounded. Her eyes were red but not too red, and her mouth was open just slightly. The noise around him seemed quieter now, as if his entire world were trapped in a bubble that just so happened to surround their two stools. He no longer cared about all the unwanted touching that surrounded him.

Then he kissed her. Her lips were wet against his, which felt dry and in need of balm. Her hand squeezed the back of his neck, then slid to his jaw and caressed his stubble as their lips merged. Darkness overtook his vision.

She pulled away first. Her bottom lip was tucked under her front teeth. A hint of lust twinkled on her face. "We should order another round," she said.

So they did.

. . . .

It was late and cold and very dark when they left. The crowd inside was still rambunctious, the party only beginning. Randolph was happy to pay the tab and go and remove himself from the scene. His head felt like a bowling ball on his shoulders.

He drove to divert his focus away from the pain. Sheila partially dozed off beside him, their arms interlocked. There was a motel a couple of miles west; he was in good enough shape to make it there without incident. When they arrived, the man inside wore long, greasy hair and thick glasses and a mysteriously stained polo shirt. A TV with an old-fashioned antenna sat cockeyed on the corner of his high-top desk, and a steaming microwavable dinner cooled in front of it. Something that portrayed itself as mashed potatoes and peas and a sorry excuse for meat spewed toxins into the air. The man hardly acknowledged them and recited monotone instructions and policies, of which there was only one—just clean up after yourselves and do not bring trouble. It was a no-tell motel in every sense. Randolph paid for two adjacent rooms in cash.

Sheila seemed bothered but accepted the key to her room, and she disappeared inside without saying goodnight. Inside his own, Randolph flipped on the lights and yanked the curtains closed and tossed his bag on the bed. The room smelled of must and dander and lacked a satisfactory level of cleanliness he was accustomed to. A standard double bed failed to tempt him with its sunken pillows and a wrinkled comforter that had a floral design straight from 1985. He did not think he would have the nerve to sit on it, never mind attempt to sleep. He could only imagine the things that had happened in this room, on this bed, in this bed. When was the last time the sheets were changed? Was there even a cleaning crew for a place like this? He did not want to know.

One thing he failed to pack was ibuprofen, and he regretted it. He wondered if it was possible for his head to spontaneously combust from the pressure. Too much Scotch, not enough food. Amateur mistake. Against his better judgment, he sat on the edge of the bed and rubbed his temples with his forefingers, begging the pain to dissipate. The mattress bounced above the springs with every movement. Dehydration lurked.

He got up and searched the room for something that may offer relief since his fingers could not. Near the coffee pot, he found an individual plastic cup sealed in another layer of plastic, which he tore off and brought to the bathroom. He flipped on the light and prepared for the worst. It was ordinary but not as repulsive as he imagined it might be. The tile was off-white and dirty, the grout blackened, but without cracks or roach carcasses. The sink was surprisingly clean. A single window above the toilet shone with starlight from the night. Randolph cranked the handle on the faucet and filled the cup with cold water, which he guzzled. Then he repeated it. The headache would get better.

Back in the main room, he sat on the bed again. He felt dizzy, saw stars, but not the ones from outside the bathroom window. It had been hours since the bar nuts and even longer since the club sandwich, and he wondered if eating would help. It had been a while since he drank that much and he was feeling the effects of coming on too strong. His body revolted. He lumbered outside to find something, anything, to put in his stomach.

The chill of the early morning whacked him like a fist and stole his breath, and he was temporarily nauseous. Thankfully, it quickly passed. A vending machine with individually wrapped cookies and sleeves of crackers and small bags of chips and nothing with any nutritional value hummed from the far side of his room window. Into the machine, he fed two singles and entered the corresponding codes that released the packages to the metal door at the bottom. A quarter spat out from the coin release slot, which he left behind, a gift for the next.

Exhaustion came—physical mostly, but also emotional. It had been a long day and he was clueless as to what he was doing or where he and Sheila were going. He hoped tomorrow would bring clarity. In front of Sheila's room, he pinched his fingers into a loose fist and rapped his knuckles on the door.

"Sheila?" he called.

No response.

The light was dim behind the curtain. Perhaps she was in the shower or already asleep, though he acknowledged that would have been fast. Had she even had a bag with her? He failed to notice. His mind was jumbled, his thoughts a blur. He rapped on the door a second time and called out louder than the first, but with the same results. With nothing further to do, he moved on and retreated to his own room.

He tossed the extra sleeve of cookies on the table and tore open his own. They were stale, but the chocolate was still sweet, and his eyes rolled into darkness while he chewed. He pushed in one cookie after the other, chewed as a cow would hay. When he opened his eyes to remove his shoes, he noticed the pile of crumbs on his crotch, which he brushed to the floor without a care.

He fell backward onto the bed. His eyes were heavy.

But he could not sleep.

The day replayed in his mind like a film reel, and he saw the images over and over—the hospital and the text message from Sheila, then O'Reilly, and the diner and bar. And the kiss. Oh, the kiss. The sweetness of the vodka lingered on his lips as he thought about it. He licked it away, but it returned with a vengeance, on the attack against his psyche. The responses flamed within him—the physical rolling in his gut, the tingles in his legs, the ecstasy that swam through his brain.

He thought of Sheila. He pictured her lips sucking his, imagined her tongue rolling through his mouth like a tidal wave. He wondered what it would be like to feel her, to touch her, to have her. He wanted her. He reached down and unzipped.

Part of it was mental—he knew that and he was working on it. But the physiological part was hard to overcome, and there was not much he could do about it. He had seen his doctor about the problem but refused to medicate. At the time, anyway, it seemed unnecessary. Emotionally, he was engaged, ready to give his mind to the process, but he was sheepish about his physical limitations and the restrictions it put on this part of his life. He ached for release—a full release, not the kind he could achieve with direct, concentrated stimulation. The experience was nowhere near the same as it once was.

He lay not limp but only moderately erect in his hand. It was the best it could get and the most disheartening and depressing experience he imagined any man could withstand. It felt as if his manhood was gone, stripped away seemingly overnight. One day he had full function, the next he did not. Without this portion of him working as it should, he struggled to persuade himself he had something useful to offer a woman.

It was part of the reason his relationship dissolved with Patricia, he imagined. Emotional and financial support only went so far, and when the physical part was all but lost—though not completely, but it was difficult for him to accept what the changes entailed—a relationship suffered. Over years, it was inevitable. In some ways, he blamed himself, though he knew it was not his fault. If he had only taken better care of himself when he was younger, or if he had monitored his health more closely throughout the years, perhaps he would not have this issue.

Sheila.

How would he explain it to her? When was the right time, or how? A physical connection was not the only thing that mattered, but he would be a fool if he thought it did not. Someone as young as Sheila deserved to know what she was getting into before getting too deep, did she not?

Randolph huffed. He stuffed himself back into his pants and zipped the front. He rolled on his side. The headache was no better, which he figured did not help. Sober or not, the problem would not disappear overnight, and he had to do something about it before it got any worse. But even that was an impossibility. It either got worse—maybe permanently—or it stayed the same. The odds of a complete recovery were low. This was just who he was, take it or leave it, like it or not.

CHAPTER ELEVEN

After the longest eight hours of his life, Benji slid into his car and peeled out of the coffee shop parking lot. His phone blew up with pointless ten-second disappearing videos sent from his friends and notifications he did not care about. Still nothing from Shay. He drove to her apartment.

She lived on the east side, about as far from Benji's place as possible while still living in the city. But it was worth it. She was worth it. When he arrived, her apartment was dark. It was a ground floor walkout with a singular window that faced the street, so Benji saw right in. There was no curtain. He walked around the back to the parking lot and looked for her car. The designated spot with the faded white paint with her apartment number on it was empty, home to only a crushed foam cup. A streetlight flickered on the far end of the lot.

He did not want to loiter too long, especially in the dark, but he had to do his due diligence and check it out the best he could. He was worried about her. Back in the front, he cupped his hands on the glass and looked through them as if they were binoculars. With the darkness at his back and the moonlight filtered, he waited for his eyes to adjust. When they did, he saw only the ordinary—a striped afghan neatly draped across the back of the sofa, a throw pillow displayed on the corner of the cushion, a side lamp still and lonely, the remotes aligned on the end table.

No sign of Shay.

Benji wanted nothing more than to get inside and check out the rest of the place, but it was not possible. He pressed his fingertips against the glass and pulled toward the stars, but the window would not budge. The exterior door to the building required a key. Even if he was able to get into the building, the apartment had a separate key. He had neither.

There was no way in.

Shay clearly was not home, and there was no sign of a break-in or foul play. That made Benji feel a little better, though not entirely. Why had she not called?

He checked his phone—no messages or missed calls from her. Sadness crept in. Had she ghosted him? Considering what they were up against, that explanation seemed implausible. An impossibility. There was too much at stake.

Over his shoulder, he sensed something. Someone. He turned and found an older woman with a lit cigarette in her mouth and a glare that could kill a man. She stared at him from her second floor porch. A giant smoke cloud billowed around her face like a mask. It was a miracle she could breathe at all. No words came from the porch, but Benji felt her watching. His time was running short, and he knew it. The last thing he needed—they needed—was law enforcement getting involved and asking questions. This had to be kept under the radar. Without further thought, he stepped back and dropped his hands into his pockets and walked to the curb, then slipped in his car and drove west through the heart of Cedar Rapids.

· · · · ·

He was out of scenarios. All the ones his mind conjured up were demoralizing in some form or another. Unless he heard from her overnight, he would have no choice but to trace her steps as he knew them, maybe ask around a bit. It was a risk, but there was no other alternative. Without contact, there would be problems. Big problems. And he did not have the answers.

He recognized Cheyenne's car when he pulled up to his building. It looked out of place parked against the curb—too clean, not enough blemishes on the paint. Each time it was left alone and not stolen was a good day, especially in this neighborhood. He almost did not stop because he did not want to deal with her right now, but he also knew she would not either. It could not be avoided forever, as much as he would have preferred it that way.

"Hello, lover," she said when he got to the top of the stairs. She sat on his doorstep, her knees under her arms. Her skirt was short, which meant lots of skin showed. Too much.

"I'm really not in the mood," Benji said while he fumbled for his key.

"That's not why I'm here."

That was what he was afraid of.

"Then why are you?"

"We need to talk."

Benji's jaw clenched. He did not know what he would say to her. She stood and followed him inside once he managed to disengage the locks.

He stripped off his leather jacket and draped it over the arm of the chair. Cheyenne kept her clothes on and joined him on the sofa.

"What do you want to talk about?" he said.

Her eyebrows raised. "Really?"

He swallowed.

"What happened?"

"I don't know."

"Wrong answer."

"I know it's not like it was supposed to be, but I'm handling it."

"I don't think you are. I'm starting to question if you're cut out for this."

"I am."

She eyed him. "You're lucky your ass is fine. But it's not going to save you. I want to know the details. What are you doing, specifically, to remedy the situation?"

The truth was, he did not know. He could make up a story to get her off his back, but he thought she would see right through it. He had to be upfront with her.

His pocket vibrated. It bought him a few seconds, which he was thankful for. He fished for it, reached his fingers inside his pocket, and pulled out the phone. It was a text message. He tapped the screen and the phone came to life.

It was Shay.

He knew his face lit with excitement but he tried to rein it in because he also knew Cheyenne watched him too. Further questions were not something he wanted, so he tried to be as casual as he could as he read it.

Hey! Sorry I missed your messages. My phone died. Something came up, so don't worry. I'll tell you all about it when I see you. Everything is fine.

Benji felt fifty pounds lighter, energized. He exhaled and could not help but smile. He knew she would have an explanation. He knew it! He loved that girl. They would be okay.

"Well?" Cheyenne said.

Benji looked at her. "Just trust me, okay?"

"Why should I?"

"We've made it this far, haven't we?"

She did not respond.

"Speaking of fine," he said, eyeing her now. "Why don't you bring that ass over here and show me how much you missed me?"

She stood up and huffed, then walked toward the door.

"Where are you going?"

She stopped and faced him when she got to the door. "You don't just get a piece of ass anytime you want it, you know."

He smiled until he realized she was serious.

"You better be handling this."

"Don't worry about it. It's under control."

"I hope that's true. Goodbye, lover."

CHAPTER TWELVE

The side of a fist pounding on a door woke him. At first he ignored it, thought it was meant for someone else, but then it happened again. And again. His eyes were so heavy he wondered if they were sewn shut. Blind, he managed to drag himself from the bed and planted his bare feet on the raggedy carpet and pushed himself toward where he thought the door was. His toes instinctively scrunched to protect themselves from whatever lingered that the eye could not see. He reminded himself to wash well.

Another knock.

By now, his eyes were open, though his vision was crusty. Irritation rose. Then annoyance. The clock said it was just before eight o'clock. With each toe-scrunching step he took, the more aware he became. And with it, he realized his headache had not gone away, though it dulled. He had not had that much to drink in many years, and now he regretted it. Even if it led to that luscious kiss.

Another knock, this one farther away. Then came a squeak and a voice, then another voice. A door closed. Randolph took one final step and blinked away the blur, then he closed one eye and pressed the other against the hole in the door. It was like looking down a long tunnel, through multiple layers of glass and past the scratches and particles of debris that covered them. No one was on the other side.

He moved to the left. The curtain was stained and smelled like mildew, but it was bulky enough to block the light from outside. His nose suddenly congested, he gripped the curtain and swung it open and gave his eyes a few more seconds to adjust to the brightness that now overwhelmed them.

Two pickup trucks were in the parking lot outside the window—one Randolph's, another he did not recognize with its large tires and jet-black paint and what looked like tinted windows. It had not been there last night when they arrived. Gray clouds covered the backdrop. Rain lingered on the horizon. It looked cold. What day of the week was it?

The voices came again—both inaudible but distinctly two. Outside the window to the left was the vending machine he used last night, to the right a post that held up the canopy over the walkway. After he stepped farther left, the post gave way to people, two of them—the sources of the voices.

A man's back faced him. He knew it was a man by the short haircut and the way he lacked any figure at all—flat hips, a droop under where his backside should have been, a bulky frame no woman he had ever seen could support. A brown jacket covered the man's back—one, Randolph imagined, of those zip front types—and gave way to pleated brown pants. Facing him was Sheila, whose lips occasionally moved then stopped. She did not smile.

Randolph stepped back toward the door and unlatched the chain and reached for the handle. The brass stuck to his palm as is if it were covered in adhesive, but he tore it away once the morning entered the musty room. He popped his head outside. Sheila's eyes darted toward him. The conversation with the mystery man halted. The man turned then too, and Randolph saw his face.

O'Reilly.

"Look who it is," O'Reilly said.

"Nice to see you again, Gary," Randolph said, though it was not.

O'Reilly smiled. "I'm impressed you remember. After such a long night, especially."

Randolph froze. Words were stripped.

"How do you two know each other?" Sheila said.

"We go way back. Isn't that right, Randolph?"

Randolph said nothing. He was shook.

Was he watching us?

Silence.

"So glad you could join us," O'Reilly said, his attention still on Randolph. "Sheila and I were just talking about—"

"I don't think he cares," Sheila said.

"If you're old friends, which I've been led to believe you are, then I disagree."

"Randolph,"—Shelia looked at him, her angry eyes full of intention—"will you go back inside, please?"

"Why don't you stay?" O'Reilly said.

"Everything is okay," Sheila said. "Please go back inside. This doesn't involve you."

Randolph looked at her. While her complexion had become pale, her eyes were focused on him, and the tension around her creased lips indicated she meant it. He scanned back to O'Reilly, who looked amused with a pointed grin like the Joker's, then back to Sheila. She nodded at him, urged him to do as she asked. He kept his attention on her for a beat longer, just to make sure he had not missed something— a clue or a sign she was in trouble—then retreated. He backed into the room and closed the door.

His chest pounded.

With his back pressed against the door, he listened. The voices were inaudible still, the volume low. The pulsing in his ears overwhelmed his auditory awareness, and everything blurred together. He could not focus. He crossed the room and sat on the edge of the bed and dropped the bowling ball that still replaced his skull into a basket made of his hands.

Was he doing the right thing?

There was something about O'Reilly he did not like—whether it was his smugness or the way he attempted to hijack the two conversations they had or the way he domineered Sheila just now. Or worse, the way he subtly indicated he knew Randolph and Sheila were out late the night before—Randolph found that distressing. Who was this man?

The way Sheila acted toward him unsettled Randolph too. She was not afraid—Randolph determined as much in that regard—but he sensed there was something deeply personal she and O'Reilly shared. Their relationship had a history, maybe emotions were involved. How did the document O'Reilly had at the hospital play into it, if at all?

A knock on the door startled him, caused his shoulders to leap. The reflection against the window cast a shadow behind the curtain which gave the illusion of an intruder in the room. Randolph tensed and clutched onto the edge of the mattress. But then the shadow passed and the illusion disappeared, and he felt foolish. Another knock on the door came.

He stood and crossed the room again, peeked into the glass hole on the door. Sheila was alone. She looked down at her feet, and she knocked once more as he watched. Without hesitation, he opened the door, stood to the side, and let her in. She walked past him and closed the curtains and leaned against the window. Her breaths were heavy. Randolph kept by the door and debated whether he should flip the deadbolt.

"I'm sorry," she said.

"About what?"

"About that."

Randolph nodded. "Is everything all right?"

She looked away, did not respond.

He flipped the deadbolt. There was no harm in not. The table on the opposite wall still held the extra sleeve of cookies from the vending machine, so he went to it and grabbed them.

"You hungry?" he said. "You must be hungry." He walked toward her and handed her the sleeve.

She took it and thanked him.

Now what?

His lips parted. As they did, so did Sheila's, and her words came out first, "Can we get out of this place?" Unfledged, pleading eyes looked at him.

Without hesitation, he said, "I'll get changed."

CHAPTER THIRTEEN

He splashed water on his face and used a towel to clean his feet and combed his hair and brushed his teeth and quickly shaved, then he changed clothes. Sheila met him outside under the canopy. Her hands were empty, his question from the night before answered. The clothes on her back were the same as they had been.

Randolph returned the keys and joined Sheila in the truck. The black one from earlier was gone from the parking lot—O'Reilly's, he figured now. The west ramp was not far from the no-tell. The rain that spat against the windshield was the only sound for a while. Suddenly, there was nothing to say. Randolph merged onto the freeway and got in line with the other vehicles, hovered steadily around the posted speed limit.

"Ex-boyfriend?" he said.

"Who? Gary?"

"Am I wrong?"

"Why would you assume that?"

"Just because of the way he acted around you. And you around him. It felt like he tried to intimidate you. Yet, you looked comfortable enough, like you know him."

She looked at him.

"I was glad to see you didn't back down. Is he someone to worry about?"

"He's a pompous ass, if that's what you mean."

It was not, but he left it.

"Tell me again how you know him," she said.

He told her about their chance meeting at the hospital.

She nodded but did not comment.

"What did he mean by that?" Randolph said. "That I don't want to get involved."

Her gaze was straight ahead, disengaged. "You'd have to ask him yourself, I guess."

"What about the document he had? He said he was investigating something and wanted to ask you some questions. What's that about?"

"It's nothing."

He grunted in frustration. His face warmed and he sensed the anger boiling within him. The vagueness in which she spoke told him nothing. While her mysterious persona was attractive at first, it had worn thin. He needed answers from her—real answers, not these superficial responses that did nothing but heighten the mystery and raise more questions. He wondered if she was not who she claimed to be, though when he thought about it further, she had not claimed to be anyone. Which was the problem. He still knew nothing about her.

The mirrors were clear, so he flicked his wrist and changed lanes. Droplets of water spat against the glass and smudged underneath the squelch of the wipers. The interstate sign indicated lodging and food and gas were accessible off the next exit which was a half of a mile ahead. He merged onto the ramp as it came upon them.

"Why are you getting off?" Sheila asked.

He ignored her.

A red light turned green, then another. A half-empty municipal parking lot lingered up ahead, across from an IHOP. Randolph pulled into the lot and parked, then killed the engine.

"What are you doing?" Sheila said.

He unbuckled and faced her. "I've been patient with you. You experienced a traumatic event at the supermarket and we hardly know each other, I get it. But I've been forthcoming with you. I told you my story. Yet, I know nothing about you. I'm the one who's gone out of my way here. I could easily turn back at any time, you know, and forget this whole thing.

"Your phone's attached to you. You won't tell me who this O'Reilly guy is. You don't even have a change of clothes or a bag. You have nothing. I want answers, Sheila. You owe it to me."

He exhaled. He felt bad about going off on her, but had to let his feelings be known. Whatever their situation was, it was unfair for her to remain so closed off. He put himself out there to her, for her, and she had not reciprocated.

Sheila unbuckled and reached for the door handle and pushed the door open.

"Where are you going?"

"You want answers? Fine. But I'm starved."—she pointed to the ginormous blue sign across the street—"If you want answers, follow me."

"We dated for a while," Sheila said, referring to O'Reilly. She forked a buttery buttermilk pancake into her mouth. Syrup dripped and landed on the edge of the plate. Powdered sugar kissed her lips.

Randolph picked at a spinach omelet between sips of hot coffee, black, but hardly ate. "What happened?"

"I broke it off. It just wasn't working anymore."

He sipped.

"But that was a couple of years ago. He still pops up in my life from time to time."

"Is he dangerous?"

"I'm not sure. I mean, I don't think so. He never hit me or anything."

"What does he want with you?"

"Beats me. It was only a fling, nothing too serious."

"What did he say this morning?"

"Just that he misses me. I told him off and he left."

Randolph leaned back in the booth. The cushion squeaked against his back. The tiny potatoes on his plate were bland and the omelet was mediocre at best, but he was not hungry anyway. His stomach was still queasy from last night. "Have you informed the police?"

"About what?"

"About Gary. About him stalking you."

She laughed. "I wouldn't go that far. And no, I haven't."

"Why not? If he's bothering you."

"They wouldn't do anything anyway."

"Why do you say that?"

"He's buddy-buddy with them. I'd stand no chance."

"He told me he's not a cop. Is that true?"

"No, he's not. More like a private investigator."

"He's a PI?"

"He's like one, not exactly."

"What does that mean?"

"I really don't know. He never would share many details with me. But that was how he phrased it: 'like a private investigator.'"

It did explain a few things—the paper he showed to the receptionist at the hospital, how guarded he was when they first met, how he kept popping up into Sheila's life; he would have the means and resources to do such things. The reasons for why, though, were worrisome. Randolph thought Sheila was being naïve about it, though he did not tell her that was how he felt. She was blinded by innocence. Maybe it was an age thing. Young people trusted too much.

Randolph grabbed the mug and slid a finger through the loop. The steam billowed into his face. "So let me see if I have this straight. Your ex-boyfriend—the not exactly a private investigator, but kind of a private investigator—watches you and follows you, and yet, you're not concerned. Is that right?"

She forked a bite and let the question sit. "When you put it that way, it sounds worse than it is. He's just a lovesick puppy dog of a man, if you ask me."

Randolph considered that, but something did not add up. "Okay."

"Okay? That's your response? Okay?"

"I just don't get it, I guess."

"It's because you're sheltered, is why."

He was not amused.

She forced a smile and dropped a hand on his. "I'm just teasing you."

He smiled back because he thought that was the right thing to do. But he still did not buy it.

"Full disclosure, though," she said, "Gary does have a bit of a jealous streak."

CHAPTER FOURTEEN

Back on the interstate, the rain tapered off. Gray clouds threatened to give way to white ones and open blue sky was ahead. There was hope, it seemed, for the day to turn around. Sheila was curled up with Randolph's jacket and asleep next to him. Her rhythmic breaths offered him relaxation while he drove, an opportunity to clear his mind. The NPR radio host chatted with a guest with an east coast accent about the state of the world. Randolph did not pay much attention to the conversation, though; it was just noise. His head finally felt better.

The hum of the open road gave him time to think, without interruption, about all that had happened. He tried to analyze his conflicted emotions. The quest with Sheila had been more adventurous than he imagined. His expectations were high going in, and now he wondered if that was naïve of him. He imagined an instant connection, a tryst, something easy. While there was a flicker of romanticism between them, it was anything but easy—probably more of the spirits talking last night than anything else, if he was honest with himself—and it was a reminder of how long he had been out of the game.

The woman next to him was an enigma. For as welcoming and charming as she was when they met, a shroud of uncertainty surrounded her. It could have been a personality quirk, but if that were the case, he must decide if that was something he could live with. Yet, she seemed to enjoy his company. And for someone with her rousing cachet, that was no unimpressive feat. He wondered about that. What was it about him that attracted her? Then he wondered further if he was fair to assume she was—again, the only evidence she might have been was alcohol-driven, so it could have meant nothing. He offered her an escape from whatever troubles life had brought her—O'Reilly, for one—so maybe that was enough for her.

Was she using him?

The way she kissed him—aided by alcohol or not—was not a hoax. It felt so genuine, so real. And the way she looked into his eyes with an inferno of passion told him what he felt then was not faux. Not to mention how disappointed she acted—or embarrassed, he wondered—at his subtle rejection when he paid for two rooms instead of one. None of that was bogus. There was a spark between them. He felt it.

He looked over at her while he drove. The vulnerability in which she peacefully slept, the trust she had in him to bring her safely to their next destination—even the destination itself, which was entirely his decision—said something. When he considered all she had been through with the ex-boyfriend who still tracked her, he thought differently about the situation. Despite her downplaying it, stalking was not something to be taken lightly. Maybe the man had not done anything to harm her yet, but that did not mean he could not do so. Randolph admitted he hardly knew anything about the situation and would likely never gain a full understanding—and that was okay. The past was the past. But still, he had a pressing desire to protect her from this man.

Then this hit him: Maybe she was the one who needed him. She trusted him enough to go with him—that had to have meant something. He boasted at the idea. He longed for not only someone to care about him but also to need him. It was not about control—quite the opposite. To need someone was to be vulnerable, and to be vulnerable was to expose emotions that led to powerful connections. And that opened the door for a new love to blossom.

But it was too early for that. Much too early.

He reached across the seat and pulled the arm of his jacket over her forearm, which was uncovered. She repositioned herself and groaned but remained asleep.

He thought sexual thoughts about her as he drove, one hand in control of the wheel while the other wandered. A small bulge formed in his pants, but not enough for him to reposition himself—which was the same problem he had become accustomed to. The emotional aspect had not dissolved, nor the desires, but his body was not aligned. His prostate ached sometimes, desperate to cleanse itself. The daily struggle challenged his masculinity, made him feel like less of a man.

He would have to tell Sheila about it before long because she deserved an explanation for his behavior last night. It pained him to consider the hurt he caused her. His only hope was that her memory was foggy because of the inebriation she had experienced. Being rejected was the worst kind of pain—he knew it well. It was not that she was not desirable, because she certainly was. Far more desirable than any woman he had ever been with, frankly. He had to explain that to her, wanted to, when the right moment arose.

A single buzz interrupted his thoughts, brought him back. Then another one pulsed. He recognized it as coming from a mobile phone, but his was in the cup holder in the center console and powered off, the screen as black as midnight. Another buzz.

Sheila's phone was in her hand, her fingers wrapped around it as if it were her lifeblood. The screen lit up. Her grip was just loose enough for Randolph to pinch the leathery case around it and pull it up, which he did, enough to see the screen. His eyes darted between the flashing white lines on the pavement and the phone that dangled between his fingertips.

Guilt set it. It was unlike him to invade someone's private life this way, but his curiosity got the best of him. He tried to think of a way to justify his actions but could not. But he did not stop, either. If Sheila woke up and questioned him, he did not know what he would say to her. The name on the screen: Griff. A nickname, Randolph gathered. Unique.

The call screen disappeared and the phone turned to black, and he was relieved. He slid it back into Sheila's hand without waking her.

Another buzz quickly followed and the phone lit up again. Still Griff. Who was Griff? A friend, maybe, or a family member. Women had male friends, right? The call stopped and a new voicemail symbol popped up. Whatever Griff wanted—this acquaintance of Sheila's—must have been important. Young people did not leave voicemails these days, or so he heard.

Randolph left the phone. He did not use his much, but he knew enough to know messages often required a password or a scanned fingerprint to access. So even if he wanted to listen to the message, he would be unable to. It was better if he did not, anyhow; nothing positive could come from it. Boundaries.

He turned his attention back to the freeway, peeked at his mirrors. He heard it and felt it before he saw it—the thundering roar of the exhaust, then the rumble under his feet. Before long, the speck in his rearview grew larger and became clearly visible. It was a pickup, black and with enormous tires, and it made up ground quickly.

Randolph switched lanes to let the truck pass, except it did not. It rode his tail as if the two trucks were connected. Its horn blasted. It looked similar to the one he saw in the parking lot of the motel this morning, but he could not be certain. It could have been a coincidence—those lifted trucks were not unusual. But if it was the same, that meant one thing, and it was not good.

O'Reilly.

CHAPTER FIFTEEN

The neighbor's wi-fi password was freebyrd44—like the song, just with a y. Benji did not know what the 44 stood for. He used the network in exchange for weed. He thought it was a fair barter.

Some nights he would not sleep. The insomnia he acquired as a teenager manifested itself in times of crisis. The current situation could be described as just that—a crisis. While Shay's text offered comfort that she was all right, it still left him unsettled. The job was not done and he did not know why, and he was concerned. She refused to answer his phone calls still, or respond to his texts.

Being an insomniac was not always a burden. His body required less sleep than most, which was a gift. The amount he could accomplish in twenty-four consecutive waking hours was remarkable. Through countless hours unwrapping the depths of the dark web and reading books from the library most people would be shocked to know even existed, the skills he acquired were in abundance.

He was a techie at heart. The capabilities of a computer, if you knew how to use it, were beyond what any user's manual would ever say. He was self-taught on how to write code and disassemble and reassemble the guts of a machine, and how to use batteries and static electricity to never be without power, and how to get access to information the general public was not privy to. The capacity of one's brain was far more than short- and long-term memories.

Benji was not a genius, though his IQ was higher than average. He could not apply his skill of retaining much of the information he chose to learn to the real world and instead chose to apply it to personal endeavors. He could have gone to college if he wanted, but that did not interest him. He preferred to learn on his own accord rather than through a lecture based on an outdated textbook by a person who knew next to nothing about the topic he or she lectured about. He lacked tolerance for a classroom setting.

His workstation was his classroom. His laptop was equipped with the fastest processor on the market and storage and memory that exceeded industry standards. The retina scanner was top- notch. The fingerprint sensor was precise and foolproof. The passwords he kept were at least fifteen digits long and completely randomized—he knew them all by muscle memory. He always protected himself.

He did not trust cloud services. The wi-fi network he accessed was far from impenetrable, but it helped he used someone else's rather than his own so to stay off the radar. He wrote custom software to detect possible intruders and external threats before the off-the-shelf software could. And while he had not ever planned to use it, he installed a kill switch that would wipe all his data in minutes if the situation ever arose where that was necessary—though the time required to rebuild everything again would be devastating. But he had to be prepared for the unexpected.

His latest project was put into action—field-tested, so to speak. The design worked, as proven by the results. But the execution was flawed somehow, and he wanted to know why. He waited long enough for answers without any, so it was time he proactively investigated himself as best he could from a safe distance.

He flipped open the laptop and pressed the circle in the corner, and the machine booted up. He kept his eyes open wide and did not blink until the lens on the machine authorized entry. The command prompt popped on the screen, the cursor blinking, and Benji used the trace-route command to find the IP address he was after. Most surveillance systems used standard HTTP port numbers, and this one was no different. He knew the WAN IP address from prior research. After that, all he needed was login credentials, which was not as difficult to guess as one might imagine. The username was one of the standard administrator ones and while the password was trickier, it did not take long. It was why his passwords were so long and randomized; you never knew who was watching.

He was in.

It sounded simple, but it was not. He spent countless hours researching and had spent years honing his skills. More often than not, he was not successful. The more advanced the setup, the less likely it was he could access the network. Which was why the plan had been perfect—this system was far from technologically advanced. Which he knew.

Yet, somehow, the plan did not work.

And now, behind the security of his laptop, Benji could find out what happened.

The security footage was grainy, but the wide angle of the camera showed everything. Shay was there, in position. An exchange happened. She seemed cool. Everything appeared to be in place, the execution flawless. So what happened? He kept watching. Two minutes passed. Then the footage flashed and went to black. The rest of the video was the same.

Benji rewound the file and watched it again. Same thing. Then again. This time, he stopped the reel and clicked frame by frame and adjusted the degree of zoom. He slid close to the screen and squinted at it, the heat of which warmed his face.

It seemed unfathomable. As closely as he looked, as many angles as he tried, he could not tell what happened. The flash appeared out of nowhere as if a brilliant LED was flipped on then off. Shay was on the screen then she was not, and that was that. Vanished.

He signed out and closed the laptop and groaned. The information was not helpful. What went wrong? Cheyenne would ask again, and he would have to tell her what he knew. Which was nothing. Unless Shay reached out again or answered his calls so they could chat, he would not have any answers. Frustration came. He had the sense Shay was up to no good by straying from the plan, but he did not know how or why. Was the flash her doing?

There was only one way to find out.

He made a call.

CHAPTER SIXTEEN

Randolph gripped both hands on the steering wheel and clenched hard. The truck was still on his tail. Headlights flashed in his rearview and paralyzed his vision. He was temporarily blinded while his eyes adjusted, but he tried to remain calm—though, on the inside, he was near panic. The seat vibrated under him as the tires rattled against the rumble strips, and he worried he was too close to the guardrail. His hands and wrists and forearms shook as he struggled to regain his composure and pull the truck back onto the freeway, back to safety.

A horn blasted. Randolph leaped, blindly swung the wheel left then right. When his vision returned, he realized he was closer to the rail on the shoulder than he thought—close enough to touch it if the passenger window was cracked—and he eased back into the lane. The truck was still behind him, practically on top of them. His heart pummeled his ribcage.

Sheila stirred next to him, grunted as consciousness returned. He felt her look at him, tasted the sweat that formed on his upper lip.

"What's going on?" she asked. "You're drenched."

Was he?

He looked down at his armpit and saw the stain. "Some asshole is on my ass."

Sheila spun in her seat. "Let him pass."

"I tried."

She spun back around and looked at him. "What?"

"What, what?"

"What's wrong?"

He peeked in the rearview at the pickup which was still close but not quite as. "The truck."

"What about it?"

"I've seen it before."

"Okay." She spun again, then back.

"This morning. At the motel."

She unbuckled and spun fully this time, faced the rear window.

"Is it O'Reilly?" he asked. His eyes quickly shifted between the road and the mirror. He felt somewhat in control of the situation finally now that he had control of the vehicle. He was glad Sheila was awake.

Sheila turned back and re-clipped the lap belt. "No, it's not him."

"Are you sure? How do you know?"

"Positive."

"How do you know?"

"I just know, okay? Let him pass."

Randolph shook it off. A pull-off was up ahead. He pushed harder on the pedal, felt the roar of the acceleration rush through his toes. Getting to the pull-off felt urgent. He flicked his directional to the right and yanked the wheel in that direction. The rapid clicks seemed louder than usual, like the way the hands of a grandfather clock sang as they landed on noon in an empty house. They drowned his thoughts.

He decelerated and coasted off the road, allowed himself a second to breathe. On the freeway, the pickup flew past, its exhaust rumbling. A vocalist screamed through the speakers as though it hurt to do so. The truck disappeared into the horizon before long and took the rumble with it, the pained voice too. Randolph exhaled.

What is wrong with me?

He jammed the transmission into park, unbuckled, and slid out. He needed air. He shook himself out through the mist and ran his hand through his hair. It was not misty enough to need wipers, but still enough to dampen his fingers. He was rattled and he did not know why. Paranoid. It was clear he was out of his element.

A hand landed on his shoulder and startled him. He whipped his head around and felt the joints in his knees tense.

"Are you okay?" It was Sheila. She kept her hand on him as she stepped closer.

His shoulders dipped and his head fell.

"Do you want me to drive for a while? You look exhausted."

Maybe that was it. Maybe he was just overtired. It was a long night after all, and he was awoken earlier than he would have liked. Her driving for a while was not the worst idea he ever heard.

"I'll drive," she said.

As he walked around the truck and climbed into the passenger seat, he was touched by Sheila's tenderness. She saw something in him that he failed to himself and took control of the situation to ensure he was all right. It had been a long time since someone had done something like that for him. It was the little things that mattered the most.

"Thanks," he said as he climbed in and closed the door. The seat was warm.

"For what?"

"For noticing."

She leaned toward him and placed a hand on his forearm. She smiled at him through a yawn. No words were needed.

Back on the freeway and steadily cruising, Randolph's eyes were heavy. The lids felt weighted, and the balls behind them ached. But then he remembered something and said, "Griff called."

"Excuse me?"

"Griff. That's what your phone said."

She looked at him but kept two hands on the lower half of the wheel.

"It rang when you were asleep. I saw the name on the screen."

She nodded, moved her attention back to the road.

"A friend?"

"Something like that."

"Do you need to call him back? I think he left a message."

"It's not that important."

"Are you sure? He left a message."

"It's fine," she said. "Why don't you rest? You drove for a while. Relax."

That sounded nice. His body would not argue, he knew that. It needed more time to recover from the adventure from the night before, which felt like an eternity ago. He closed his eyes. Exhaustion suffocated him. Where they were headed, he did not care, not at the moment. He trusted Sheila to make the decision, just as she had done with him. Whatever would happen would happen, and he would adapt. Together, they would figure it out. Everything would be fine.

CHAPTER SEVENTEEN

He slept for a while. When he awoke, it was to the smooth rhythms of Dan Fogelberg's mellow harmonies. Dan told a story about the time he ran into an old girlfriend and she spilled her purse and they shared a few beers and laughed about old times. The girlfriend was warm and safe and dry, but unhappy still. It felt like a story based on reality—the harsh reality of mundane life. Dan's calmness made it seem more manageable, though. Randolph admired that.

With his eyes closed and the piano chords spectacularly easing him awake, Randolph felt relaxed. The grates on the dash blew a stream of lukewarm air on him, just the perfect amount to keep him cozy. The window near his ear hummed with a pinprick of cool outside air, which, juxtaposed with the warmth, played tricks on his body temperature—too hot one second, too cool the next. He stretched his back and sat up.

"You don't have to listen to this, you know," he said. Sheila was that much younger than he was, so he thought there was no way she would be interested in mellow classic rock.

"I like it."

Randolph laughed. "No, you don't."

Sheila smiled at him.

Before long, the snow turned into rain, but only inside the truck— outside, the sky was gray but clear, and the moon hovered just below the canopy of trees. Randolph felt wonderfully refreshed. It was five o'clock. He had slept for hours.

"Where are we?" he asked.

"Not sure, to be honest. Somewhere in eastern Nebraska. We crossed the state line some time ago."

"Thanks for driving. I guess I was exhausted."

"Don't mention it. You hungry?"

"Starved. You?"

"Let's eat."

.   .   .   .   .

They ate and they talked, got to know each other better. Sheila smiled often and laughed. They shared stories. They learned about one another's lives—their backgrounds, their interests, their hopes and dreams. Randolph learned a lot about her. She enjoyed fish and tacos, but not fish tacos—something about the combination of the smells misled her taste buds; she believed in love but not destiny, and definitely not fate; she thought friendship was important but its significance was overstated; she tried but could not understand the infatuation with The Beatles—she was more of a Doors gal herself; she disliked the taste of all green vegetables, except for Brussels sprouts, but only when doused in garlic butter; her least favorite chore was cleaning the shower. Her favorite? Singing while cleaning a pile of dishes. Also notable—and he was not sure if this was good or bad— was that she was not a fan of French onion soup. It really was a new beginning any way he sliced it.

She once broke her arm playing beach volleyball, which still ached sometimes when the temperature dipped too low; she had been to the island of Palau thrice and it was by far her favorite place on earth— nearly 350 islands made up of sandy beaches and palm trees, small populations, and beautiful, sunny skies twelve months of the year; her favorite animal was a tortoise. Worms terrified her. While she did not talk much about her childhood, she did tell him she had an uncle she looked at like a father. She did not say anything about her real parents, and Randolph did not ask. He got the sense it was a sore subject, saddening.

He shared his life with her too—about his career as a mechanical engineer, about the breakdown of his marriage, about what drove him to pursue her. She acted curious about his job—she asked probing questions he would expect someone who did not know anything about airplane engines to ask—but he got the sense she was just being polite. It was difficult to understand for someone who thought differently than he did, he knew that. But he appreciated her for trying.

About his marriage, she trod lightly. He shared more than he thought he would, but when she interlocked her fingers and rested her chin on her thumbs and looked him in the eye and nodded, he kept going. He wanted to. It was nice to talk about it, to get all the anger and resentment off his chest. The story was simple, really—boy met girl, they fell in love; boy married girl, they lived; they argued and they disagreed, but they loved until they did not; then they lived together but separately until eventually not at all—that part was still forthcoming, though very soon. Even still, Randolph had not talked it out enough, so he felt better for doing so.

Randolph reached across the table and grabbed Sheila's hand. She let him. "Thanks for listening."

"Thanks for sharing."

Silverware clanked.

"Tell me a secret," he said.

Sheila smiled, partially laughed. "What?"

"About you. Something not many people know about you."

She pulled her hand away and leaned back. Randolph picked up his glass and poured an ice cube into his mouth, embraced the chill against his tongue.

"I'd have to think about it for a minute," she said.

He shrugged with smugness, waited.

After a minute, she said, "Okay, I've got something."

Randolph leaned forward. "Let me hear it."

"I, um...wow, I'm really anxious about this. I've never told anyone this before."

Randolph folded his hands, waited her out.

She took a deep breath. "Okay, here it goes. One time—well, not just once—I had a relationship with a woman."

He waited for more, for a reaction, for anything. But nothing came. "And?"

"A sexual relationship. An affair."

Randolph's chest thumped. "Oh. Oh wow."

Sheila crinkled her forehead and covered her face with her hands.

He thought of something to say, quickly. She was embarrassed and he did not want her to be. "Well. I don't know quite what to say."

She uncovered her face, though not entirely. "I'm sorry, that was too much. Are you mortified? I shouldn't have—"

"No, it's quite all right. I'm glad you felt you could share that with me. I'm sorry I didn't know what to say. It caught me off guard is all."

"You're not upset?"

"Of course not. We all have things we regret in our pasts."

"Oh. Is that so?"

"I mean, sure. Nobody is perfect. That's life, right?"

"It's just...I never said I regret it."

Randolph let that sit for a few seconds. "I'm just going to put my foot in my mouth over here, don't mind me."

Sheila laughed. "Don't worry about it. I'm just saying, I don't regret the experience at all."

"No? Why's that?"

"Have you ever heard that women are better kissers than men?"

"I wouldn't know, but I have heard that."

"Well I would know, I do. And I can tell you, it's true. No question about it. Women are superior kissers."

He leaned forward. "Is that so?"

So did she. "Definitely. And our lips are so sensitive, so when a good kisser kisses you passionately, it flows down our bodies and sparks desire in all the right regions. It's a natural reaction. We're wired that way as mammals."

He thought about the kiss from the night before, about how he felt the tingle from lips to toes, about what it did to his body. It almost felt like it was happening again as he remembered. The restaurant suddenly felt very warm. He was hyper-focused on Sheila as if the two of them were alone, everything else on the periphery insignificant. He smelled the lust on her, and he knew what that meant.

Her lips were spread. Behind them, her tongue peeked. She leaned back. "But what do I know?"

He felt something in his gut. It twirled, spun out of control, rode waves through his system. His heart sprinted as the thoughts of him and Sheila together tormented him, teased him in every way possible. "We should get out of here. Do you want to go?"

She folded her arms but smirked. "I thought you'd never ask."

CHAPTER EIGHTEEN

"How many rooms?" It was the young man behind the counter at the motel. It could have been the same man as from the night before, the similarities striking.

Randolph looked at Sheila, who stood within an arm's reach. His bag was on the floor between them. "One room," he said as he looked back to the counter.

Sheila slipped her fingers in between his and smiled while the man smashed away on the keyboard. Randolph's stomach rolled again. The man told them the price and accepted Randolph's credit card without the least bit of hesitation. Sheila stepped closer and interlocked her arm with his, rested her chin on his shoulder. She smelled like a rose.

"Here you go, sir," the man said as he handed Randolph his card and their room keys. "Check out is ten o'clock."

Outside, the moon hung high above them, almost full. Stars littered the darkness and illuminated him and Sheila as if the universe were watching. Randolph was confident, his shoulders held high. He felt strong. Sheila's arm stayed linked until they found the room.

So much of it was similar to the no-tell from the night before, and that was to be expected. The motels off the highway were made for quick stops and a place to crash, not to impress—they did what they were supposed to, no more. The rate was reasonable. Frankly, he was surprised they accepted his credit card and were not a cash-only establishment, though he supposed it was the way of the world these days. He made a mental note to check his statement when he could to assure everything went through as expected and he was not overcharged. He dropped his bag on the carpet and stepped aside, locked the door, and connected the chain. Sheila sat on the end of the bed.

He grabbed the curtains and yanked, shutting out the starlight, blocking out the peepers. He breathed in hard and pushed it out quietly. He suddenly felt less macho, not as confident. Nerves crawled within him. His body shook. Sheila looked at him when he turned toward her, her shoulders straight and her necked craned. A fire burned in her eyes. He smiled and walked toward her, stopped in front of her. She looked up at him and bit the inside of her lip.

"What now?" she said, then she stood.

A hand landed on his hip, and it was not his own. It slid to his front, then to the back. Sheila walked around him, her fingertips swiping across his belt. His everything stiffened when her lips pressed against the back of his neck, then his collar. She smelled beautiful.

Soft, moist lips on his neck.

Soft, moist lips on his earlobe.

Soft, moist lips on his jaw.

On his cheek.

On his lips.

Then he felt her tongue on his and he tensed.

Her hands crawled south, stopped at his belt. Then she pulled away, bit her lip, and bent her knees. Her eyes stayed on his as she descended.

But he was anxious. Petrified, even, of how he would perform. He slid his hands under her armpits and stopped her, pulled her back up. The eroticism fell from her face in an instant.

"What's wrong?" she said.

"Nothing, nothing's wrong." Though that was not true. He knew it was a lie, and so did she.

"Something's wrong." —she sat back on the bed and her head fell—"Is it me? Do you not find me attractive?"

He sat next to her on the bed, which bounced just like the one the night before. "No, no. That's not it. You're the most beautiful woman I've ever met."

"Then what, Randolph? I've thrown myself at you repeatedly. What's the problem?" She was angry now.

His head dropped and he sighed. She had to know. He had to tell her before it was too late, before she was gone for good. "Okay, so here's the thing. It's a physiological thing. Well, and a psychological. Both."

"What are you talking about?"

"A few years ago, I was diagnosed with prostate cancer."

She threw her hands over her mouth and gasped. "Are you dying? Is that why you . . ."

"Oh, no, nothing like that. I'm not dying. Thousands of men live with it. More than that. It's not a death sentence. It was caught early, so it's okay. Everything is okay."

"I don't understand."

"When caught early, there may be no symptoms. I didn't have any. You know, besides....Oftentimes, the best treatment is doing nothing. My doctor's been monitoring it. If it doesn't get bigger or spread, then nothing has to be done."

"Are you impotent then?"

"Well, no, not exactly. If it gets bigger or spreads, the prostate may need to come out. If that happens, then I may or may not be. Hard to know."

"And now?"

"I have a difficult time performing, let's say that. The prostate issue has made it difficult to, well, you know."

"But you still can?"

"I haven't. Not in a while. But, in theory, yes."

"In theory?"

"There's nothing physically stopping it, per se. It can be more difficult, but not impossible. I'm told a big part of it is getting past it psychologically. To say it's caused some problems is an understatement."

"In your marriage, you mean?"

He nodded and looked away. He was embarrassed, felt ashamed. A hand landed on his thigh.

"Thank you for telling me," she said.

"I guess we both have some things of significance that have happened to us."

"Everyone has a past."

He looked at her, met her eyes. "And a future."

She smiled. More, she glowed. Her eyes lit up and welled with tears. Dimples formed on her cheeks. When she leaned in and kissed him, his eyes faded to black and his world flooded with emotion. Instead of fighting the overpowering feeling he felt, he relinquished control and swam with the waves. He wished it would last forever.

Clothes came off. First his, then hers. Her lips pressed against his clavicle then his chest then his torso while he laid on his back and let the sensations suffocate him. He squirmed and convulsed and groaned in ways he was usually uncomfortable with. But Sheila made him feel powerful and desired and therefore put him at ease. He blocked out the negativity from his mind and lived in the moment, and in doing so, his body was free. Vulnerable.

Before the night was over, every square inch of his body had been kissed, including parts that had not been in an exceptionally long time. And it was amazing.

CHAPTER NINETEEN

Benji knew a guy who knew a guy who worked in the call center for one of the major cell phone companies. In exchange for information, he arranged a drop of a top-tier grade of weed—not the best, but the next level down. Turned out, the information was incredibly useful. Precisely what he was after. It was a record of all Shay's phone activity over the last week.

It told him a lot.

Yet still not enough.

If nothing else, his suspicions about her were correct; she was up to something. The reason her apartment looked like it had not been touched in a while was because it had not. It was difficult to fathom why that might have been.

Who was Shay, really? He hardly knew her. They had dated for a while, a few months—he lost count how many. Time flew these days. They had been emotionally intimate at times, though as he thought about it further, he wondered if that was the truth. He had not been entirely truthful with her, so why should he assume she was with him?

The information he shared about himself—about his parents and his childhood and his insecurities—was true, and he had no reason not to believe Shay's stories were anything but. And the connection he felt to her—the love, dare he say—was real. Or at least he thought as much. Until now.

But the other stuff, he may have fibbed a bit. Withholding certain information was not a lie, per se, was it? He did not think so.

He pushed those thoughts aside, felt guilty for having had them. Shay would have an explanation for why she had not been home, just like before—as she said in her text message, something came up. He trusted her. Not because he wanted to, but because he had to. They were in this together. That was what being in love was about, was it not? He was still learning. An amateur.

Despite the trust, he could not wait any longer. He was well beyond anxious about what had happened, and answers were needed. Cheyenne would be back with demands, and he would need to comply. He had to think proactively if he was going to salvage this situation before it got out of hand.

He went to his bed. Underneath was the one travel bag he owned—gray and worn and stained with coffee that was not his. He bent over and wrapped his fingers around its straps, then pulled it out. He spread it on the bed and filled it with the necessities from his drawers.

Just then, there was a knock on the door. He froze at first—a natural reaction—then relaxed. His online activity was untraceable, so he had nothing to worry about. He had mastered the art of being a digital ghost, so whoever knocked was not there for that. Anything else he could easily explain away. He left the bag on the bed and went to the door.

"Guess who?" Cheyenne said when he opened it. A genuine smile enveloped her face.

"Why are you so happy?"

"Why not?"

Benji stared at her.

She came in. "I have something for you."

A black duffel bag hung from her shoulder. When she let go, it slammed to the floor like a sack of sand.

"What's the occasion?"

"I thought I'd try a different approach. Something is wrong, I can sense that. I'm not stupid, you know. So I thought if I came bearing gifts—an incentive, perhaps—we could get back on track."

He was suddenly itchy all over. Extremely uncomfortable. "Okay."

"Okay? That's it? Just okay?"

"What do you want me to say?"

He watched her eyes scan the room behind him and land on the bed.

"Going somewhere?"

He said nothing.

She stepped toward him, got really close. Her perfume burned his nostrils, sucked the air from his lungs. He was glad she could not read his mind.

"Listen to me, and listen good, because I'm only going to say this once. I know there's something you're not telling me. So you're going to tell me exactly what you're hiding, and we're going to fix it. If you hold out on me, things will get very bad for you. Do you understand?"

He lifted his chin so he was taller than her. It was important that he appeared to remain in control of the situation, even if that was not the reality.

"So tell me what's going on. Now. Or I'll castrate you."

He did. All of it. Because what other choice did he have? It was not out of fear she would actually snip off his manhood, but because she was right—he had not told her everything, and if this was to go down the way everyone needed it to go down, they had to be forthcoming with one another.

Okay, he told her most of it, not everything—some things were better kept to himself. Just like with being a digital ghost, he had to protect himself from the unexpected. Life was unpredictable. Especially his.

When he finished, Cheyenne looked neither upset nor disturbed and remained surprisingly calm. "See, that wasn't so hard now, was it?"

A hand clamped between his legs and squeezed. A jolt of anguish blasted through his gut.

"Speaking of not being so hard." She smiled at him and twisted before eventually releasing him.

He groaned as he keeled forward.

Cheyenne reached down and grabbed the duffel she brought in, slipped her shoulder through the straps. "Get your shit, come on."

He looked up through the agony. "Where are we going?"

She looked at him like he was a fool, the way a mother might scold a child who should know better. "Where do you think?"

CHAPTER TWENTY

For the first time in longer than he could remember, he came last night. Not just a drip or a partial ejaculation, but a full release—an explosion, a cleansing. Rapture. It had been so long, he forgot how euphoric the experience was. At the moment, he thought he was going to detonate with the buildup of the ecstasy. As for Sheila, he was officially head over heels for her. She seemed satisfied.

His body ached. He used muscles he forgot he had last night, but the soreness that engulfed him was more than welcomed; it was celebrated. It reminded him he was still alive, still a man with testosterone flowing through his veins, still desirable. He still had it. It changed his outlook on what he conceded his life to now be. Psychologically, it changed everything. There was still a sliver of hope for him to be the man he once was, for the man he longed to be. His confidence was back.

He rolled over and leaned on his elbow and slid a palm under his chin to support himself. Sheila looked like an angel next to him, unclothed with the white sheet tucked against her jaw. A small pillow formed a cocoon basket around her skull. Sunlight peeked through the curtain and shone against her buttery complexion, reflected against the carpet of freckles that trickled around her shoulder like skin art. She breathed easily, happily. Randolph smiled at the sleeping beauty. He felt amazing.

Something real was forming between them. He had been in love more than a few times, and he knew the feeling well. But he also knew infatuation came first, as did lust. Both were dangerous. He considered himself to be a strong-willed man, so he was determined not to make impulsive decisions about anything significant until his feelings settled. That was the responsible thing to do.

But damn, Sheila.

He wanted her again. The bitterness of the salt from her skin on his tongue was still fresh, and he craved more. The prick of her nails against his back stung like it was happening all over again. He heard the fervor in her voice, imagined the darkness that surrounded them the night before. He felt himself harden.

He closed his eyes and kept his hands off, daydreamed about her.

When he opened them, Sheila was awake and focused on her phone. He was not sure how much time had passed, but he was now as limp as a deflated balloon. She saw him and rolled over, placed her phone face down on the end table. The sheet pulled away when she did and exposed her nakedness. He looked without hesitation.

She turned back and smiled at him, then slid her body in close and snuggled against him. Her skin was as warm as wool, and he draped his arm around her shoulder as if it were normal. She smelled like perfection.

"Morning," she said with her face buried in his chest.

"Morning. Sheila, last night was—"

"Amazing, I know." She pulled her neck away and looked up at him. She beamed.

"I feel like I should be thanking you."

"Thanking me? For what?"

"For understanding and for helping me break through the wall I apparently had up."

She did not respond, just gazed into his eyes.

It felt like the perfect moment to tell her how he felt about her, about the things that were happening within him. But he remembered his commitment to himself and stopped. It was too soon. Much too soon. They ogled at each other in silence for a while instead.

Eventually, they got up and showered and dressed and turned their key into the front desk just minutes before his card would be charged for another night. The same man from the night before offered them a map of the local area, made some recommendations on where to fuel up their bodies. There was a shopping center nearby which had something for everyone, he said. After they ate and filled the truck's gas tank, they went there and shopped. Randolph insisted. Sheila's clothes were creased and dirty and in need of washing, and her phone's battery was nearly dead.

After, they found a laundromat. The patrons around them stared as they laughed and covered each other while they changed clothes in front of the machines. Sheila slipped on the new and washed the old; Randolph changed into one of the outfits he brought from home. A gray-haired woman stood in the corner and eyeballed them, crossed her arms and shook her head. A mother covered her young son's eyes and pulled his head into her chest as if seeing a fellow human being in their underwear was the most traumatic event that could happen in the child's life. If nothing else, they made the best of the mundane activity, successfully killed the time it took to complete the spin cycle and a quick tumble dry. Randolph immensely enjoyed her company and could not have cared less about the patrons who disapproved, which was a new experience for him.

By late afternoon, exhaustion set in after another half-day on the road, and the sun began to set. The exhaustion was more than about another day of driving, but rather what was to come. With an early start, they could be in Wyoming tomorrow. With that meant the end of their journey, or at least an arrival to their unspecified destination. Further decisions would have to be made then. At the time he proposed it, it felt like an unobtainable goal, a fantasy land they would fail to reach. Maybe he doubted himself that he would actually go through with it.

Yet, there they were. One day away.

A sign welcomed them to Valentine, Nebraska. It felt appropriate, like fate. Sheila must have felt that way too—minus the fate part—because she slipped her fingers into his and squeezed. Valentine for lovers. Life was good.

Greenery surrounded them, along with miles and miles of flat, paved roads. Other vehicles were few and far in between. Farmland lined the terrain. Corn stalks and rolled-up hay bales stood taller than people. A handful of cattle grazed in the pasture in the distance. The smell of manure crept its way into the cabin through the air vents to the point where they closed them and the windows. A gigantic tractor inched slowly along the side of the road.

They finally came upon civilization. Or at least Valentine's version of it. Main Street stretched no more than a mile. First, a Baptist church with a farmer's porch shared a tiny lot with a mom-and-pop hardware store, which had a handwritten sign on the lawn offering a steep discount on overstocked lawnmowers. Across the street, the fire station housed a single garage. Further down the strip, the sign above the pharmacy lacked complete illumination, the remaining letters forming a word that was not actually one. A corner store looked decrepit with cracked paint and a splintered front window, but promised beer and cigs for the locals. It was all about the important things, the essentials.

Randolph pulled into the lot of a garage that offered full-service. Refueling was not necessary, but directions were. The wireless network had been spotty for a while, so Google Maps was no help. They were lost. A bell rang when Randolph drove over the rubber hose that strung across the pavement. He held his finger against the button on his door and his window descended, and he waited. Sheila smiled at him.

Another bell rang. He peeked in the rearview and saw a man walking toward them, a slight limp in his step. Oil stained what remained of his overalls. The man arrived at the window and leaned in, twirled a toothpick between his lips. Black holes filled his mouth where teeth should have been. His hands were colored similarly.

"Whatcha need?" the man said.

"Hi there."

"How much you need?"

"Oh, we don't need fuel, actually. Just directions."

"How much?"

"As I said, we—"

"You ain't from around here, are ya?"

"No, in fact, we're not." —Randolph offered his friendliest smile— "Which is why, you know, the directions."

"How much?"

Randolph shot Sheila a look as if to ask what he was missing. She shrugged. A few seconds passed, then she leaned forward and reached into her back pocket, came out with a crinkled ten-dollar bill. She held it out, offered it to toothpick. He took it and disappeared.

Randolph felt the clunk of the gas nozzle before he heard it. He cringed as the liquid sloshed in the tank, thought only the worst thoughts about its impact on the truck's engine. Was the grade of fuel up to snuff in these parts? Where did it even come from? It was not long before the nozzle clicked, which was a relief. The machine read nine dollars even.

Toothpick reappeared at the window and leaned against it. He spat a brown liquid at his feet. The toothpick twirled between his triangular teeth. Randolph thought about asking for the change but reconsidered.

"About those directions," Randolph said.

"What about 'em?"

"Is there anywhere we crash around here? Maybe get a bite to eat?"

The man looked between them and grinned, then spat again. The blackness in his mouth reminded Randolph of charcoal.

"There," he said, and pointed straight ahead.

Randolph turned and looked and saw it.

A Comfort Inn.

How about that?

"Thanks," he said to toothpick, who backed away from the truck and held up a hand. Randolph drove off without another word. He could not have been happier to get them out of there.

CHAPTER TWENTY-ONE

It was morning. Glorious morning. His phone rang, but he could not find it twisted in the sheets with their bodies. He could not recall when he had it last or where he left it. Sheila was asleep next to him, breathing softly, unresponsive to the jingle. He slid out of bed and followed the sound, which led him to his bag on the floor near the bed. Dirty clothes were strewn everywhere—his and hers. Their shoes were nowhere to be found. It was a wild night. He bent over and unzipped the bag and shuffled through the pile. The volume of the jingle increased as he did. He grabbed it when he found it and blinked away the morning blur. But the name on the screen stayed as it appeared the first time, and he knew it could not have been good. He picked up.

"Patricia?"

"Where have you been? Where are you?"

"I could ask you the same thing."

"When will you be back?"

He thought about it. "Not sure."

Patricia grunted through the phone. He knew her eyes were rolling. "Do you know what today is?"

He felt for his watch but was not wearing it. "Should I?"

"The mortgage is due."

"I'm surprised you know that."

"I'm not stupid."

"Never said you were."

A brief silence.

"Well?" she said.

"Well, what?"

"Are you going to pay it?"

"No, I don't think so."

"Excuse me?"

"It's about time you took some responsibility for your life, don't you think? Why don't you pay it?"

"With what money, Randolph?"

"That's part of independence, darling. Figure it out."

"Don't be an asshole. What has gotten into you?"

He looked over his shoulder. Sheila rolled over, snuggled close to the comforter. She looked peaceful and content. Happy. That was something he had forgotten all about—the look of happiness. He went into the bathroom and pulled the robe off the hook on the door, admired his old but not too old yet reasonably fit body for his age in the mirror, then crossed the room and slipped onto the porch. The hotel overlooked the flatlands, so there was not much to see. The service station with the creepy toothpick of a man lurked on the other side of the swamp in the field. Randolph's stomach growled as he inhaled the morning and tossed the robe over his bare shoulders. His prostate ached.

"Are you there?" Patricia said into his ear.

"I'm here. What?"

"Are you listening to me?"

He was not, but she kept talking anyway.

"Listen," he said, cutting her off, "I've been thinking. About the divorce. I think now's a good time."

Silence on the other end.

"Patricia?"

"What?"

"Did you hear what I said?"

"I thought you didn't want it?"

"That was before."

"And now?"

"Did I not just say I'd sign?"

More silence.

"Do you still have the paperwork for me?" he asked.

"Well, yes—"

"Good then. I'll call Larry and have him contact your lawyer, get it all figured out."—Larry was his attorney—"Same guy?"

"Yes."

Patricia seemed off. Not as confrontational as usual, less angry. It was almost as if she no longer wanted the divorce, despite her years of badgering about it. It must have been the surprise of it, finally getting what she wanted. Reaching the pinnacle was oftentimes less gratifying than the journey itself; he wondered if that was what was happening to her.

"I've got a connection at the courthouse," he said. "I've spoken to him about this in the past, and he said there's a way to have this expedited so we can both move on as quickly as possible. Shouldn't take much longer than a few weeks, I'm told, depending on how many cases are ongoing."

"Okay."

She was definitely off. "What? What is it?"

"Nothing."

"It's not nothing, Patricia. We've been married for thirty-two years; I know when something's bothering you. What is it?"

"Thirty-one."

"Wrong. Maxwell was born the same year we hit the thirty-year mark. I remember it well. And he's two now."

"Fine."

Score one for Randolph.

"So, tell me," he said. "What is it?"

"Well, I wasn't going to tell you like this. But you've left me no choice."

He waited.

"Don't you think you might want to handle your other legal matters first? One thing at a time, as they say."

What was she talking about?

"What are you talking about?"

"I take it you haven't heard. I'm surprised Larry hasn't called you."

"What? What is it?"

"The supermarket. The explosion. There's video footage of what happened."

"And?"

"And you were there."

"So were hundreds of other people. So what?"

"That's not what the police are saying."

His chest pounded with a dash of adrenaline. "What are they saying?"

"That you're involved. With that woman you're with."

Patricia's verbal fist knocked the wind straight out of him. He felt weak and out of breath and leaned against the rail for support. How did she know who he was with?

"You still there?" she said.

"I'm here."

"You can do whatever you want, but if it were me in this situation, I'd make this priority number one."

His chest felt tight. He sucked deep breaths and exhaled to fight the pain, but he managed to keep it together long enough to say, "This is important, Patricia." —the pain twisted, but he fought back; he would not let her hear him struggle—"What are the police saying?"

She sighed an exasperated sigh. "Are you not hearing what I'm saying to you? If you just listened to—"

"Patricia!"

"They're saying you're a suspect! Is that clear enough for you? Get your shit together, Randolph. Clean this up. I don't want this embarrassment in my life. I've got a reputation to live up to, you know."

She disconnected.

CHAPTER TWENTY-TWO

He pulled the phone away from his ear and stood back, tried to catch his breath.

What just happened?

None of it made sense. Why would Patricia call him, and why would she care who he was with? She seemed off, hurt that he had moved on. Was that it? Sometimes the grass was not always greener on the other side, so maybe that realization hit her. Maybe she realized watering their own grass was a better path forward than the one she thought she desperately wanted. But it was too late for that. He had moved on. And dare he say it, his feelings for Sheila were real.

But then he considered something else. He made a promise to himself to not make an emotional judgment until his feelings settled. Did he fail himself by not following through with the boundaries he set? Was it too soon?

Nonsense.

The heart wanted what the heart wanted. When it knew, it knew.

Patricia wanted out for longer than he could remember. If it took feeling desirable again for him to find the courage to let it happen, to let, what they once had, go. Then so be it. If it failed to work out with Sheila, then it did. It changed nothing between him and Patricia. That phase of his life was over.

That was before.

Now was after.

Sheila.

Was he wrong about her? What if what Patricia said was true? Patricia did have a motive to muddle his psyche—jealousy, perhaps, or spite—and she knew the ways to rattle him. So that had to be considered. But why would she say anything at all? That was the most difficult part to justify. It was as if she wanted to delay the divorce or was having second thoughts, which seemed entirely out of character for the new version of herself he still did not recognize. If there were dots to connect, he failed to do so.

He felt settled now, breathed easier. His toes were cold against the wooden panels beneath his feet, so it was time to go back in. He would confront Sheila, though he did not know how. He wanted to tread lightly.

He leaped backward and squeezed the phone in his hand, felt a pinch on his skin. Sheila stood on the other side of the glass with the afghan from the bed draped over her shoulders like a shawl. Her eyes pierced his like a scythe, and he felt the fire. But her lips were parted and her teeth showed, and the indents in her cheeks greeted him.

The door slid open. Sheila's hand grasped the frame and she pushed herself past the threshold and stepped toward him. He relaxed his grip and sunk back into normalcy.

"Hey," she said.

"Hi."

"Everything okay out here?"

He nodded and lifted his phone. "Phone call."

"Anything important?"

Here it was: the fork. Decision time. He could shrug it off and move on, make his own judgment and keep it to himself. Or he could tell her who it was on the phone and what she said and respond accordingly, based on what Sheila's reaction might be.

"Actually," he said, "that was Patricia."

She looked at him blankly.

"My wife."

Her face fell. "Oh."

She looked hurt. Or disappointed. Or heartbroken. Sad.

"We had some details to discuss about the divorce, that's all."—she perked up—"Everything's fine. It'll be over soon."

She smiled and walked toward him, rested her head against his shoulder. He wrapped his arm around her and pulled her close, the smell of sweet romance very much in the air.

"Did she have anything else to say?"

He pulled her tighter, planted his lips on her forehead. "No, nothing important. That was it."

· · ·

They went back inside, made up the bed, and showered. Packed their things. She carried a bag now, full of a clean new wardrobe, thanks to their shopping trip and shenanigans at the laundromat the day before. It was nice to see her in something new, something fresh. One thing he noticed: She looked amazing in anything and everything she wore. Why she was with him still baffled him beyond belief.

The morning was early enough to partake in the continental breakfast the hotel offered, so they did. Stale muffins and cold coffee and fresh fruit, though not much of it. The toaster worked to warm a slice of white toast from the loaf, but it smelled of burned raisins and ash. They pieced together enough to fill their bellies for a few hours at least. For the price of the room, it was about as satisfying as he expected.

Check-out was ten o'clock, which came fast. By ten past, they were in the parking lot and loaded into the truck and already sluggish. He wondered what their next move was. They could be in Wyoming by dark, but then what? Anxiety flooded him at the thought, about what they would do, where they would stay. What were they doing? They could not hop from cheap motel to mediocre hotel and back for the rest of their lives. They needed a structured plan.

The excitement had worn off—not about Sheila; the fondness for her grew by the day, but of the journey. Headaches lingered because he was so liquored up. He was exhausted. He wanted to be home—not home in the sense of Cedar Rapids, Iowa, but rather in the sense of a place to lay down roots. Permanence. It was not clear if Sheila wanted the same thing.

"You okay?" she asked. She smiled at him, but he saw the concern in her eyes, behind the facade. He would have loved to know what was on her mind.

"I'm okay."

"Penny for your thoughts."

He looked down and smiled. The ignition key was in his hand, which rested on his knee. He turned his hips so he faced Sheila, then he looked up. "Can we be direct with each other?"

Her face dropped. "I thought we were."

"What happened at the supermarket?"

She hesitated. More so, she did not respond. Her mouth opened as if she were about to speak, but she stopped. He waited, tried not to analyze her silence and open his mind to all the possibilities that may follow.

"I don't know what happened," she said.

He was disappointed. While he was not convinced it was a lie, he felt as if she held something back. It was just a hunch, though. Nothing she had said or done made him believe otherwise.

"I don't remember much. You came, we chatted, you left. Another customer came in line, who I helped. Next thing I knew, I was in the hospital. What happened in between...it's blackness."

He studied her face, kept his neutral. For him, it was difficult to tell if someone was being dishonest or not. Tears welled in Sheila's eyes as she relived the trauma, and he thought it looked genuine. But what did he know? He was just an engineer; he knew nothing about the psychological aspect of people and if faking such a thing was even possible. All he had was his instincts, and those told him Sheila was an honest soul.

"I'm sorry," she said as she wiped a tear away. She took a moment to regain her composure and shake off the emotion. When she did, she looked him in the eye and said, "Why do you ask?"

He felt terrible, like he wronged her. It was a sensitive topic because it was still so fresh in her mind. It must have been traumatic for her, being inside when the supermarket exploded. He could not understand what that must have been like. The guilt he felt about his lack of sensitivity weighed heavily on him.

"I'm sure it's nothing," he said, "but I was told there's a tape. Footage."

"Okay. And?"

And what? Did he want to tell her? He had no choice. "And the police think we had something to do with it."

She pushed away, leaned against the door. She studied his face, sized him up. He did not like the look in her eye; he felt judged by her.

"But as I said, that could just be hearsay."

"Who told you this?"

"Patricia."

She relaxed, then smiled. "Ah-ha. That makes sense now."

"What does?"

"You. Since you talked to your wife this morning, you've been off."

"Well, I—"

"Hold on a second."

"What?"

"Did you say 'we'? The police think we had something to do with it? As in you and me?"

"That's what I was told, yes."

"They know we're together then. How do they know?"

"I was wondering the same thing myself."

Sheila did not respond. She looked around the cab, frantic. She spun around and fumbled in the back, unzipped her bag. When she turned back around, her phone was in her hand. It shook as she pressed her finger on the screen harder than needed.

"What are you doing?" Randolph asked. He was alarmed by her reaction, but he did not know what about.

She toyed with the phone for another minute before tossing it on the back seat. "Damn."

"What? What's the matter?"

"I was hoping for a wi-fi network to connect to, but nothing."

"Still no network?"

"I tried. Still nothing."

He retrieved his phone and found the same thing. The network data quality was very poor and had been for quite some time.

They sat in silence.

"What were you looking for anyway?" he said.

"I was going to try and see if it was online. If it was on the news or something."

Good idea. He was embarrassed he had not thought of it himself.

Her eyes lit up. It was like a lightbulb—an idea that sparked in real time. Before he could ask what she was thinking, she whipped around again and grabbed the phone from the rear seat. She pried the back of the phone case off, removed the battery, and pulled out a tiny computer board. Randolph knew nothing about any of that stuff.

She tossed the board on the dashboard and dropped her phone into the cup holder. "It makes perfect sense."

"What?"

She faced him. "Gary."

O'Reilly! Right!

"It must be him," she said. "How else would anyone know we're together? He saw us together."

Randolph thought about it. It made sense, except for one thing. "But what about the footage?"

"Don't you see! He's a private investigator, right?"

"You said he was like a private investigator."

"Don't parse my words. That's what he told me. But look, he has connections, okay? Good ones. Men in uniform. Government officials. He could have easily got his hands on that tape."

"Say he did, what are you suggesting?"

"He found out we were together. He's infatuated with me still, right? He got jealous. So he looked you up."

"How, though?"

"You told him your name, didn't you? He greeted you by name. Cross-check that with your license plate, and easy. It's not hard to find someone."

"I still don't understand. What does one thing have to do with the other?"

She dropped a hand on his, captured his focus. "Gary got the tape and tracked me down at the hospital, just like you did. Then he followed us. Then he looked into you, found out you were married, contacted your wife. Do you think it's a coincidence she called you?"

He considered that. It made sense.

"He thought he'd use her to drive him back to me."

He remembered the phone call. *Where are you?* "My God. I bet you're right."

"We must have lost him somewhere. The cell service has been spotty."

"You think it's the phone?"

"What else? He's a psycho, I'm telling you. You can track someone's SIM card so easily. Too easily."

That must have been what she removed from her phone. The SIM card. The term was familiar.

Then a gasp, and an, "Oh no!"

"What?"

Sheila wrapped both hands around his wrist and squeezed. He winced and tried to pull away, but she quickly released him before he had to fight to save it.

"He might be here," she said. "Or close. Who knows when we lost him? Maybe we didn't."

"We haven't seen anybody. We would have seen him again by now."

She shook her head. "You don't know him like I do. This guy, he's a fucking lunatic, okay?"

He realized his heart was beating quickly, jolted with nervous energy.

"Trust me on this."

"Okay, I trust you. What do we do?"

"We have to leave. And we have to leave now."

"And go where?"

"Doesn't matter. Anywhere but here."—she reached over her shoulder and grabbed the seat belt and buckled in—"Please, can we just go?"

He looked at her, peered deep into her eyes. There was fear there, and panic. She was scared of this man. Petrified. Randolph wondered if that meant he should be too, but he was not. All he wanted to do was protect her, to keep her safe. Whatever that took. If that meant they had to leave right away, then leave was what they would do.

"Okay," he said. "We can go."

CHAPTER TWENTY-THREE

The amazing thing about being a digital ghost, about doing all his work from behind the protection of a firewall and several aliases, was Benji had a clean record. Aside from a speeding ticket a few years back and a handful of parking tickets, he was as clean as a whistle. An upstanding citizen. Which meant flying using his real identification was not only possible but also much safer.

He and Cheyenne waited in line and bought tickets at the counter at the airport. Their flight boarded an hour later. Benji's gray, coffee-stained bag contained all he needed—and nothing illegal; he left most of the weed at home. He was not proud of how he smuggled the ounce or two past the security gate, but it was what it was. He was just an ordinary guy taking a leisurely flight across the country. Nothing to see here.

Cheyenne sat in the chair next to him at the gate. Despite a lengthy, loud, embarrassing disagreement with the ticket agent, her oversize duffel bag was too large to be carried on. Cheyenne belittled the agent, spewed obscenities, and demanded to have a conversation with the manager about the situation which happened. The manager was friendly but not accommodating, and if Cheyenne wanted to board, she must check the bag. No exceptions. The manager promised to personally take the bag to the tarmac and see to it with her own eyes that the bag was safely secured underneath the airplane.

Liar.

But Cheyenne took the bait—she had no choice. Not unless she wanted to stay back, which Benji knew she did not. And so she radiated with hatred next to him while they waited, angry at the world for not accommodating her every desire. A much smaller carry-on sat on her lap, her knuckles white around it. Outside the window, the plane was being fueled. The bags were already secured beneath, the airstairs gone.

Cheyenne huffed and stood, walked away without saying a word. It made no difference to Benji. She would either get over herself or would not, and he put her out of his mind. He thought instead about what lie ahead. It was not clear to him what they might find, if anything.

Before long, Cheyenne returned with a hot coffee and a cooler head, and she sat back down and sipped. Their knees touched but their eyes did not meet. A crowd filled in around them—folks with bags over their shoulders; folks with luggage on wheels; folks with packs on their backs. There were solo riders and vacationing couples and families who regretted bringing their young, obnoxious toddlers along to ruin their vacation but had no choice but to. It reminded Benji to always wear a rubber. Always. A line of these people formed near the gate. VIPs were let through.

Their group was called and they stood, made their way to the back of the existing but moving line. He waited behind Cheyenne, who tied her hair into a ponytail. The strap of his bag dug into his shoulder and yanked on the collar of his shirt, so he readjusted. As he did, a voice came from behind him, a man's.

"Excuse me," the man said.

Benji turned toward the voice and the man.

"Are you Benjamin Griffin?"

"Who's asking?"

"Come with me, please."

Benji turned to Cheyenne, but she ignored him, looked away. Bitch. Hers were the only eyes not on him at the gate.

"Come with me, before I force you."

He did not know what to say or do, so he obliged. The man was not dressed like a police officer and did not offer a badge or his name or his credentials. His button-down was pressed and tucked into his slacks, and he stood taller and more well-built, fuller, than Benji was. Though he would never outwardly admit it, Benji was intimidated.

The man led him down the corridor, through the crowd, and into a private room through a door no one knew existed, despite being unhidden. A conference room or an interrogation room meant for TSA agents. There was a long table without chairs and plain, undecorated walls. Windowless. Stuffy. Sweat formed on Benji's neck.

"So, Benjamin—"

"Let me stop you right there. Nobody calls me Benjamin except my mom. It's Benji."

"Fine. Benji. Tell me, what—"

"Who are you?"

"That's not important right now."

Benji disagreed. He stepped toward the door and stretched for the handle, but the man held a hand up against Benji's chest and stopped him. Benji did not like it.

"Don't touch me."

The man removed his hand.

"Now move. Please. I'm leaving."

"I can't let you do that."

"Are you a cop?"

"No."

"Are you security?"

"No."

"Do you work for an airline?"

"No."

"Then I'm leaving."

"I know who you are."

Benji froze. He was not sure what that meant, what the context was.

"And I know what you're doing, what you've done."

Not good.

"Look, man. I'm not hurting anyone. It's just a little grass. Half the states in—"

"I don't care about that. That's not what I'm talking about."

"Oh. Well, I think you have the wrong guy. I've done nothing wrong."

There was a long silence. The man towered over Benji, folded his arms, flexed his jaw. Benji breathed deeply but shallowly, tried to ground himself, to stay calm and relaxed, to not give in. He braced for the beating he was certain to receive.

"Who's that woman you're with?" the man said.

"Nobody."

"Nobody?"

"Just a friend. We fuck sometimes, that's it."

"Do you fuck all your friends?"

Benji shifted his weight and sighed, looked at the clock and watched as the hands ticked. "What do you want, man? I'm going to miss my flight."

"I want to know why you were looking at the security footage of the supermarket explosion in Cedar Rapids from earlier this week."

Benji stiffened, felt his throat parch.

The man stood and waited, flexed his jaw again.

"Who are you?" Benji said.

"Why were you looking at the tapes?"

"Who the fuck are you?"

The man stepped closer, looked down at him. Benji smelled what he thought was whiskey on his breath, but it also could have been Listerine.

"I won't ask again."

"I wasn't."

Two hands grabbed Benji's collar and shoved him against the wall. Rage boiled in the man's eyes as he pressed against Benji's chest with what must have been all his might. The veins in his neck stuck out like tripwires ready to snatch a perp. Benji's back cracked as he was flattened against the wall like a pancake. A *mancake*.

"What the fuck, man!"

"I know you were looking, so don't bullshit me! Now I want to know why."

"She's my girlfriend, okay? That's why!"

The man released Benji's collar and stepped back. Confusion swept over his face. "Who's your girlfriend?"

"She's one of the cashiers. I hadn't heard from her after the explosion, so I was checking on her. That's all, man. I swear."

The man reached into his hip pocket and fished around for something, scrunched his forehead. Panic rose within Benji. He eyed the door, thought about making a beeline for it, wondered if he could make it before getting shot. What would he do if he did make it, where would he go? Chaos would ensue if he made a scene at the airport. He would be put on a watch list—or worse, blacklisted. The last thing he needed was attention from the federal government.

He had to wait and react, do nothing.

If this man, whoever he was, was able to track his activity online, Benji questioned if he was not as smart as he thought he was. Or as careful. What went wrong? He followed all the standard protocols for invisibility. Obviously, as proven by his current situation, he needed to step up his game, refresh his skills. Maybe he had gotten complacent.

The man pulled out something compact and dark, thrust it in Benji's direction. He flinched but stayed cool, then relaxed once he saw what it was. A phone, just a phone. It had a video queued up.

"Which one is your girlfriend?" the man said.

Benji took the device and watched the screen. His hands trembled, but he squeezed the phone tightly so the man would not notice—he could not, would not, show fear; that would give the man the upper hand. The footage on the screen was the same he saw before—the grainy overhead view, the wide angle. Shay was there, just like before. Despite the grain, she was still beautiful. Just stunning.

"There," he said. "That's her."

The man took the phone back and paused the feed. He pointed to the woman on the screen, to Shay. "That's your girlfriend?"

"That's her."

The man grinned, then smiled. "I'll be damned."—he looked up and at Benji—"Well then, my friend. Benji. I think we may be able to help each other out here."

CHAPTER TWENTY-FOUR

Despite Wyoming being so close, they could not go there. Not anymore. Too predictable. It was disappointing, yes, but he was not bitter. Sheila needed him right now, so he had to react appropriately. Route 20 would bring them there, to the border of Wyoming, to nowhere in particular. But they detoured south on Route 83 instead, the final destination just as unknown as before. He hoped the sudden change in direction would throw off the tail.

O'Reilly.

Sheila was rattled. Whatever he did to her in the past left a lasting impact, and despite the separation between them, he still had control over her. Whether Sheila would admit it was another matter—her stubbornness was not hard to identify. But O'Reilly knew and actively took advantage of it. And now, Randolph knew too. Though he did not know what to make of it. Or worse, what to do about it.

Sheila sat quietly and fidgeted. Her phone was still off and in a cup holder in the center console. The chip she removed bounced around beneath it each time the truck abruptly changed lanes or veered around a corner. Randolph heard his thoughts as if they were spoken aloud.

While the need to know irked him, he would not ask Sheila for more information about O'Reilly. If she wanted to tell him, she would. He considered the idea that she wanted to forget about that time in her life, so to bring it up would be insensitive—Randolph could empathize with that desire. As much as he wanted to know everything, it ultimately did not matter. Everyone had a past; the past was where it should be left.

Speaking of the past, how about Patricia? What was that all about? Everything about her—her persona, her vibe, her sudden opinion change about the timing of the divorce—was so strange and unlike her. Though admittedly, he hardly knew who she was anymore. Some days it depressed him to remember who she used to be, of what they used to have. But then he thought about all the events that happened over thirty-two years and wondered where they went wrong. How much of it was his doing, he would never know. He would not ask her because it did not matter anymore. The past was the past, right? Everyone had one; that was where it should stay.

What about the tape? Was it true? He still had not heard from Larry—his attorney—which he would have by now if something was up. Bizarre.

The road was clear. Traffic was moving, weather a non-issue. A good travel day. Randolph took his free hand and felt for his phone, grabbed it from the console. The network was still poor.

"You okay?" he asked Sheila, who nodded without words. He slid his hand across her leg, to send his love, then pulled away. Further dialogue felt both unnecessary and inappropriate. The moment called for nothingness. Self-reflection.

After several miles, they returned to civilization—not Valentine's version of it, but actual civilization. More vehicles to count and vibrant billboards along the interstate and road signs indicating food and gasoline and lodging options were off the exits. It was a relief. Randolph's phone chirped with notifications and alerts and missed calls as the network reconnected. And a voicemail. He picked up the phone and thumbed the screen, kept an eye on the road. He navigated to the voicemail and pressed play. Listened.

"What is it?" Sheila said shortly after the message began. Apparently, his expression told a story that did not require a verbal response to indicate something was wrong.

"I need to make a phone call."

"Is everything okay?"

"No. Not exactly."

He flicked his wrist to engage the directional and pulled off at the nearest rest area. He unbuckled and stepped out, left the truck running. He found the number in his contact list and dialed it, waited for Herm to pick up. He did.

"Randolph?"

"Herm, I got your message. What's going on?"

"I was looking through your accounts earlier—routine check-up, you know?—and I saw something strange. So I called you right away."

"What did you find?"

"Did you authorize another withdrawal from the safety account? It's your money, but you asked me to flag this account."

"That's right, thanks for monitoring it. And to answer your question—no, I didn't."

"Is everything all right? That makes two large sums in a short time."

"I haven't touched this account. You know I wouldn't."

"Right. Which is why it seemed off."

Randolph's stomach twisted with dread. He had a bad feeling about what might come next. "How much are we talking?"

"Twenty grand."

The wind was sucked out of him. A gut punch. His worst nightmare. "Uh, okay. Which one was that?"

"Both."

"Twenty grand total, then?"

"Afraid not. Each."

Each!

He had to think. And not panic. There had to have been an explanation. It was a mistake, a clerical error. That was all. Nothing to worry about.

"Randolph?"

"I'm here. Just thinking."

"I feel terrible. I feel like this is on me. I was out of town with the family for a couple of weeks. Then by the time—"

"It's not your fault, Herm. Let's just figure it out. What do you know?"

"Thank you." —he sounded relieved—"Two weeks ago there was a withdrawal. I was out of town then. Then two days ago another one, same amount."

"Am I being robbed?"

"No."

"You're sure?"

"I am. I looked into it. The money, both times, was taken out in cash."

"What? That's not possible."

"It was Patricia. She's on the account too. And as a joint account holder—"

"I get it."

Silence.

"Are you sure you're okay?" Herm said. He sounded concerned. Like a friend.

"It's a long story."

"I understand."

"Can we stop her from taking more?"

"To remove her from the account, you'll both need to come in and sign a few things."

Damn.

"What if that's not a possibility right now?"

"I could freeze your account, but it'll only be temporary. I can flag it under suspicious activity."

"Let's do that. How long will that last?"

"Hard to say. Out of my control, I'm afraid."

Randolph nodded, though he knew Herm could not see. "Okay, okay. That gives me some time to figure out what's going on."

"I must warn you, though. If I freeze the account, you'll be unable to access any of the funds either. I don't know what you've got going on, but if that will be a problem—"

"It's not."

"Well good. I'll set that up when we hang up. If you need anything, Randolph, on or off the record, you can call me. You know that, right?"

"Thank you. I mean that."

"Take care now."

They hung up.

Patricia.

What was she up to now? First her awkward phone call, now this. He did not know what to believe, if what she said was fact or fiction. But he had a way to find out.

He quickly scrolled through his phone and made another call. Larry would know what was up.

"Hello?"

"Larry, it's Randolph."

"I see that. What can I do for you?"

"Fine thanks."

Larry was a bit of a prick, but that was why Randolph paid him. For matters where an attorney may or may not be necessary, he knew he could count on direct, unfiltered, unbiased advice. Not free, though; $200 an hour, one hour minimum. Worth it? Usually not, but sometimes yes. He had gotten Randolph out of a pickle or two over the years—nothing serious; a domestic issue here, a land surveying issue there—so he was forever grateful. More so, he was an expert in family law, which was something Randolph had always closely protected himself with.

"I'm right in the middle of something," Larry said. "Can you make this quick?"

"Patricia called me earlier this morning, told me the local law enforcement are looking for me."

"Regarding?"

"Did you hear about the explosion downtown?"

"At the supermarket? Yeah, I heard. What, do you think I live under a rock?"

"That."

"Did you do it?"

"No! Of course not."

"Then what's the problem?"

It was another long story. One he did not want to get in to. "She said there are tapes. Surveillance footage."

"I'm sure there is. Nothing I've been made aware of, though, regarding you or any other of my clients."

"I'm on the tapes."

"I thought you said you didn't do it?"

"I didn't."

Papers shuffled. "What do you want me to do?"

"Look into it."

"What am I looking for, exactly?"

"To be frank, I don't know."

Larry sighed. "All right, I'll make some calls, but I'm not happy about it."

"Thank you, Larry."

"Don't thank me yet. Just wait until I bill you."

Randolph smiled. Fucking Larry.

"All right," Larry said. "I've got to run now, but we'll be in touch."

CHAPTER TWENTY-FIVE

Sheila stared at him as he climbed back into the truck and wiped his brow. A headache pulsed in the back of his skull. He rubbed his eyes. He sensed everything was beginning to crumble around him, that the jig was up. His life had spiraled out of control—he knew it and watched it happen in real time, yet could do nothing to stop it. He felt helpless.

"Do you really think making a phone call right now is a good idea?" she asked. "Considering everything."

"Why wouldn't it be? It's not like he's tracking me too. It's not me he wants."

Sheila turned and faced the window, crossed her arms.

"What? Am I wrong?"

She did not respond.

He fumed. About everything. The bullshit from every direction had worn him thin. He slammed the truck into gear and floored his way back onto the interstate. Once he merged into the lane and kept pace with traffic, he took some time to cool off, to decompress. None of this was Sheila's fault—he knew that. It was not fair he took it out on her, or anyone. It was not about what happened to him, but about how he reacted to those events that made the man. He regretted his reaction.

"I'm sorry," he said once the guilt set in. "I didn't mean to snap at you."

She stayed quiet.

"It was my accountant on the phone. And then my attorney. There's something troubling going on."

She faced him.

"I think my wife is cleaning me out."

Nothing.

"I've made a careless mistake. She—Patricia, my wife—has been talking about a divorce for years. I kept pushing it off and pushing it off, hoping it would get better. Hoping she'd change her mind."

"I wouldn't call that careless."

"No, not that. That's not what I'm talking about. I should have been prepared. I should have taken care of certain things, but I didn't. I blinded myself with hope."

Her focus was on him, urging him on.

"My parents died. Many years ago now. A house fire."

"I'm so sorry. That's terrible."

"It was a gas leak. They were asleep when it happened. I've comforted myself through the years with the thought that they didn't suffer, that they were killed instantly. But there's no way to know, so . . ."

"If this is too difficult to talk about, by no means—"

"I want to. I want you to know."

She nodded.

"Long story short, they were frugal. My dad, he refused to buy a dishwasher."—he smiled at the memory—"I can't imagine how frustrating that must have been for my mother. But it was just the three of us, so I get it. Now at least. Then—no, not then. I thought he was being ridiculous. The funny thing is, she never let him forget it. When they would disagree about something completely unrelated years later, the dishwasher always came up."—he smiled again, chuckled— "Anyway, he worked hard and they lived within their means. Less so, probably. So they had a sizable nest egg.

"And as I said, it was just the three of us. So I inherited all of it. It was a lot. I could have stopped working then, if I wanted. But I didn't want that. I enjoyed working. Until I didn't. Then I just stopped.

"Everything I inherited was put into a separate account, away from my own investments and retirement and whatnot. I made enough to support our lifestyle, so I didn't need the money. We didn't need the money. Needless to say, Patricia was my wife—is still, legally. I'd left her on all accounts, hadn't gotten around to taking her off."

"Because you thought you still had a chance to reconcile."

"That's right."

She reached across the shifter and placed a hand on his knee. "I'm so sorry."

"I don't know if she didn't think I'd notice, or what. I don't use the money, so maybe that was a fair assumption. But my accountant handles the rebalancing and reinvesting and all that, which maybe she didn't know. It was never her deal. She was on the account simply because she was my wife. The beneficiary defaults to your spouse."

"I get it."

"She's not technically stealing, either because she's on the account. But that's exactly what she's doing."

"What are you going to do?"

He told her about his conversation with Herm and how he would temporarily freeze the account. When finished, Sheila looked at him blankly, confused.

"What's that face for?" he said.

"You don't see it, do you?"

He flicked his eyes between the road and Sheila. "I guess I don't. What am I missing?"

"Her phone call earlier. Now this. It all makes sense."

He thought about it but failed to see a connection. What did the tapes have to do with the missing money from his inheritance?

"About the divorce," she said. "She must have realized she had access to that account when she was able to take money out. And as long as you're married, she has access. Which is why she suddenly wants to wait."

It did make sense. How had he missed that? But there was something that did not fit. "What about the tapes? She had no way of knowing you and I were together. So the part about the tapes existing must be true. Right?"

She pulled her hand away and sat back. "Maybe."

"And what you said before about O'Reilly—your theory about him being the one to initiate all this—how does the money play into it?"

She shook her head. "I don't know."

Him either. "Well, my attorney is looking into it. He's good. He'll get to the bottom of it."

"Your attorney?"

"I told you I spoke to him."

"What's he looking into?"

"Whether the tapes exist or not."

"Why do you want to know?"

"You don't?"

"No, as a matter of fact, I don't."

He could not understand this. "You mean to tell me you're not curious about what happened after you blacked out?"

"Why would I be?"

"How are you not?"

"Some things are better left unknown. Why open up that can of worms if you don't have to? I'm here, you're here, we're fine. No damage done. Let it be."

He could not disagree more. That mindset could not be further from his, and it bothered him. More, it frustrated him. How could she feel that way? How did she not want to know what happened to them, especially if there was lost time? It shocked him. Unfathomable. "Sheila, I—"

"Please drop it."

"Can you at least—"

"Drop it."

"Just tell me—"

"Randolph, drop it!"

He leaned back, tightened his grip on the wheel. He was angry. Agitated. Annoyed. And while he would stop talking about it for now, he would not drop it. Not now, not ever. He was going to see this through. He would find answers about what was happening, whether Sheila wanted him to or not. It was his life at stake, and his livelihood. And his future.

CHAPTER TWENTY-SIX

There was no sign of O'Reilly, no imminent threat. The detour seemed to have worked. Still, Randolph remained flustered. What Sheila said rang true—Patricia was unquestionably up to something shady. And the issue about the security tape and its connection to Patricia and the money situation irked him. He checked his phone every hour to see if Larry had called back with any news, but he had not.

What did that mean? Was no news good news, as the saying went? He did not know. Patricia's motivation for falsifying the story about the tape seemed to be a disconnect for him, something beyond his comprehension. There was no way she could have known about his excursion with Sheila. Impossible. There had to have been a tape.

But what if there was not? What if what Sheila said was all it was? He would not put it past Patricia to thieve from him; she had nothing of her own. The evidence certainly pointed in that direction. She did not come from nothing, but her upbringing was not luxurious either. When they married, they drafted a loose prenuptial agreement that dictated financial terms to protect Randolph and his assets, but it was not airtight. A provision was never made to include his inheritance, as it was not something projectable at the time. Nor had he known about his parents' net worth then.

The court may force him to pay alimony because of that, which was something he was prepared for. But what that figure would be, or if he and Patricia could sit down at a table with their attorneys and come up with an agreeable number before that happened was one of the details to figure out. She would get half of the proceeds of the house, once it was sold, and she would be entitled to half of all their physical assets. The cash was a separate issue.

That part of the process did not bother him. They were happily married for many years. They arranged that he would work and she would not, and though Bruce had been out of their home for nearly a decade and without the need for parental support for longer, the arrangement never changed. It was what it was. Frankly, he thought she deserved support for her years of being a homemaker. What they accumulated over the years together—regardless if the togetherness was earned in equal parts or not—was theirs to split. He had no issues with that.

It was not entirely about the money—it never had been. He had plenty of it to sustain how he wanted to live. Frugalness was a trait he inherited from his parents, along with their assets. His net worth was in the low millions and growing every day with compound interest—his parents' portion was at least half of that, maybe more. He could easily live on just the interest alone. But Patricia stealing from him, dipping into the money inherited from two people she barely coexisted with, was a problem. She was not entitled to that money in his view, nor was she the two-thirds of the cash the prenuptial stated was his.

Two-thirds was more than enough for him. He could scale back and live smaller, and he planned to. His portion would cover him through his death with attentive financial planning. Patricia would not walk away with nearly as much. But the money from his parents' estate was rightfully his, as it had nothing to do with Patricia. She had no right to that money.

If only he had been smarter about it. He should have been more proactive when the talk of divorce first arose.

While Patricia and his parents did not dislike each other, they only associated because they had to, because of the union. His mother never thought Patricia was good enough for him, and while his father did not outwardly express his concerns, Randolph sensed the man's dissatisfaction too. They stayed at an arm's length from one another but did find common ground when it came to Bruce. Good not great was how Randolph would have described the relationship if asked.

That was before.

Now was after.

They were gone.

Now he wondered if perhaps his parents were right, if they saw something about her all along he failed to. Maybe his instincts were not as good as he thought.

Bottom line: He would fight for the inheritance money.

But that was a problem for another day. Larry would be on it—that type of family dispute was his specialty. He would assure Randolph got what he was entitled to. The bleeding had to stop, though, before it got further out of hand. Before there was nothing left.

Randolph phoned Herm to check in on the situation with the account; he was told it was set, frozen. No more cash could be withdrawn. Herm reminded him it would not last forever. At least it bought him some time, which was all he needed right now.

It was the same routine: he and Sheila drove, stopped, and ate; they drove, they fueled up, they swapped seats; they drove. A light illuminated on the dash to indicate the truck was due for an oil change. It was a reminder of how many miles they had covered in the past few days. And yet, there was still no solid plan for what came next.

Daylight turned into darkness. Another night in a musty room—though this one was a hotel which felt like a serious upgrade. Another darkened sexual rendezvous. He did not ask, nor could he make a judgment about Sheila's emotional state, but he found himself disconnected from the experience. His mind wandered. His stiffness was flaccid. He did not climax. He was sure Sheila did not either.

He hated to disappoint her. She rolled onto her side and pinched her knees together and pushed her backside toward him. He sat up in the bed and pushed his back against the headboard, sighed in frustration. It was reminiscent of all those nights with Patricia, of all the times he left her unsatisfied. The buzz from the self-pleaser she would use afterward rang in his ears, reminded him of the emptiness he felt as a man who could not meet his wife's needs.

"Sheila?" he said.

No response.

"Sheila? I'm sorry."

Her weight shifted. The bedsheet tensioned against his waist as she rolled over and faced him. "I'm sorry too."

"Listen, I—"

"It's my fault. I'm sorry. My mind is preoccupied today. I'm a little anxious is all."

"O'Reilly?"

She nodded.

He sighed. "Yeah, me too."

"I feel terrible for getting you into this. I feel like it's my fault."

"It's not. I'm a grown man capable of making my own decisions."

She looked away, pulled the sheet over her sternum.

"Is something else bothering you?"

She looked at him with damp eyes but said nothing.

He leaned in, smelled her flowery skin. "You can tell me. What is it?"

She looked uneasy, nervous. Uncomfortable. Randolph felt guilty for making her feel that way around him.

"Do you still love her?"

He smiled and snickered, but sat back when he saw it was a serious question. It shocked him. "Patricia? Do I still love Patricia?"

Her eyes were on him.

"Patricia and I loved each other for a long time. Many years. But at some point, the love died. Fizzled out. Went up in flames. A natural progression, maybe? I don't know. It wasn't how I drew it up when we married, I'll admit that. But when your spouse stops loving you, you eventually become hardened toward them. You put up a wall. The point of no return—it's real. At least from my experience."

"Randolph—"

"To answer your question—no, I am not in love with Patricia. Upon reflection, I've come to realize I haven't loved her for quite some time. I was hanging on to something that was dead, something that was hopeless."

Sheila was no longer looking at him. He slid closer to her, close enough to reach her face with his hand, which he did. A finger on her jaw gently turned her gaze toward him. Sadness filled her eyes.

"I am in love, though, Sheila. But not with her. I'm afraid to admit it, but here I am, putting myself out there. Being vulnerable."—he stopped himself, caught the lump in his throat—"The person I'm in love with...I'm looking at her."

Tiny droplets of water fell from her eyes, danced down her cheeks like ballerinas. He let go of her jaw and thumbed the tears away, felt the dampness against his skin. She lifted her hands and wrapped her fingers around his wrist and cried.

"Why are you crying?" he asked. Though he was not sure to whom—himself or her.

"It's just...I've never been in love. Not with someone who loves me back."

His heart fluttered. Then he pulled her toward him and pressed his lips against hers, determined to challenge the notion that women were better kissers than men.

CHAPTER TWENTY-SEVEN

What the actual fuck? Benji missed his flight. The airline would not allow for a transfer, so he was out the cost of a round-trip ticket. The next flight would not be for twelve hours. There were plenty of seats available, the clerk said with a smile as forced as the one he returned to her as he handed her his credit card.

He took an Uber home to not lose his parking spot and be forced to pay a second time. He napped, got high, made a phone call, texted Cheyenne an update on his situation, jerked off, and funneled an entire bag of Cheetos into his mouth as if he had never eaten before in his life—but not in that order. Later, he took another Uber back to the airport, passed through security a second time, waited at the gate, then in line again, and finally boarded.

The man in the seat next to him was grossly overweight and unapologetic, and while the window seat should have been a blessing, it felt like a claustrophobic nightmare. Benji sipped room temperature water from a plastic cup not much larger than a Dixie, nibbled on a bag of no more than six pretzels, and tried to focus on the in-flight entertainment but was unable to. He was tired and grumpy and too warm. The behemoth of a man next to him snored like the wild animal he was.

He could not get the mysterious man from before out of his mind—the creep from the first trip to the airport. The man remained nameless, which was an undesirable arrangement—he knew Benji's name but it was not reciprocated. Benji was left without a choice in the matter—either work with the man and his digital ghosting would remain unknown, or refuse and be exposed. Twenty years in prison stared him in the face.

So he agreed to help. A simple transfer of information for the exchange of his continued freedom. The man was equipped with pages of questions and a blank notepad. Benji sat with him for over an hour. The questions ranged from Benji's relationship with Cheyenne to his sudden influx of troubling dark web searches. The man wanted to know who Shay was and how Benji knew her, and how they met and where. He asked about Benji's skill set and his sudden travel plans to a location void of any substantial leisurely sightseeing ventures. The man was relentless. Benji was humbled by all the man knew, embarrassed he was not as sly as he thought he was.

Benji answered all the questions as openly and honestly as he could—except for when he did not—though he later questioned his reasoning for doing so. He could have called the man's bluff instead, but with the information he knew about Benji's life—you never ask a question you do not already know the answer to, the man had said—and a copy of the footage Benji had already seen and dug through himself, he sensed the man was not someone to toy with. He had no leverage.

Once the man was satisfied, he clicked his pen and pocketed it, then slammed the notepad shut and stood. Benji was free to go. If more information was needed, the man would contact Benji directly. Benji hurried out with his head down.

But now, as he sat wedged between the buffalo to his left and the humming glass to his right, he wondered what it all meant. Was it truly as simple as telling the man what he knew and moving on with his life? It seemed unlikely. But with no name and no contact information to dig around with, he had nothing. His only choice was to try and move on and forget about it.

The plane finally landed. The muscles in his lower back were stiff and his legs were in serious need of stretching. The pretzels from hours earlier did nothing to quell his hunger. He craved a smoke.

Buffalo Bill took his time unpeeling himself from the seat—whether out of necessity or not, Benji could not say—and struggled to unclip the lock on the storage bin above the seat.

Benji grew anxious, found himself getting angry—or worse, *hangry*. It had been a long, stressful day, and the current situation was not conducive to Zen. If the fat man did not get his shit together soon, Benji might lose it. Chubby laughed when he finally got the storage door open, only to remember that was not where he put his bag. Someone smiled at the man's ineptitude, another offered her assistance. Benji felt the steam rise within him.

"Fuck!" he yelled and instantly felt everyone's eyes on him. "Can somebody please help blubber get his shit so I can get out of here?"

All the chatter on the plane stopped. A man in a seat near the wing told him that was not cool, man. But nobody acted. So Benji pushed porky out of the way and stood on his toes and pulled all the storage doors open, yanked all the bags toward the seats. People grumbled and cursed and yelled hey, but nothing happened. One of the flight attendants glared at him from the front of the plane but said nothing.

Benji pushed his way through the line—most people let him through, though some were not as willing; every group had the stubborn ones who had to protest to prove a point or disagree with the majority for the sake of an argument. Some people got off on that shit. But now was not the time. A mother masked her child's face with her hand; a different man told Benji to stop being a dick. Finally, a flight attendant angrily stepped forward and cut off his line to the exit.

"Sir!" she said. "The way you're acting is entirely inappropriate. Please be—"

Benji lifted a hand to cut her off, and she gasped as if he had used a racial slur. She was white. She eventually stepped aside and let him through, and nobody tried to stop him as he power-walked through the jet bridge. He rushed through the gate, past the baggage claim, into an open corridor that was maddening with people who were clueless about where to go or what to do with themselves. He thought he might explode if he did not get outside soon and away from the chaos and the people who stood in the center of the walkway with their shit strewn about as if they were the only ones in the airport with a connecting flight to catch or somewhere to go. He followed the signs that led him out of the building and into the departure terminal and into the fresh air, which he sucked in as if he had been smothered without it. Which he kind of was. The moon hung high above.

He found a bench and threw himself on it and screamed into his hands. The energy pent-up within him roared out, and he felt the tension let go as he released it. Drool hung on his lips, but he did not care. He was exhausted. When he looked up, a black man with a funny hat and a bitter grin flashed his eyes at him. Benji looked back and wiped away the saliva, and the man walked off. Benji wanted nothing more than to not be around people anymore. Too many for one day.

He sat alone for a few minutes. The tension fell further away with each passing moment, and so did his energy. His eyes were heavy. The chaos of the surrounding noise faded into the night.

A black sedan with dark windows rolled up to the curb and stopped. Benji watched it but did not react. He could barely hold up his head anymore. A mugger could have had his way with him, and Benji would not have put up a fight—take whatever you want, man, just make it quick. The passenger side window of the sedan rolled down and he immediately thought of the man from the airport in eastern Iowa, but he was too fatigued to care about the idea of that too.

"Hey," a voice called from inside the sedan. He recognized it.

"Hey," he said.

He forced himself up and shoved his hands in his pockets and stepped toward the vehicle. The door opened from the inside and he slid in. The cushiony seat enveloped him and he felt weightless against it.

"You look like shit," Cheyenne said. "What happened to you?"

"Please shut up," he said. "Don't talk. Just drive."

Cheyenne smiled and shifted the car into drive and peeled away.

· · · · · ·

It was later. He napped in the car and ate real food and smoked away his stress with the singular joint he smuggled in his rectum. The baggie that held it was immediately discharged, his hands washed, after he retrieved it. His fingers passed the smell test. Cheyenne would not stop talking. He heard about her flight and how anxious she was about her luggage getting lost—which it did not, thank the heavens, or he would not have ever heard the end of it—and about how she killed the afternoon awaiting his arrival. The details were lost on him. She had grabbed his bag too when she landed and brought it with her to the hotel—a surprisingly friendly gesture, he thought, and not one he would have expected from her. He was sure it was for selfish reasons.

By the next morning, his back still ached from the crummy sofa cushion Cheyenne forced him to sleep on, which neither made sense nor bothered him. She awoke him in the night to ride him then quickly fell back asleep in the ginormous bed by herself while he fought to get comfortable on the tiny sofa. He thought about suffocating her with a pillow while she slept so she would stop snoring, but he somehow restrained himself, though the prospect was tempting.

Cheyenne woke up, blew him, then showered alone. Benji ravaged through the mini-fridge for anything edible. He was not paying the bill, so he ate everything—the cookies, the candy, the singular brownie that was outdated by more than two days but still tasted like a volcano of chocolaty goodness on his tongue. The sugar rush went straight to his head and manifested itself in a splitting headache, so he guzzled both bottles of water and threw back the shot of Jack. Relaxation eventually caught up and outwilled him.

When she reappeared from the bathroom—a white towel around her head, another barely covering her lady parts—she asked him not to lay on her pillow because he stunk.

"They're going to wash them," he countered, and she retreated into the steam cave with disgust.

His balls hurt. And he could smell himself—the sweat where the antiperspirant should have been, the staleness of his breath. So he stood and dropped his pants, lost the shirt, and stumbled into the bathroom. Cheyenne was nude in front of the mirror, examining herself.

"You're disgusting," she said when she noticed him, though she did not take her eyes off herself.

"Thank you," he said. Then he cranked the shower handle to the red zone and stepped into the water.

Beads of liquid heat pelted his skin like magma. A shiver ran through his pores and warmed him from the toes up. He closed his eyes and let the steam take him away.

"What happened to you yesterday?" Cheyenne asked from the other side of the curtain. "Who was that guy?"

The man from the airport. "I didn't catch his name, actually."

"What did he want?"

He considered not telling her but was not prepared to devise a lie. "Just some dude, poking around for information."

"What kind of information."

Silence.

The curtain whipped open and Cheyenne stood in front of him, her hands on her naked hips. Two bags of sand hung from her chest. "What kind of information?"

"Hey, psycho, relax. Just about some stuff I've been up to. And about where I was going. And . . ."

"And what?"

"And about you."

"Me! What about me?"

"I'm sorry, but can you close the curtain? You're letting all the steam out."

She leaned in close—but not too close; the magma pellets made a wall between them. "Do you forget who you're talking to? What exactly did he ask about me?"

"He wanted to know who you were, how we know each other. That's it."

"And what did you tell him?"

"That we're friends. And we fuck sometimes."

She looked down at his manhood and smirked, then back up. The smirk was gone. "What else?"

"That was it."

Her eyes pierced his and held. He was first to blink.

"Benji? Sweet, sweet Benji. What else did the man have to say?"

"Well, he did ask about the footage."

Her expression changed. Anger. Rage. "That footage?"

"That footage."

"And what did you tell him?"

He knew his answer was bad. Really, really bad. Thankfully, Cheyenne did not have a weapon at her disposal; if she did, he would have been in serious trouble, afraid of what she might do to him. "I told him what he wanted to know."

Benji grunted as a stabbing pain rushed through his gut. Cheyenne's shoulder was wet now, and her hand squeezed as if his manhood were a stress reliever. He was all but incapacitated.

"Meet me out there in five minutes."—she motioned to the sleeping space—"You're going to tell me exactly what you told him. And then you're going to tell me how the fuck you plan on getting us out of this mess."

She released him and walked out.

He pressed his back against the tiled shower wall and nursed himself. All the while, water splashed against the floor on the other side of the tub and soaked the mat. His balls hurt too much to think.

CHAPTER TWENTY-EIGHT

The sun was awake and peeking through the curtain. Randolph was up and had been for a while. Usually an early riser, the last few days of sleeping late were unorthodox for him. As his body settled into his new workless routine, not arising in the darkness appealed to him. But he was restless already, and it was only nine o'clock.

Sheila was curled up in a ball and asleep, unmoved by the intruding light or the disturbance of his shower in the next room. He was starved. Before pocketing the room key and slipping out, he jotted a note for Sheila in case she awoke and wondered where he was and left it on the bedside table. He placed a hand on her hip just to feel her, then left.

He remembered seeing a coffee and doughnut shop on the drive in—some non-franchised joint, which was usually the best type. He hit the main road and took off the way they came in, filled up his gas tank. The line at the coffee shop was long but not absurd; the employees were friendly. The dough smelled fresh and the display cabinet teased him with treats reserved for a special occasion. He ordered two bottles of water and onion bagels for old time's sake—or what felt like it. They had only known each other less than a week, but it felt like forever, as if they had gone through hell and back. He was not sure if that was a sign the bond they had formed was strong, or if it was a bad omen for the future.

He paid for the breakfast and offered his pleasantries and stepped toward the door, but as he reached for the bar, his attention was stolen. High in the corner of the wall, mounted above a shelf with a cable box, was a small television. The morning news was on, and the female anchor teased stories that would follow after the break.

No, not possible.

He could not have heard it right.

He released the bar and retreated inside, stood under the television with his arms crossed, the brown paper bag crammed against his chest.

No way.

The commercial break was as long as he could ever remember—fifteen automobile ads; six for mobile phones; another for shaving cream. The longest hand on the clock on the wall stuck as if broken.

Finally, the newsroom reappeared on the screen and he sprung up, stepped closer to hear better. The tease from before was just that—a tease about a story from neighboring Iowa that had people scratching their heads. In less than thirty seconds it was over. The full story was developing.

Oh no!

He rushed out of the shop, nearly pushed the heavy door into a pretty blonde whose head was buried in her phone. She gave him disapproving eyes and he apologized, and he hurried to the truck.

Oh no, oh no, oh no.

Patricia was right. There was a tape. If network news in Nebraska had the footage, he could only imagine the circus that was Iowa. A local supermarket exploded in broad daylight with hundreds of shoppers and employees inside, and nobody—at least not as far as he gathered from the broadcast he just saw—knew why. A supermarket he was inside just minutes before the explosion. A supermarket the woman he was with worked in at the time. A woman—might he add— whose grainy face was as clear as day to him in the footage shown.

What did it all mean?

He considered all the options without any reasonably coherent conclusions as he hauled ass back to the hotel. After he pulled in and parked, he slowed down to try and calm himself. His heart pounded to the point of him being short of breath. He clutched the steering wheel and took deep breaths.

Why was he so worked up? He did nothing wrong. He was there, but so were hundreds of others. Sheila was a victim too—far more so than he; she was inside when it happened. Relinquishing control of what felt like his livelihood made him extremely uncomfortable. But still, he did nothing wrong.

He had to call Larry and try to figure out what was going on. He retrieved his phone and dialed, but there was no answer.

Damn.

Breathe. Relax.

He took another minute until he was good, calm, ready to think and react reasonably. Inside the hotel, the concierge greeted him and welcomed him to the morning. All he could do was offer a halfhearted wave in return; his mind was preoccupied. The elevator ascended as if it were his personal chariot, opening its doors only at the floor Randolph pressed with no stops in between. He stepped into the corridor and wove through the labyrinth of identically wallpapered walls. Some had framed stock photographs of landscapes that had nothing to do with where they were hung on them, while others were bare. There was no noticeable pattern to why or where the frames were hung—some hired interior designer clearly rushed through the job to move onto the next more exciting, more lucrative gig. Randolph swiped the plastic key through the slot on the outside of the door, waited for the screen to illuminate green, and turned the handle.

The bed was empty, the sheets splayed across the floor. He walked toward the bathroom. The door was closed.

"Sheila? Are you in there?"

A few seconds passed. Then the sound of running water came and went, the hinge of a towel rod squeaked, and the door opened.

"Hi," Sheila said. She smiled at him. His shirt hung off her shoulders against a dark backdrop.

"Hi."

Her face fell. "What's the matter?"

He remembered the bag in his hand. "Hungry? I brought breakfast."

She looked at him. Her face was expressionless, emotionless.

"I got onion. You like onion, right? Last time you ate—"

"What's wrong, Randolph? You look like you've seen a ghost."

Was it that obvious? He pushed past her and flipped on the light, gazed at his reflection in the mirror.

Yikes.

Not seen a ghost, but was the ghost. He looked disheveled. Terrible.

Sheila came up behind him and dropped a hand on his shoulder. Her touch sent waves of warmth rushing through his body. The tension fell away. The paper bag slipped out of his hand and crashed against the countertop.

"What happened?" she asked with the gentlest voice he had ever heard. The voice of an angel. Or maybe just the voice of someone who actually cared.

He pressed his hands against the counter and leaned forward, dropped his head. "I can't do this anymore. I just can't."

Sheila was silent behind him but her touch remained. He eventually looked up and caught her reflection. Sadness overtook her face.

"I think we should go back," he said.

"Go back to where?"

"To Iowa."

"Why?"

He told her about the news broadcast.

"There's no reason to go back," she said. "You did nothing wrong. We did nothing wrong."

"I have to figure this out."

"Isn't your lawyer working on it?"

"I tried to call him earlier, but he didn't answer."

"Well, there you go. He has nothing to say, I'm sure. Because you did nothing wrong."

He shook his head. "No, no. That's not it. There's so much going on, I just need—"

"We can't go back, Randolph. We can't."

He sighed. "Why not?"

"Gary will kill me if we go back."

He straightened, turned to face her. "Kill you? Are you that afraid of him?"

Tears pooled in her eyes. "You have no idea."

Well, if you shared . . .

He grabbed her hand and held it, gazed into her eyes. They stayed like that for a while.

"What do you suggest then?" Randolph finally said. "If we can't go back."

"Well, I do have an idea, actually. But I'm not sure you're going to like it."

CHAPTER TWENTY-NINE

She was right; he did not. Not really. But he understood it, at least from her perspective. She seemed confident it would work. She led the way—picked the place, drove there, put her cash on the table and told the women inside what the deal was, what they wanted to accomplish. Randolph merely went along and did what he was told.

The women brought out supplies he had neither seen nor heard of, did things to him he never imagined. He sat in the chair like a doll while women spoke among themselves around him as if he were not in the room; he was nothing but a mannequin, a canvas for their artistic expression. He nearly dozed off while they waited. The final result he disliked on himself, though he thought Sheila looked spectacular.

"Ten years younger," she said to him, referencing his appearance afterward. A giant smile caved in her cheeks. She looked happy.

The man he saw in the mirror was not someone he recognized—bleach blonde hair on his head rather than dark brown; stubble and eyebrows that did not match; wrinkles that were more pronounced than he remembered. It would take him time to get used to the new him. The dramatics did not seem necessary, though he agreed it had a chance to work.

Sheila was the opposite—from short, straight, and blonde to long, wavy, fiery red extensions. Lust and seduction radiated from her, overtook the room. The other women in the waiting area stared—as much at Randolph as her, he thought. They must have looked ridiculous together—an alluring young woman with a man almost old enough to be her father. She, promiscuous. He, perverted. One of the women eyed him without hiding it, then shook her head and grunted. She did not understand; frankly, neither did he.

Sheila's fingers linked with his and captured his attention. He looked at her.

"You ready?" she said. She smiled, paid no attention to the disapproving onlookers. He loved that about her.

He nodded. He was. Anywhere but there. The judgment game was strong, and he did not like it. He was not used to being noticed, and frankly, it made him uncomfortable. Outside, they climbed into the truck and she kissed him with wet, gentle lips.

"What do you think?" she asked after they separated.

"I think you look great. Stunning. But I thought you did before too."

"What about you? Do you like yours?"

He flipped the visor and opened the mirror window. He studied himself, turned his head from left to right. "I don't know. It's not me,"

"That's the point."—she smiled—"I love it. You look...so different."

"Bad different?"

"No. Definitely not. Exotic. Confident."

"You think?" He looked again, did not see what she did.

"Sexy."

He turned to her and smiled. She kissed him again.

"I feel better now," she said. "Now it's your turn. Where to?"

He shifted the truck into gear and checked the clock. It was still relatively early. "If we make good time, we could be there by dark."

She turned and buckled, as did he. Then they were off, headed west.

It was dark when they arrived. Ten hours later. The town was called Green River, though he had never seen a body of water that color. It was a tiny commuter town but with spectacular views of the frosted mountains on the horizon at its highest points. What few people resided in the neighborhoods were generally quiet but friendly, from his experience. He thought they would blend in fine, just until he could figure out their next move. All he knew was they could not keep doing what they had been—it was neither sustainable nor realistic. He still had not heard back from Larry, which ate at him.

The house at the end of the short drive was ranch-style—one-floor living at its best. It was hard to make out the features in the dark, but Randolph knew its shutters were the same color as the roof, and the vinyl siding was bright and cheery. The gutter on the front of the house was cracked near the base of the downspout the last time he was there—he remembered the crawl space underneath the house being dank and muddy because of the runoff. He wondered if it had been fixed since the last time when he pointed it out. He hoped so.

He woke Sheila, asked for her opinion. The time zone had changed, but it was still late. Closer to ten o'clock than nine like the dashboard said. Too late? It seemed so. But he had not seen anywhere to stay on the way in, and he also did not have the energy to try and find one at this hour—not to mention the lack of desire to spend yet another night in a strange bed with unusual smells and a shortage of worthy towels. Sheila said it was up to him.

Great.

Should he call first? He did not want to cause alarm, though—the phone never rang after nine o'clock with good news. He could send a text message, but what if they were asleep? A call would get their attention at least.

He sent a text.

No more than sixty seconds later, the porch light flipped on. Randolph felt a jolt of excitement, but also angst. Showing up unannounced was inappropriate for anyone, especially this late. But what choice did he have? They were there now.

The front door opened and a man stepped onto the porch. Loose sweatpants drooped from his hips, slippers on his feet. Sleeves covered his arms. He hurried to the truck and stood with his arms crossed, his expression not one of joy. Randolph lowered the window.

"It's late, I know," Randolph said. "I'm sorry."

"And unannounced."

"I'm sorry."

The man looked between Randolph and Sheila but did not say anything.

"This is Sheila," Randolph said.

"Hi. Nice to meet you," she said.

"This is Bruce," Randolph told her. "My son."

CHAPTER THIRTY

Benji was still wet but wrapped in a towel as he sat on the edge of the mattress. The drips from his hair landed on his shoulders and he shivered, missed the warmth and solidarity of the liquid magma. Cheyenne stood in front of him, fully clothed, her arms crossed. He felt like a child about to get scolded.

They had been through the details—he relayed as much as he could remember about his conversation with the mystery airport man, told her about the tape, what he saw. He failed to mention he had seen it already because it seemed irrelevant. She did not have to know everything.

"What exactly did you agree to?" Cheyenne asked, referring to the agreement between him and the mystery man.

"He had a list of questions about the girl on the tape, so I answered them."

"What's in it for you?"

"Freedom."

"Freedom?"

"No prison."

"Should you be in prison?"

"It doesn't matter. I don't want to talk about it."

"It matters to me."

"Too bad. It has nothing to do with you and me, so forget it."

She was quiet. Her arms were still crossed while she eyed him.

He thought about her question. Should he be in prison? While it was true, he was not a law-abiding citizen, he had not hurt anybody. His crimes were digital only, never personal. Hacking, security footage retrieval, the occasional editorial manipulation. Nothing worthy of prison. He was simply a kid who meant no harm—he was pleading ignorance.

"What aren't you telling me?" she asked, bringing him back.

There was a lot. For starters, Cheyenne thought the girl on the tape was an associate—a hired hand with a role in the game, someone without a stake. And it would stay that way. Cheyenne could not know he and Shay were lovers; she would be devastated. He would wait until this was all over before breaking the news to her about them—that this was all it would ever be between them. There was no scenario in which he saw a future with Cheyenne. None. He did not trust she would react well to this revelation.

"What if we get caught?" he said.

"You assured me we wouldn't. That's why you're here. That's why we're here."

"I used to believe it, but now, I'm not so sure."

She stepped toward him. "Don't let this prick bring you down. You're dynamite. You hear me?"

"He said he'd be in touch if he needed more information."

"And?"

"Which means he's watching me. Us. He'll figure it out before long."

She backed away and crossed the room, reached for her obscenely large bag. "I don't have time for this shit."

"Where are you going?"

"Where do you think I'm going? We came here for a reason. I'm following the trail with or without you."

"You're not afraid of getting caught?"

She shook her head. "It's too late for that. I'm in too deep."

"It's not too late. If we stop now, no one will ever know."

"Wrong. You wouldn't understand. I'm going to make this very simple for you, okay? Either you put some clothes on and join me in the car in five minutes, or you're on your own finding a ride to the airport. And I think you can figure out what that means for you."

She left.

He stayed on the bed, still dripping with water, stuck at a proverbial fork in the road—go along and do what he knew was wrong, or change his ways and make a good decision for the first time in his life.

He missed Shay.

Once a bad boy always a bad boy. Right? It was too late for him to change his ways now; as Cheyenne said, he too was in too deep. Fuck that guy from the airport. Fuck everyone. He was dynamite.

He rode in the passenger's seat, window down, arm out, his overlong hair sweeping through the air. The list of Shay's communications was in his other hand—the list he bartered from the guy from the call center, the one he traded a bag of his good not great stash for. A more recent list was traded for a stack of green he could not smoke, in the form of a small fraction of a Bitcoin. Benji transferred the currency an hour ago.

The lists did not make sense. Shay may have been in trouble, despite the most recent text message, which said the opposite. But how easy would it be to forget that? He had no hard evidence she was the one who actually sent him the text. It could have been anybody. This was not part of the plan, and her safety was now priority number one. Once he found her, he would get the answers that ate at him, and they would have a path forward to execute the plan as previously established.

That was before.

Now was after.

Things were different now. The stakes had changed, had risen. Benji was involved now too—even deeper than before—thanks to airport guy. His investment was personal. And he knew Cheyenne would feed him to the wolves if it came down to it to save herself. He was not as ignorant as she thought, or as he pretended to be. He was stealthy, fully aware of the danger in front of them. One false move could mean the end. And prison. Airport guy had no idea what he did not know.

They were in the middle of nowhere. It could not have been farther from the bustling city life he was accustomed to and enjoyed. His phone worked, but barely. The signal flipped between one bar and none. He was glad he downloaded the lists ahead of time. More than simply a record of the phone numbers Shay called and texted, Benji's list had full details.

Cell towers had four unique identification codes attributed to them, which shared data about which mobile devices used it. The mobile country code said which country the tower was in; the mobile network code offered insight into which wireless provider's network it was; the location area code broke it down further into the tower's general geographical location; and the cell identification number homed in on the specific location. Contrary to popular belief, this information was not accessible by the police only; if someone had this data, they could easily find out the precise location of the cell tower. Which meant, in Benji's situation, he knew Shay had been within roughly 45 miles of the towers on his list at one time—the average radius of a standard cell tower.

In short, Benji traced Shay's movements from the time she left Iowa. But instead of following her from location to location, they simply went to the location of her most recently registered mobile network connection. They were a day behind, maybe less, at worst. Airplanes were a beautiful thing.

Benji was wired. Even as Cheyenne pulled into the gas station and groaned about something he ignored, his focus was strong. He tried to put himself into Shay's shoes. If she were in trouble, what would she do? He thought about it. Sadly, he did not know. He realized he did not know her very well. On the surface, sure, but not at her core—not as a human being. How might she react during a time of crisis?

He suddenly felt very uneasy. Almost queasy. Was she playing him? He considered what her motivations could be, how doing so could benefit her, but he came up blank. She had nothing to gain. Not at this stage.

The car stopped. Benji looked around, saw a rusty gas pump and a crooked sign, a hotel across the street. A pickup idled at the light on the street, though it sounded as if it may stall out if the light did not quickly turn to green. Cheyenne's window lowered.

A man walked up—a dirty, filthy man. He wore a faded mesh trucker hat with a torn rim and badly stained denim overalls. Oversize work boots clunked against the pavement with each step he took. He was like a cliché out of the deep south—except they were not in the deep south. The dirty man leaned on the window frame and flipped a toothpick between his rotted teeth. His lower lip was fully packed.

"Whatcha need?" the man said. Then he spat.

CHAPTER THIRTY-ONE

Bruce led them into the house. Randolph kept Sheila close but with still enough distance between them so to kill the negative energy. The vibes were bad. Bruce was not happy. Randolph understood why. He should have called first.

It did not hit him until he saw Bruce's face—the thoughts that must have gone through his mind. As far as Bruce knew, Randolph and Patricia were happily married. Little did he know—and why would he?—about the reality about all that had happened throughout the years. He and Patricia tried to maintain some semblance of normalcy whenever Bruce and Max were around, and he was proud of that. But what he had not considered was how abrupt it may appear for Bruce when it came to a head. For that, he misjudged the situation. Badly. He needed to speak with his son in private.

He caught up to him. "Bruce, can we talk?"

"Not now. It's late."

And that was that. Randolph would have to sleep on it. Somehow.

"Everything okay?" Bruce's wife said when he approached. Her name was Janet. She was generally reserved and always kind. She looked like someone's mother—she gave off that vibe, had that motherly feel about her. Maxwell was a lucky boy to have her for his mother. Randolph liked her very much.

Bruce whispered something to her in passing and she disappeared into the house. He held open the door for his guests and they entered into the living room. It was just as Randolph had remembered, just more chaotic—children's toys piled in one corner; a thinned bookshelf on the far wall; a tower of DVDs racked near the television. A giant container of jumbo Lego was on its side on the carpet. The wick of a candle flickered on the end table, though it smelled nothing like the pomegranate pictured on the label.

Randolph stood with Sheila at his side, unsure what to say, unsure if he should. Bruce clicked off the television and swept the invisible crumbs off the sofa and gathered the mess from the floor and shoved it into the corner with the rest. Randolph thought to offer his help but kept the idea to himself as to not overstep.

Janet returned with an armful of pillows without pillowcases and a large, fluffy, squarely folded quilt. She smiled at Randolph when their eyes met, but did not say anything. Bruce took the makeshift bedding from his wife and laid it out over the sofa.

"This is the best we can do, sorry," Bruce said. "Spare bedroom is more of an oversize closet at this point."

"This is more than adequate," Randolph said, and he meant it. "Thank you."

He watched his son for a while longer. He looked older. The shadow on his face was dark, but not more than the bags under his eyes. The full head of hair he once had now showed more forehead than it ever had. His belly protruded out further than Randolph had ever seen. Dad life.

"Would you mind if I used your bathroom?" Sheila said. "Long ride."

"Of course!" Janet said. "Follow me."

Sheila did. She crossed the room and disappeared into the darkness of the hallway with Janet.

"Son?" Randolph said when they were alone.

Bruce tucked the edges of the quilt under the cushions before straightening his back and facing Randolph.

"I should have called. I'm sorry."

"Yeah, Dad, you should have."

"I'm sorry."

"What are you even doing here?"

"It's a long story. But I'm happy to tell—"

"Who is this woman you're with? And where's Mom?"

"Bruce, there's something we need to talk about."

"I'd say so. But not tonight. I'm tired. Max has been fussy so it's been a long week. I'm going to bed."

"I understand."

Bruce stepped toward the hallway but stopped before he got there and turned to face Randolph. "Please be quiet. Max is asleep. He'll be up early, so I expect you'll be too."

"No problem."

Bruce scanned him from head to toe, shook his head. "What's up with your hair?"

"Long story, like I said."

"I'll say."

They stared at one another for a few seconds before Bruce broke it and turned away.

"Goodnight, Son."

But he was already gone.

* * *

Aside from a small side lamp, the house was dark. And quiet. Not a sound from anywhere. Eerie almost. Randolph was exhausted. He and Sheila faced each other on the sofa, their legs intertwined, their backs against opposite armrests. They both wore the clothes they had on before, their bags still in the truck.

The pressure of the situation weighed heavily on him. Randolph knew Bruce was pissed, and Bruce knew Randolph knew he was pissed. Which meant Janet, the sweetheart she was, should be upset with Randolph too. Sheila was not happy either. He had played this all wrong.

"Sorry about the setup," he said to Sheila, whose arms were crossed so tightly he thought she might get stuck. "I guess I should have called first."

"You have a son. When were you planning on telling me?"

"It never came up, I guess."

She laughed. "Please, Randolph. Don't patronize me."

"Listen, I'm sorry if—"

"He's my age!"

He snuck a peek toward the hallway. "Please, keep your voice down."

"Why, so I don't wake up your grandson, which I also knew nothing about? Goddammit, Randolph!"

"Please, Sheila. I said I was sorry. I wasn't trying to hide it from you."

"Yet here we are."

He sighed. "I never brought it up because it didn't matter."—she laughed again, but not a real laugh—"Bruce is a grown man with his own life a thousand miles from my own. I did my job. I raised him, and now he's gone. That's it."

Sheila shook her head, but Randolph could tell the tension in her muscles had loosened.

"I have a son, yes, and a grandson. But they live here and I live there. I see them once a year if I'm lucky. But I should have told you. I was wrong. And I'm sorry."

He watched her for any signs of the lowering of the shield she held in front of her. He felt bad, but he could only imagine how she felt—an obviously unwanted houseguest in a place she knew nothing about with a man who lied to her about the son and grandson he had. When put that way...yikes. He messed up bad.

"This was a bad idea," he said. "I don't know what I was expecting. I haven't seen him in over a year, haven't called in months, and yet I expected him to welcome me into his home with open arms in the middle of the night. I was a fool."

"You're not a fool."

He looked at her.

"Okay, you're kind of a fool."

He laughed, then so did she. The tension faded.

"Should we leave?" he said. "We can go right now if you want."

"Then what? How will you explain that? We're staying. You and your son obviously have some important things you need to discuss."

She was right. "What about you? Are you going to be all right? I've put you in an impossible situation—which wasn't my intention, just so you know."

"I know it wasn't. Your heart's in the right place. But don't worry about me. Janet is a peach. We'll get along just fine."

He leaned back, felt more relaxed. "Well, all right. If you're sure."

"I'm sure."

"But you do have to promise me one thing, though. Deal?"

"Anything. What is it?"

"No more secrets. We've got nothing if we don't have trust. Am I right?"

"Completely."

She smiled. "So what else do you got? Spill your guts."

He thought. His daily life was basic, simple. No addictions or bad habits. No secret stash of anything illegal. No foreign bank accounts in the Cayman Islands. He was up to date on his taxes and his vaccines. No criminal record. She knew everything else there was to know.

"There's nothing," he said. "I promise."

She nodded, satisfied.

"What about you? Anything you're not telling me?"

O'Reilly.

"No," she quickly answered. "There's nothing."

You sure?

"Well, all right then," he said. "It's settled. No more secrets."

"No more secrets."

She leaned forward and crawled across the sofa and kissed him. His eyes involuntarily closed as a frenzy of feels overtook his lips and ran through his core.

"I love you," she said after she pulled away.

He had no choice but to believe her. About everything. "And I love you."

CHAPTER THIRTY-TWO

Randolph was the first one up. Not because he felt well-rested, but because he could not sleep. His mind roared with thoughts he could not turn off. More than anything, he wanted to sit with Bruce and explain everything that had happened. Needed to. The look on his son's face was not one he ever wanted to see—the hurt, the pity, the betrayal. He owed him a truthful explanation. Most importantly, he did not want to force a wedge between Bruce and his mother—that was not what it was about. But sometimes the truth hurt, and Bruce would learn that. He was man enough to handle it and make his own determination about the situation once he heard the facts.

Randolph slipped outside when the sun came up. Sheila was asleep, though with a crooked neck that could pose a problem later in the day. The rest of the house was dead quiet as if it were a monastic silence. He needed air.

Clouds lined the sky with melancholy. It was going to be a dreary day in all iterations of the word. It smelled like rain. A headache pulsed behind his eyes where the sleep failed him. He sighed and rubbed his temples. What was he doing?

Where would he start? Trying to find a balance between being fair and honest and spilling the truth without shredding the character of Patricia was important to him. She was not all bad. Part of him knew he would always love her. Being in love was different than loving, and while the latter was typically more than enough, that only lasted for so long. Was it okay if he still missed her sometimes? He struggled with the answer. They spent most of their lives together—many good years, countless happy moments. They made and raised a beautiful, intelligent, courageous son who was a great husband and father and even a better man; from that, there was another beautiful, intelligent smaller version of that man who would one day become like his father. There was so much to be proud of.

He did not want to admit it to himself, but he missed his old life. He wanted to cry about it sometimes, just to let it out. But then he thought about what Patricia was up to—the shady business with the money—and the sadness quickly fell. Anger rose with ferocity and he wanted nothing more than to strip her of everything, to leave her with nothing. Part of him still loved her, but another part despised everything about who she had become.

The air did not help.

He retreated into the house.

Sheila was gone from the sofa. Gentle voices emanated from the kitchen. Randolph folded the quilt into the best, most precise square he could and stacked the pillows on top. Then he smoothed the sofa cushions to remove the wrinkles and joined the chatter in the kitchen.

Sheila and Janet shared a pot of coffee, each with a steaming mug at their fingertips. A plastic tray of fruit-filled supermarket Danish sat between them. Napkins caught the crumbs that missed their mouths. Janet saw him when he entered and smiled, and she made her way toward him. She wrapped her arms around his neck and pulled him into her. She felt so warm and comforting, and it was exactly what he needed—it must have been that motherly instinct, even though the roles should have been reversed. He felt a tug on his belly from Janet's as he hugged her back. The urge to never let go was fierce.

Janet released him and pulled away. "It's so good to see you. I'm sorry we didn't get to chat last night."

"No, please," he said. "It's my fault. We showed up unannounced. I put you in an awkward position. I'm sorry."

"Nonsense. You're family."

He smiled at her. "Thank you."

"So, are you hungry? We have coffee and Danish. Blueberry."

"No coffee for me. But don't mind if I do indulge in one of these things here." He leaned over the counter and snatched a Danish from the tray.

He chewed. The women sipped. The quiet was peaceful, not at all uncomfortable.

After the Danish disappeared, he wiped his face with one of the napkins on the counter and used his tongue to pick chunks of blueberry from his teeth.

"How are you, Janet?" he said. "What's new?"

"Tired. But very happy. You raised a good man. He's so good to us."

That warmed him. Though it hurt too, because he felt so disconnected from Bruce these days. Distance tended to do that to relationships.

"The cravings are so strong this time," she said, laughing. "Maxwell was nothing like this."

Huh? Is she?...

"This time? How do you mean?"

Janet gasped and threw her hands over her face. "Oh, God! I thought he told you. Oh no! I'm so sorry!"

The gut punch almost took his breath away. Janet was pregnant. He was going to be a grandfather again, and he did not know until now. He forced a smile to hide the hurt he felt. "How far along?"

Her hands were still over her mouth. "Twenty-four weeks."

He was angry. Not with Janet, with Bruce. Why had he not told him? Did Patricia know?

"I'm so sorry," she said again. "I wouldn't have said something if I knew Bruce hadn't told you yet."

He walked over to her and kissed her cheek and pulled her into an embrace. "It's all right, darling. Congratulations."

When he turned back, Sheila was hiding behind her mug, cradling it as if she would have rather been anywhere but there. This visit was a complete disaster.

Thankfully, there was a commotion down the hallway to interrupt what was about to become the most awkward three-way conversation imaginable. Janet's face lit up.

"The boys," she said.

Randolph stood next to Sheila and placed a hand on the small of her back. She set down the mug and leaned against him. He felt at ease with her.

"Hello, hello," Bruce said as he entered the kitchen. The same droopy outfit from the night before hung from his widening frame.

Randolph melted when he saw Max. He had gotten so big since the last time he saw him. His back was to him, his torso draped over his daddy's shoulder. The curl of a nighttime diaper peeked above the waistline of his pajama bottoms—tiny dump trucks and fire engines and police vehicles. The last time Randolph saw Max he was crawling, just barely able to shuffle the equivalent of a step or two before toppling over. Now, he imagined he was running circles around the kitchen island. Sammy and Max must have been the best of buds— Sammy was the family dog, a gentle and lovable Irish Setter. She must have been ten or eleven now.

Speaking of, where was Sammy? He had not seen her yet, or heard her. Nor had he seen a bed in the living room, or any toys. Dare he mention her?

As much as Randolph wanted to rush over and squeeze his grandson, he held back. Would Max even recognize him? A photo of him and Max from last year hung on the refrigerator door, which surprised him, and he wondered if children could place the real thing after only seeing someone in photos for so long. He did not know. It had been so long since Bruce was a boy; his knowledge had gotten rusty.

Bruce kissed his wife and offered his good mornings. She smooched their son after, who was still content hanging onto his daddy. Randolph was proud of how well Bruce did with him.

"Coffee?" Janet asked him.

"Please, thank you."

She leaned in and whispered something to him, then he turned and faced Randolph and Sheila.

"Hey," he said. "Good morning."

"Good morning," Sheila said.

"Good morning, Son."

Bruce shifted his body so Randolph could see Max's face, which was sick with sleepiness.

"Maxy," Bruce said with a calm, soothing tone. "Do you know who that is?"

Randolph felt the smile overtake his face.

"It's Grandpop. Remember?"

Max looked at Randolph for a few seconds but quickly dug his face into his daddy's shoulder and grunted.

"It's okay," Randolph said. "It'll take him a bit to warm up." He smiled to show he meant what he said. But he did not. Not really. His grandson did not recognize him. And it hurt.

CHAPTER THIRTY-THREE

The three remaining Spiers males—Randolph, Bruce, and Max—were outside gathering grassy dew on the bottoms of their footwear, or in Max's case, his bum. It was three generations together again, as if it were just another day. Except it was not, because the tension was high. It weighed on Randolph as if it were an impending avalanche that would inevitably give way before long.

Max had loosened up. His daddy was no longer his sole protector but instead a hindrance to exploration. He giggled as he ran in circles in the lawn, occasionally slipping where the dew was most slick. The rain held out so far, but Randolph sensed it was only a matter of time before that changed. A dull gray loomed overhead. They did not have long. The women were inside doing whatever it was women did, probably gossiping. As much as Randolph genuinely loved Janet, the imminent conversation was best had without her—a heart to heart between men, father and son. Max helped bring levity that was sure to be needed.

"Can we talk now?" Randolph said.

He and Bruce stood on either side of a makeshift box, their not so nimble limbs the walls that would keep Max from straying too far beyond Bruce's comfort zone.

While Bruce's attention was on Max, he said, "What do you want to talk about?"

Everything.

"There's so much, really. To be honest, I'm not sure where the best place to start is."

"How about with that strange woman half your age who's inside my house right now?"

It was fair. Not the beginning, per se, but it was somewhere to start. "Her name is Sheila."

"I know."

"And she's not strange. Be nice. You don't know her."

"Do you?"

He thought about that, as he had on many other occasions. Perhaps for the first time, he felt comfortable with the word yes. While it was not possible to know everything about someone else, he knew her in her heart. Understood what made her tick. Shared love with her.

"Your mother and I are getting a divorce."

Bruce looked at him. "Does she know this?"

"It was her idea."

Bruce studied him. For a lie, perhaps. "Why is this the first I'm hearing of it?"

"We've been unhappy for many years."

"You haven't seemed it. Every time I've been around, you've been fine."

"That was the idea. We didn't want you to notice."

Bruce looked away, refocused on his son.

"I admit Sheila and I haven't known one another for very long, but we have a strong connection. I know this may be difficult for you to hear, but it's the truth."

"It's not about her, Dad. It's really not. She seems nice enough."

"Then what is it about?"

Bruce leaped to his right and redirected Max, who tried to wander too far. "It's that you didn't tell me. And that the way I find out is by you bringing your new girl...or woman...or, what should I call her? Your new someone to my house without so much as a courtesy to give me a heads up about what's been going on."

"I'm sorry about that. It was a lapse in my judgment."

Bruce looked at him again, and Randolph thought he knew what he was thinking. *It's not the only lapse in your judgment.*

And maybe he was right.

Max slipped and fell and giggled about it. Randolph watched with pure joy as his grandson popped to his feet and smiled through a surprisingly full set of teeth. He saw Bruce in Max's expression, and Janet. But he also saw Patricia in his eyes—deep emerald and enthralling. Max was going to break someone's heart one day with those eyes, just as Patricia had done with hers.

"I'm sorry we didn't tell you," Randolph said. "We didn't want to worry you."

"I'm not a child. I could have handled it."

"You're right. It doesn't make sense in retrospect. You would have found out, eventually. I guess we weren't sure how to tell you."

Not like this.

Rain began to trickle. The gray clouds surrounded the house.

"Are you happy?" Bruce asked.

It was a simple question, and not one he expected. Coming from Bruce meant he wanted to know, which meant he cared, which meant all was not lost—which meant maybe, just maybe, Randolph had not screwed up too badly.

"I am happy. Exhausted, but happy."

"Why are you exhausted?"

"Short version: Lots of driving, lots to figure out with the divorce, lots of newness."

"You drove all the way here from Iowa?"

"Sure did."

"When do you go back to work?"

"Oh, I haven't told you. I don't."

"Pardon?"

"Early retirement."

"When did this happen?"

"About the same time as everything else."

Bruce looked at him good. This time with less anger and judgment; more concern instead. He bent over and scooped up Max, who had started to dig in the lawn.

"Are you all right, Dad?"

"What do you mean?"

"Are you having a midlife crisis or something?"

Randolph laughed, though even he thought it sounded dishonest. That was the second time he had been asked that question. What was up with that?

"Well?"

"No, I'm not having a midlife crisis. Just a lot of changes all at once."

"Isn't that the definition of a midlife crisis?"

"Trust me, I'm fine. I appreciate your concern." It came out sharper than he intended.

"It's just...the divorce, and now a new woman—who, might I add, is half your age—"

"You mentioned that."

"And now your job. You love your job. And your hair. And you showing up unannounced and expecting everything would be okay."

"What about my hair?"

"It looks ridiculous."

"Sheila thinks it looks nice."

"Of course she does! She's my age. Why would she want to be with someone your age? No offense."

"It's not like that. You know nothing about our relationship. And you know nothing about her."

"You're right, I don't. But I suspect neither do you."

Randolph was getting angry. "Watch yourself. You're overstepping."

"How long has it been? How long have you two known each other?"

A week. Almost.

"What does it matter?"

"How long?"

"Long enough."

Bruce scoffed. "You're too embarrassed to say it out loud, aren't you?"

"Stop it."

"Come on, Dad! Open your eyes. Don't you see what's happening here?"

"Bruce, I'm warning you."

"She's using you! You have to see it. Why else would someone like her even think about getting involved with someone like you?"

"Enough."

"How stupid can you be to—"

"I said that's enough!"

Bruce stopped then, let it sink in. Max squirmed in his arms.

"You don't know what you're talking about," Randolph said. "So I would appreciate it if you stopped pretending like you did."

"Dad, I'm—"

"I'm going in the house. You should put a jacket on that baby before he catches a cold."

CHAPTER THIRTY-FOUR

The filthy hick with the toothpick stared at them, unblinking. Benji's stomach crawled just looking at the man. He smelled like feet, even from the distance between them.

"Just fill up the tank, man," Benji said. He covered his nose with his shirt and coughed.

Toothpick nodded and disappeared.

"Don't be a dick," Cheyenne said.

He coughed again. "Roll up the window, will you? Guy's nasty."

She did, though it did not take a genius to figure out she disapproved. Nevertheless, it was true; the hick was repulsive. After a couple of minutes, the gas pump clicked and shook the car. Then as if he had not moved at all, the toothpick man reappeared again at the window. Cheyenne lowered it.

"Twenty-nine fifty," the guy said.

Cheyenne looked at Benji and motioned toward the back. He unbuckled and leaned over the seat, reached for the black duffel Cheyenne had been carrying around. Inside were stacks of green, each bundled and wound tightly. He slid a finger under one of the straps and yanked until it snapped. He discarded the strap inside the bag and fingered out a couple of twenties. He zipped the bag and spun back, handed the cash to Cheyenne.

Toothpick's eyes were locked on the bag in the back. Benji got a bad feeling; he did not like the look in toothpick's eyes. He wished Cheyenne would hurry up and give the man the money so they could move on and get out of there before toothpick started trouble. For all they knew, there was a relentless gang of toothpicks ready to attack at any moment's notice. People motivated by greed did things they were not proud of—Benji knew—and he could only imagine what this disgusting man might be willing to do. Toothpick pocketed the cash, though his eyes did not shift.

Until they did, back to them, as if he were released from a trance. "Where ya'll comin' from?"

"Iowa," Cheyenne said.

The man smirked. His mouth opened when he did, which exposed the teeth that were charred so black Benji did not think it was possible. He thought he was going to be sick.

"Why do you ask?" she said.

"Oh, jus' wonderin'. Is there a festival or somethin' I don't know about?"

"Just passing through. Why?"

"Oh, ya know. It's not every day we get out-of-towners in these parts. Though lately, this makes two."

"*Two what? Out-of-towners?*"

"*Iowinians.*"

Cheyenne shot Benji a look. He caught on to it too.

Shay.

"There was another person from Iowa here? When?" Cheyenne said.

"Oh, I can't say I quite remember." His eyes darted back to the bag in the back.

Cheyenne did that thing with her eyes again and Benji sighed. He retrieved a hundred from the stack in the back and passed it over.

"Come to think of it," toothpick said, "I do remember something. Not just one person. Two of 'em. Guy and gal, just like you."

Benji felt his eyes bulge. He was right. Shay was in trouble. "The girl," he blurted. "Did she appear in any trouble?"

"Oh, you see, I don't really remember much else—"

"For fuck's sake," Benji said. He reached behind him and grabbed an entire stack, shoved it toward the gross man. "Tell me everything you know."

The man's eyes were huge. He pushed the stack toward his nose and inhaled, then laughed like a hyena that had just made a fresh kill.

"Dude?" Benji said. But there was no response. "Hey, dirtbag!"

The laughing stopped. "Huh?"

"Stop fucking with me. What else do you know?"

"No trouble. Both of 'em sitting there just like ya'll. Got a room there." —he pointed toward the Comfort Inn across the street—"And that's all I know."

"When was this?" Cheyenne asked.

"Day before yesterday, I'd say."

"Thank you."

The man smiled. Huge. "Come back anytime!"

The window rolled up as the man shouted in celebration. Cheyenne locked onto Benji.

"Has to be her, right?" she said.

"Can't be a coincidence."

But then Benji thought of something. He quickly unbuckled and yanked on the door handle and stood up, looked for toothpick. "Hey, one more thing."

Toothpick turned, still smiling.

"How do you know they were from Iowa?"

"The license plate, brother."

. . . . .

Night fell. They were locked up in a second floor end unit, stumped on what to do next, where to go. The front desk would not share any information about any of their previous guests—hotel policy. They would neither confirm nor deny anyone matching the person in the photo Benji shared was currently or had ever been a guest. The woman got angry when Benji offered her a cash bribe.

Fuck.

The phone records stopped there. Benji checked in with his source at the call center again, but no additional calls or texts had been made from Shay's phone. And yes, he was sure. The trail had gone cold. Like ice.

Shay had vanished.

Was the dirty toothpick man fucking with him? How would he even know if Shay was in danger? What could he possibly determine from seeing two people fuel up anyway? Benji felt cheated somehow, as if the man had been holding back. But why? On the contrary, it was difficult to imagine a motive for withholding information. All he knew was he wanted Shay to be okay. He would do whatever it took.

He paced a rectangle in the room because he did not know what else to do. His contact would alert him right away if activity showed up on Shay's phone—for a price, certainly—but there were limitations to that. In secrecy, for one, and during normal business hours. The contact was not willing to risk getting caught doing something he was not permitted to do. Understandable. But not comforting. For all Benji knew, Shay had reappeared on the map already but there was no channel to communicate the information to him.

He screamed in frustration.

Cheyenne, who was resting on the bed, sprung to attention. "What? What's wrong?"

He screamed again.

Fingers went into her ears. "For the love of God, will you stop screaming?"

He stopped, but not because she asked him to.

"You're drawing attention to us," she said. "Just stop. Cool it."

"How are you so calm about this? We have nothing!"

"And you think losing your shit is going to help? Calm yourself, take the edge off."

"But she's out there! She's been here. We're so close I can taste it."

"Just relax. Sleep it off, see if anything updates overnight."

He stopped pacing and shook his head. "You don't understand. There will be no updates overnight. We're going to be stuck here holding our dicks in our hands, waiting for something to happen."

She scoffed. "Speak for yourself."

"We can't do nothing."

"Then do something."

He wanted to pull his hair out. "That's what I'm trying to tell you. There's nothing we can do."

"I thought you were some big-time hacker? Can't you...hack into something and figure it out?"

He stared at her. "That's not how it works."

"Well, how the hell should I know? That's your job, not mine."

He did not know what to say. He began to pace again. She was right, ultimately, but their situation had changed; it was not supposed to go down like this. Their roles should be adjusted accordingly to reflect this new situation, which meant Cheyenne would have to do more. To make matters worse, they were being watched now too. Airport guy. It felt like everything was hanging by a thread and threatening to crash down at any moment. Things would end badly for all of them—very, very badly.

A phone rang, but it was not his. He kept pacing.

"Shut up," Cheyenne said. "I'm serious. This is important. Be invisible."

He nodded but kept pacing. And he listened.

"Hi, honey," she said into the phone. Then she waited, then responded. Waited, responded. Said nothing that indicated who it was on the other end. "Yes, of course. As soon as I can." Waited. "No, you did the right thing. See you soon."

Then she hung up.

A devilish grin crept onto her face.

"Who was that?"

"So little faith in the universe, you have."

He grunted.

"Our luck just changed."

"How much?"

"A lot."

"How much is a lot?"

"Airport a lot."

CHAPTER THIRTY-FIVE

Randolph isolated himself in the back bedroom—or what used to be a bedroom; now, it was partially a playroom for Max, partially a storage locker for an absurd quantity of non-essentials. A functioning hoarder was a trait Bruce sadly inherited from his mother.

He tried to calm himself. His skin was warm and his brow was wet with perspiration, his heart rate elevated. His hands trembled with anger. What, exactly, was he angry about? He repeatedly asked himself that question. Was it really as he said it before—that Bruce had overstepped—or was the reality that Bruce said what he did not want to hear, that the truth hurt?

Was he losing it?

Or worse, had he already lost it?

Deep breaths. Inhale, exhale. Relax. Be logical.

Logic—that was the key. As an engineer for twenty-five years, the bulk of his adult life was built around the mindset. An economical home, an affordable vehicle—okay, the truck was a bit of a splurge, but a man could treat himself once in a while, no?—and a hefty safety net for unforeseeable future events life threw his way. A slow build of wealth to ensure a happy and fulfilled and sustainable retirement. Everything had been so scripted, so perfect. Where did it go wrong?

He thought about what Bruce said—that Sheila was using him. Well, for what? She did not know about his fortune until recently—

though the word fortune felt like an exaggeration; it was more of a heavily padded net—long after they met and formed feelings for one another. He ran through the timeline in his head—the supermarket, the hospital, the night at the bar, and the kiss that ensued. Then the nights in the no-tells and the countless hours stuck together in a box on the open road. And O'Reilly.

O'Reilly.

It did not make sense. Money had not been a topic of conversation, not until after Patricia's call. The more he thought about it, he realized he still did not know about Sheila's financial situation. She was employed at the supermarket—or at least used to be, before it exploded—but whether that was out of necessity or to avoid boredom, he could not say. Whether she had a hundred dollars or a million or ten times that amount did not matter. The money did not matter—not to him, and not to her. Bruce was dead wrong about that.

What else could she have been using him for? He thought hard about that but drew a blank. Nothing. He was who he was. She loved him for him. And the hair? That was simply to help protect him, as her own was for her, in case O'Reilly came back. She was looking out for him. Because she loved him. That was how those things worked.

So what was the problem? Bruce misunderstood the dynamic for what it was—which was not difficult to imagine if Randolph flipped the roles and envisioned himself in his son's position. That was all. He could not understand what Randolph was going through. Maybe one day, though hopefully not. It was unfair of him to judge his father for decisions he was unable to fully comprehend the motivations behind.

"Hey," a voice said. A woman's.

He had not heard anyone knock or enter, and he was startled back to focus. Sheila's head poked through the doorway, the door cracked just enough.

"Hey," he said.

"You okay?"

He nodded.

"Didn't go well?" She meant the conversation with Bruce.

"Quite the contrary."

She walked toward him, placed a hand on his forearm, and massaged it. "I'm sorry."

He nodded once but did not speak.

"He'll come around eventually. It'll just take time. It's all still new, you know?"

She was right. Right? Bruce just learned his parents were splitting up, and he had to come to grips with that in his own way. While he was a grown man, it still changed things for him too—holidays and birthdays and conversations that either should or should not be confidential; he was going to have to figure it all out. The guilt saddened Randolph and reminded him of why he had tried to push off the inevitability for so long.

This. This was why.

The impact was far greater than on just him and Patricia. Their son and his family would be affected too, and other less important relatives and many joint friends. Who would take whose side? Did they have to choose sides? Randolph did not know the protocol for these types of things; he had not gone through it himself. Life was so much easier when everyone held up their end of the bargain and fulfilled their part of a commitment.

That was before.

Now was after.

He felt saddened. Run-down. Unhappy and depressed. It was still something he was trying to get used to, too. "I'm okay," he said. "Thanks for checking on me. I'll be out in a minute."

She smiled, though it was sad. She walked away and out of the room and closed the door behind her.

It was more than a minute; it was many minutes. The rain had picked up outside. Droplets pelted against the glass like bullets, paralyzing Randolph's focus and withdrawing him from the moment. He thought of nothing as his vision blurred. The longer he stared at the glass, the wetter it got. The rain soothed him, washed away the negativity that enveloped his psyche. Everything would be all right.

There was a rap on the door. He turned to investigate, but before he could answer, the door opened. In walked Bruce, who closed the door behind him.

"What are you doing in here?" he asked.

"Just needed a breather is all."

"Have you caught your breath yet? Your guest is dying out there." *Sheila.*

"Is she all right?"

"She's fine, but she's alone."

"I thought you didn't care about her?"

"That's actually not what I said. Not at all. I specifically said it's not about her."

"I know it's—"

"Listen, Dad. I'm sorry. For earlier. Everything has been a little shocking. You know? I should have handled it better."

Randolph did know. More than Bruce knew. "I get it. I'm sorry too."

Bruce nodded. So did Randolph. Everything was good.

"So, what do you say?" Bruce said. "Join us for a game of Rummy? For old time's sake."

Randolph smiled at the memory. He and Bruce used to play often—that, and chess and checkers when he was a boy. It was how they bonded, talked about men stuff. They chatted about puberty over a game of chess, and the birds and the bees. Bruce told him about the first girl he loved during a game of Rummy during his senior year of high school. He later married that girl, but not before he told his father about his cold feet beforehand. It was normal, Randolph told him at the time, though it was not something he experienced himself, but he thought it was what he was supposed to say. Whatever he said that day worked out because Janet was still around. And they were happy. And she was having another baby.

"I'd love to."

They joined the women on the sofa. Max played with a pile of miniature cars on the carpet, completely entertained as if they were the most thrilling toys a boy could have. Randolph felt better. He sensed Bruce did too. The energy in the room felt good, like a happy home. Sheila draped her arm around his shoulder and pulled him in close. He let it happen and leaned into her.

"I think she's lovely," Janet said, a childish grin on her face.

Sheila laughed. "You're a sweetheart."

"I don't know where you found this girl, but she's a keeper."

Randolph smiled, though he hoped the question was purely rhetorical; he did not want to get into it right now. He wished he had something to occupy his hands.

Max played independently so well, complete with mouthed sounds of his interpretation of cars and trucks—far better than Bruce ever did as a boy. His lips rattled as he drove a pickup truck in a circle around his little body on the carpet, leaving a dark ring like a racetrack. Randolph could not help but smile while he watched.

"I hate to ask because I don't want you to get the wrong impression," Bruce said from the far side of the sofa, "but what's your plan?"

It was a reasonable question—one Randolph had expected. "I know we can't stay for long, I get that. If I'm being honest, we don't really have a plan. Ridiculous, I know."

Bruce nodded. "Can I ask why?"

He let out an anxious sigh. He supposed it was time for an explanation. "That's only fair."

Bruce leaned back, folded his hands in his lap. He was all ears. Where to start?

Then Randolph's pocket vibrated.

He leaned back and reached inside and somehow managed to squeeze the phone out of his pocket without tearing the seam that tightly hugged his thigh. The screen was blurry at first, but when his eyes adjusted, he saw the name.

"Hold that thought," he said. "I need to take this." He swiped the green button and held the phone to his ear, then got up and stepped into the short hallway. He kept his voice low. "Where the hell have you been? I've been calling you."

"Shut up and listen for a minute," Larry said. "We've got a problem."

CHAPTER THIRTY-SIX

They were on an airplane—Benji and Cheyenne. Thankfully, it was Cheyenne next to him this time rather than the Buffalo from before. Though if he was honest with himself, he had grown tired of Cheyenne's company and wanted her gone just as much as he had the Buffalo man. But that would have to wait. Business first.

He leaned toward her and whispered, "When we land, what's the plan?"

Her face was buried in the in-flight magazine that lived in the net behind the seat in front of her. Many of the pages were dog-eared. She did not look at him.

"You know what the plan is."

That was true. He did. No sense in rehashing what had already been discussed more times than he could remember, although the affirmation would have been nice. He slipped earbuds in, reclined the seat, and closed his eyes.

This would all be over soon.

CHAPTER THIRTY-SEVEN

"What kind of problem?" Randolph said into the phone as he creeped deeper down the hallway. "Did you find the tapes?"

"I'm still working on that. But fuck the tapes. We've got bigger fish to fry."

"What is it?"

"I've been poking around, making some calls," Larry said. "And shit's about to go down."

"How so?"

"With your wife."

"Explain."

"Do you have an accountant?"

"I do."

"Has he made you aware of what's going on?"

The forty grand.

"I'm aware."

"Are you, though?"

"Patricia made two cash withdrawals for twenty grand each. How do you even know about that?"

"Don't worry about that. It's my job to know these things. The money—that's only the tip of the iceberg."

"What's going on?"

"Did you know she has two one-way tickets to Sweden? Purchased three months ago. Scheduled to leave two weeks from today."

"Sweden? No, I know nothing about that."

"Did you know she's opened up three separate individual offshore bank accounts since January? Or that she put a down payment on a condo in Fiji?"

"Fiji?"

"This is bad, Randolph. Really, really bad."

His head spun. What did any of this mean?

"It's clear as day what's going on here," Larry said. "Do you not see it?"

He did not know what he saw. He was beyond confused. How did he miss these things?

"She's cleaning you out while you're still married. She's bleeding you dry, slowly but surely. She'll take as much as she can before the divorce is final, stash it away where the government can't get it, and still take her third of what's left." Larry knew about the prenup and the two-thirds, one-third split; in fact, he wrote it.

Bitch.

"Well, shit."

"Well, shit is right!"

Randolph's heart pounded. Adrenaline shot through him like fire. He tried to focus. "What do I do?"

"The freezing of the account was a good start, but it's only temporary."

"How do you—"

"As I said before, don't worry about it. Don't ask questions."

"Okay."

"Good. Now, this is what you need to do. For all the credit accounts where you're the primary, have her taken off immediately. For your joint accounts, it will take longer, but we can file for a motion to freeze all joint assets. With the evidence we have, it'll be granted, no question. But we need to file the divorce paperwork first. I took it upon myself to make some adjustments to the agreement your wife's attorney sent, just so you know. You'll appreciate the revised terms. Are you somewhere I can fax it to you?"

"I'm afraid not."

"Can you come in?"

"Not possible. I'm out of town."

"Well, wherever the hell you are, you need to come back right away. If we don't get these papers signed and filed, Patricia's going to keep chipping away. Anything over ten thousand will be flagged by the bank. If she's smart, she'll start taking smaller amounts at a time."

"What about the frozen account?"

"It's just temporary. In a few days, at most, it'll be unfrozen and she can withdraw up to ten grand every day. And as a joint account, there's nothing you can do about it."

"Fuck. This is bad."

"You honestly have no idea. Get your ass over here as soon as you can so we can stop the bleeding."

Randolph nodded to no one, knew what he had to do. "I will. I'm coming back."

"Good. Oh, and one more thing."

"What?"

"Just remember that Patricia is your life insurance beneficiary while you're still married. Once the divorce is final, you need to change that right away. First thing you do. I'll have the documentation ready, you just need to give me a name to put down."

What?

"Let me think about that. I'll get back to you. Do you think I'm in danger?"

"I didn't say that."

"Then what are you saying?"

"All I'm saying is people do weird shit when they're going through a divorce—I've seen it all."

"Have you seen this?"

"I've seen it all."

He thought about that, let it sink in.

"You think you know someone until everything's being taken away," Larry said. "You just never know what people will do when money's involved. Watch your back, Randolph. That's all I'm saying."

"Thanks, Larry."

"I've got to get off now—the wife's on the other line. Do what you have to do and get back into town sooner rather than later. Got it?"

"I'm on it."

"I'll get all the paperwork ready. Talk soon."

.   .   .   .   .

He took Larry's advice. Of the handful of credit cards in his wallet, two were solely his. Patricia had been added as an authorized user many years before. He called the number on the back of each card and pressed one for English and waited in a short queue to talk to a live person who he asked to remove Patricia from the account. On one of the joint accounts, he paid off the remaining balance over the phone and closed it completely. The other two had zero balances, so he closed those too.

There was nothing he could do about the cash accounts. The asset accounts did not concern him, as they required signatures from each party to do anything; nothing could be sold or transferred without his consent. He considered Sweden and Fiji and how they were possible, and he concluded Patricia must have had individual accounts all along, or had opened new bank loans to get access to additional cash. Where the money came from if it was the former was hard to figure. But then he remembered something else Larry said and he felt a pinch in his gut. There was only one way to confirm.

He quickly dialed his accountant. Herm, being the man he was, answered straight away.

"Hello, Randolph. How are things?"

"Not good. Are you in front of your computer?"

"I am. Something I can do?"

"Can you check for additional large withdrawals under ten thousand?"

"What's large? Two grand? Three?"

"I'll check. Hang on."

He waited, anxiously paced. The pain in his gut worsened with each moment that passed.

"Um, Randolph?"

"How bad is it?"

"I'm so sorry. Anything under ten—"

"I understand, Herm. It's not your fault. Just tell me how bad it is."

"Three grand here, four there. Seven and a half. Six. It's all over the place."

"Since when?"

"The first of the year. January second was the first one."

Randolph felt sick.

"It's been every couple of days, sometimes daily. I'm so sorry."

It made sense. He would see all the year-end tax statements, but not until a year from now. By then, the divorce would be final, the papers signed. The damage done. Larry was right; Patricia was cleaning him out. It was as clear as crystal. Sweat drenched his face.

"Randolph?"

"I have to go. I...I need to go."

"If you need anything, call me. I'm so sorry."

He hung up. Then he covered his mouth and rushed into the bathroom and retched into the porcelain.

CHAPTER THIRTY-EIGHT

Everything spun—his vision, his mind, his world. What was happening? He lurched a stream of nothingness, but the pain was real. His stomach ached where it should not, deep inside his gut. Everything trembled.

Someone knocked on the door.

"Not now," he said.

But someone entered anyway.

"Not now, I said!"

"You all right, Dad?"

Randolph reached up and grabbed the handle, pulled it down. Water and phlegm swirled and spun before disappearing, which did not help his vertigo. He closed the lid and pressed his back against the bowl.

"Was it something you ate?"

"No, nothing like that."

Bruce nodded, folded his arms. "Who was on the phone?"

Randolph swallowed, tasted the acidity from his throat and the warmth of his breath. He thought he might be sick again.

"What's going on?" Bruce said. He seemed both concerned and irritated with tight lips and tired eyes. All the drama had clearly worn him thin.

"Your mother is stealing from me."

Bruce laughed. "That's preposterous. How can someone steal something that's technically theirs?"

It was a struggle, but Randolph dragged himself to his feet, used the wall as a crutch. "There are certain things about being married that aren't always as they seem."

"Please don't give me a lecture about marriage, okay? You seem to forget sometimes that I'm married too. Happily, might I add."

"You're right."—a pause—"Your mother signed a prenuptial agreement before we married."

Bruce unfolded his arms and leaned against the door frame. "I never knew that."

"Why would you? A man's marriage is his business only. There's a lot you don't know. But to understand the scope of everything that's gone on, I think you should know."

Bruce nodded. "Okay."

"Okay."

"But can we not do it in here? I need to sit."

They moved back into the living room. Janet's motherly instincts took over, and she set Max up with a movie and a snack and a cup of juice. Sheila slid over and stayed quiet, made room for Bruce on the sofa next to his father. By now, Randolph assumed Sammy was no longer around for good since he still had not seen any signs of her. She was a good dog.

All eyes were on him. Sheila knew many of the details already, but for those she did not, she was about to. He spent the next dozen, maybe two dozen minutes—however long it took; he did not keep track—telling them everything he thought was relevant.

The moment he discovered Patricia's infidelity broke his heart. While things between them were not perfect, he thought they were in love and mostly happy. They had been sexually active just days before. She came home late one night—something that had begun to occur with a much higher frequency than was normal; out with friends, she said—and he saw it through the upstairs window. Her with another man. They embraced like lovers at the end of the driveway, smooched like friends would not. Randolph closed the blinds and sat on the bed, dropped his head into his hands.

At first, he was in denial. They were platonic friends who showed casual affection for one another—that was all. But his eyes would not lie, and what he saw was impossible to unsee. The embrace lasted longer than it would have if they were just friends. The smooch was more than a friendly peck; it was glazed with a passion she once had for him, their hands all over one another.

It was his fault—that was how he felt. His sexual performance had been pathetic in recent months. It was not just the length of performance that caused the issues; it was before the event even started. Something about him was off. He chose not to confront Patricia that night. He was not quite sure what to say to her, how to broach what he saw. Instead, he killed the lights and slipped into bed and tossed the covers over himself and pretended to be asleep. He was awake while Patricia undressed and showered and eventually crawled in next to him and fell asleep with her back facing him.

The next morning, he called out from work and made an appointment with his doctor instead. His prostate was checked. His PSA had been monitored and tracked for years without issue, so his doctor expected nothing. But a week later, once the results came back, he was summoned back to the doctor's office for further testing. Cancer was confirmed. Monitoring rather than removal was oftentimes the best course of treatment, especially when caught early.

He never did tell his wife.

Instead, he shut down—emotionally, certainly, but also physically. Sex with Patricia no longer interested him. She did not seem bothered, either, since she was getting what she needed from much younger, more handsome men than he—that part was an assumption, but he was not blind to the likely reality.

It went on that way for a few years. He did not look at her that way, and she did not care. Worse, she was happy. Sexually fulfilled for the first time in more years than either one of them could possibly remember, with no expectations to pretend to be happy being with a man who repulsed her. And without the physical connection, the rest of it became a problem. They were emotionally disconnected too, then entirely.

He was at his lowest point when he met Sheila—though met was a stretch—when he saw her. He had taken a lot of time off from work in recent weeks, had pondered retirement to move onto the next phase of his life—whatever that may have been. He was unhappy and lacked enthusiasm for anything he used to. Nothing mattered. He was at his lowest point. Rock bottom.

And then he saw her.

Sheila.

The same crimson apron she wore four days later, when he finally worked up the courage to have a conversation with her for the first time, drew his eye to her. Not to mention the way she smiled and laughed and spoke sweetly to everyone who passed through her line. He had to see her up close.

He grabbed a hand of bananas and walked up to her line, placed it on the conveyor belt. She smiled at him and grabbed the bananas by the tops and entered a code into her computer.

"How are you today?" she asked him.

That was the first time she spoke to him. And it was the first time anyone had asked him that in a very long time.

"I'm...I'm good."—he smiled—"Really good." And he was.

After, he spent the next few days pondering if he should talk to her—really talk—and what to say to her if he did. It took two more trips through her line on consecutive days before he opened his mouth and asked for what he wanted on the third. The rest, they say, was history.

Randolph looked up. Janet's eyes were filled with tears, Sheila's sorrow. Bruce was still, in a state of shock.

"You have cancer?" Bruce said. "You've had it and didn't tell anyone?"

"It's under control. It hasn't grown. My doctor's monitoring it."

Bruce jumped up and threw his hands on his head. "Jesus Christ, Dad! Cancer! You have cancer."

"It's not as bad as it sounds. Prostate cancer is one of the most curable forms of cancer in the world. Did you know eight out of ten men will have cancerous cells in their prostate by the time they're eighty?"

"What the hell, Dad? Why didn't you tell me?"

"I'm telling you now."

"Oh, come on, stop with that. That's bullshit and you know it."

Randolph did not respond. Instead, he let his son blow off steam. He understood his frustration about everything; it was hard not to. And he understood why he was upset, why he must have felt out of the loop. But in fairness, no one knew. Just him and his doctor. And Sheila.

Sheila.

It took a minute, but Bruce eventually calmed down and sat next to his wife. Janet put her arm around him and massaged his shoulder. Max was enthralled by the television, oblivious to the commotion behind him.

"What does any of this have to do with Mom robbing you?" Bruce said.

"What!" Janet said as if she had been personally wounded by the words her husband spoke. "Robbing you? Patricia?"

"Yes," Randolph said. "Patricia."

Janet shook her head as in disbelief. "My goodness."

"Well?" Bruce said. "What's the deal?"

Randolph told him. Everything. About the explosion and the hospital and meeting O'Reilly. Then about hitting the road with Sheila without a plan and about the phone call from Patricia about the tapes. Then about Herm's discovery, and Larry's, then Herm again. Janet shook her head the entire time he spoke while the disbelief on Bruce's face broke Randolph's heart. But he had to hear it if he wanted the whole truth.

"I don't even know what to say," Bruce said.

"Join the club."

"I'm sorry, Dad."

"Yeah, me too."

Silence fell. What now? There was not much left to be said. Thankfully, a distraction came. Randolph's phone—it rang again.

"Speak of the devil," he said as he retrieved it. "It's Patricia."

The room collectively gasped. Randolph put a finger to his mouth to signify quiet.

"Patricia," he said. "To what do I owe this pleasure?"

"Why are my credit cards turned off? And why are the accounts frozen?"

"I know what you're up to. I know about the withdrawals."

"I don't know what you're talking about."

Typical response. He knew she would lie about it.

"Are you going to answer my question?" she said.

"To protect myself."

She did not respond, which told him everything he needed to know.

"And I'd also like to remove you as the beneficiary on my life insurance policy. For the same reason."

Silence.

"Patricia?"

"I'm here. I heard you. We'll discuss it when I get there."

"Excuse me?"

"Pulling in now, see you in a minute."

She hung up.

"What's wrong?" Janet said. His expression must have told quite the tale.

He pocketed the phone and tried to swallow, though his throat was parched. His hand shook. "Patricia," he said. "She's here."

CHAPTER THIRTY-NINE

Cheyenne hung up the phone and pointed to the driveway on the right. Benji rolled into it without flipping the directional. The street was void of other vehicles or people. One of the neighbors had a basketball hoop set up on the street. The rental was ordinary—mid-size with low performance output and high mileage. Entirely forgettable, not at all exciting, but it sufficed. After a three-hour flight and three more hours on the road, he was exhausted and grumpy and ready for it to all be over. And it was about to be.

"This it?" he asked.

Cheyenne nodded.

He parked behind the massive truck with the Iowa plates to make a barricade should things go south. Rain showered down and smeared the glass as the old wipers failed to efficiently do their job.

"You're sure about this?" he said. But Cheyenne's door was already opened, and she was gone. He jammed the transmission into park and stepped on the parking brake, then joined her in the rain.

By now, he knew Shay was with another man—but not just any man; the man. Willingly or not, he could not say yet. Though he was about to find out. The man from the airport called to check in during the drive, and Benji told him what he wanted to know; prison was not something he was interested in inviting into his life. The man had been tracking them and knew where they were and would not be far behind, he said, so it was about to be a party. The mysteries of his existence would soon be solved. He did not even care that the man had tracked him somehow; they were beyond that.

He lingered a step behind Cheyenne as she pounded her heels into the stairs and ascended toward the door. She rapped it twice and rang the doorbell and impatiently waited with her hands on her hips. The door opened and a man appeared. The man? He could not remember what his face looked like.

"What are you doing here?" the man said.

"We have to talk."

The man looked at Benji and pointed. "Who the hell is this guy?"

"I could ask you the same thing."

The man grunted and turned and disappeared into the house. Cheyenne followed but did not motion for Benji to do the same, but he did anyway. Like a roach sneaking under the door, ready to lurk. Unwelcomed. A crowd awaited inside—two men plus him, three women, and of all things, a baby. It was a circus. Madness. Almost humorous.

The tall, thin, motherly looking woman bent down and scooped up the baby, held him tight against her chest as if he were in danger. One of the men said nothing, though he shielded what Benji assumed was his wife and baby with his body as if the cockroach would infect them if they were not careful. The other man—the older, grumpy one who opened the door—engaged in an argument with Cheyenne about something Benji could not maintain focus on. He kept his eyes on him, tried to place the face. It was the man, he was almost certain. Shit was about to go down. The third woman in the room creeped behind the old guy and hid, her fiery red hair like a flame at his back.

Was it Shay? He stepped to the right but still could not see her face.

"What are you doing here?" the old man said.

"We need to talk," Cheyenne said.

"I've heard about what you've been up to, thieving from Dad," the protector said. "What's wrong with you?"

"Oh, please. You don't know the half of it."

The third woman continued to hide.

"Well tell me, then," the protector said. "What's going on here?"

"Who's this guy?" the old guy said, pointing to Benji. It was the second time he asked.

Everyone looked at him. Except for the hidden woman.

"Who's this?" Cheyenne said, motioning to the hidden woman.

"Her name is Sheila," the old man said.

Benji got a good look at the older man's face. His features were weathered—thin wrinkles on his cheeks, bags under his eyes, unnatural bleach blond hair on his head. It was indisputably the man, though something about him was different. He could not place what it was. The redhead behind him finally stepped out and showed herself, and Benji gasped.

Shay!

"Shay!" he said as he stepped toward her. But he stopped himself after a step and retreated, unsure of his next move. She looked stunning with the red.

"Shay?" the protector said. "Who's Shay?"

Everyone looked at each other. When Cheyenne met Shay's gaze, they locked. Awestruck. Shock? What was happening?

"It's you," Cheyenne said.

"It's you," Shay said back.

They know each other?

"You know each other?" Benji said.

"How do you two know each other?" the old blonde guy added.

Silence. The two women continued to stare at one another.

"Earth to Mom," the protector said. "What the hell is going on here?"

Benji wondered the same thing.

CHAPTER FORTY

One year ago. A woman walked into a dark room. Her skirt was short and her stockings were lacy and patterned with hearts, and she was on the prowl. Music thumped around her, rumbled through her heels and up between her legs, and she shivered. Her senses were heightened.

The perimeter of the room was lined with sofas occupied by men and women, men and men, and women and women—sometimes two of one, one of another, sometimes more. Martini glasses were handed out like candy by women with skirts as short as her own, and with blouses with an extra button undone to help encourage better tips. Sex was everywhere. She smelled it, tasted it. Lusted for it.

It was the first party of this type she had attended. She heard from a friend of a friend about a group of swingers who gathered in the basement of a rundown club every Thursday. Entry required a verbal passcode which she gave the bouncer outside the entry of the main club above. The muscle man whistled and a modestly attractive woman with black leather pants and six-inch heels came out and motioned for the new guest to follow. The entrance to the basement was at the back of the club, behind a curtain manned by another bouncer and a velvet rope. The leather woman whispered something to the bouncer and he moved aside and let the women pass. They descended a set of creaky stairs toward a locked door. The weight of the damp foundation pinched her lungs as she inhaled, but she felt whatever it was on the other side of the door rush through her. Leather woman keyed the lock, pulled the door open, and let the guest in. The door locked behind her.

She stood alone in a sea of lovers. Her eyes scanned her surroundings. A small bar in the corner was manned by a flamboyant bartender with hair that stood on end and shined as if gelled by a hose. The waitresses bounced around from group to group, sofa to sofa, trays elevated above their heads, their busts exploding. A dance floor lit up the center of the room. People partied hard.

The woman watched the most freeing, most scandalous dancer she had ever seen—the only person on the dance floor at the time. Strobe lights flashed green and blue and red and bounced around the room, but always returned to the solo dancer as if she were the spotlight of the party. To the nervous newbie, the iridescence was mesmerizing. Her heart thumped. A waitress approached her and offered a martini which she accepted without acknowledgment. She fingered the stem and breathed in the fire of the gin. She sipped to calm her anxiousness.

As if on cue, the solo dancer spotted her and their eyes locked. Her dancing slowed, the focus of her movements sharpened. Arms went above her head then slowly lowered and massaged her body—first her neck, then her chest, then her hips. Her eyes closed as the rhythm of the thumping shrouded her.

The newbie put the martini to her mouth and trembled as the gin penetrated her lips. Her tongue numbed and her cheeks burned, only then did she swallow and let the flame flood her throat. The dancer opened her eyes and locked them back on hers, kept swaying. The newbie downed the rest of the liquid and handed off the glass to a passing tray, kept her eyes straight ahead. A trio of olives stuck to a toothpick, which she held onto. She ate them slowly, with more tongue than necessary, as she watched the dancer. The gin that soaked them rushed to her head.

The song ended. Another one started, but she hardly noticed. The solo dancer gleamed with sweat in all the right places. Her top was cut so low she was close to popping out; the gin woman wanted nothing more. Two olives down and as moist as a towelette, the gin heavy on her breath, she worked up the courage to approach the dancer. The other patrons disappeared in her periphery as she strode while the butterflies spun beneath her blouse.

Instead of speaking to the magnetic dancer, she invaded her space and swayed her hips and danced with her. An inferno of desire swelled between them, aided by the gin that had her feeling loopy. Their bodies touched—first over their garments, platonic; then under, far from it. Skin upon skin. Before long, the dancer was inside her on the dance floor, and it took all she had to not scream out in ecstasy in front of everyone. She came quickly and completely. After, she grabbed the dancer's hand and pulled her toward one of the sofas, which she fell onto and struggled to find her wind. She felt incredible, high on life. Her thighs trembled, but not because of the bass that rattled the floor.

The dancer continued to sway while she sat, and the two women smiled at one another as if they were old friends. They still had not spoken. Once her breath returned, she sucked the remaining olive off the toothpick and discarded the wooden spear on the floor. The gin squelched against the back of her throat as she chewed.

"Gin?" the dancer finally said.

"Yep."

"I thought so. I can smell it."

She could smell the dancer too, and herself.

"I prefer vodka myself," the dancer said.

"I prefer anything that gets me drunk."

The women laughed.

"You're a great dancer," the gin woman said.

"Thanks. I find it so freeing. Clears my mind."

"What else clears your mind?"

"What clears yours?"

Before she could answer, a man approached. The dancer seemed to know the man but did not greet him by name. He was tall and gangly but very handsome with one strand of hair that fell out of place and bounced across his face as he moved. The dancer excused herself from their conversation and retreated with the man, who spoke into her ear. Gin woman watched intently, desperate for another drink to maintain her buzz, more so for the dancer to return before long.

The dancer approached the exit. Gin woman stood up and raised her hand to steal her attention, which worked. The dancer, now alone, stared at the gin woman for a long while, but she did not turn back. Her lips pursed and dimples formed on her cheeks, then she turned and walked out the open door.

Gin woman returned to the underground club every Thursday night for a month, hoping to run into the dancer again. On the fifth Thursday, she finally did. There she was, front and center on the dance floor with that all too familiar casual deliberateness that attracted the gin woman that first night. Her heart sped up when she saw her.

Unlike the first time, the gin woman walked with purpose—a famished cheetah encroaching upon a feeble gazelle—toward the woman she could not stop thinking about and had to have. "It's you," she said when she neared her. Other dancers filled in around them.

"It's you," the dancer said back.

"I wasn't sure I'd see you again."

"Did you want to?"

"I'm here, aren't I?"

The dancer smiled. "Dance with me."

They danced. For hours. Sweat drenched the gin woman's back, and her calves ached. Her feet too. When they could not stand it anymore, they locked themselves in a stall in the bathroom and teased one another with their lips, then their tongues. Then they left—to the gazelle's place, not the cheetah's—and they fucked. It was the cheetah's first time with a woman, if she excluded the finger-fucking from five weeks prior. The gazelle showed her tricks no man ever could or would ever dream of. It was, unquestionably, the hottest, most satisfying experience of her life.

"What's your name?" the cheetah asked afterward.

"What's yours?"

"Cheyenne."

"Is that your real name?"

"Nope."

The gazelle nodded, smiled.

"Yours?"

"Shay."

"Is that your real name?"

"Nope."

"You're great with your body," Cheyenne said.

"Thanks."

"I like you."

"You don't even know me."

"I still like you. There's something about you."

Shay leaned back and covered herself with the bedsheet. Cheyenne breathed heavily, tried to analyze her new friend's thoughts. Shay was magnetic, and Cheyenne could not keep her eyes off her.

After a while of nothing, Shay said, "I haven't seen you at the club before. Up until a few weeks ago."

"I'm new to the game."

"Why?"

"Why not?"

Shay leaned forward and smiled. "I know your type."

"Meaning what?"

"It's all over your face. You have that look about you."

"What look might that be?"

Shay folded her arms and sat back again. "You're married."

Cheyenne felt an initial embarrassment, but that quickly faded. "Why would you say that?"

"I can just tell. A woman of your age, first time. Looking to spice things up."

"Are you calling me old?"

"Older than me."

"What if I was married? Would it bother you?"

"None of my business."

"Yet, you brought it up."

Silence.

Then: "Other people's marriages are their own problem. It has no bearing on me."

Cheyenne scooted toward Shay. "Let me ask you something now."

"Okay."

"I get the impression you know people."

"Is that a question?"

"True or untrue?"

"We all know people."

"That's not what I mean."

Shay nodded. "Yes, I know people."

"I thought so."

"What kind of people?"

Cheyenne stared into her eyes, looked deep into her soul. What she saw was *truth*. "You know the kind of people I'm talking about."

"I think I do."

"Well then?"

"Well, what?"

"Can you help me?"

Shay did not respond right away. Her eyes darted all over—ceiling, bedsheets, back to Cheyenne. Cheyenne did not get the impression much convincing was going to be needed, but she was prepared to do what it took. They were on the same wavelength, however rare and improbable that may have sounded having just met and barely spoken.

"Okay," Shay said. "I'll help you. But first, what's in it for me?"

Cheyenne smiled. Cheers to new beginnings.

CHAPTER FORTY-ONE

"Well?" Randolph said after there was no response from the room. "How do you two know each other?"

He did know what else to say. Patricia, his wife, was there, and she knew Sheila. But how or why, they would not say. The way they looked at one another, though—the awestruck twinkles in their eyes, the gaped mouths, the way their cheeks blushed—made it clear they knew each other. And it was personal somehow. It may not have been his worst nightmare, but only because he would have not fathomed it possible. If he were to dream up a nightmarish scenario worse than this, he could not imagine it.

Shay? The strange Benji boy called Sheila Shay—what could that possibly mean? Did they know each other too? Randolph felt like he was in a twilight zone, hovering somewhere above his body and watching the happenings from the beyond. None of this could be real.

"Who is Shay?" Bruce said for the second time.

The boy named Benji pointed to Sheila, who stood close to Randolph. He felt her heat on him. "She is."

Bruce looked at Randolph and laughed. Randolph wanted to too, but everything was such a cluster he failed to react at all.

"I'm sorry, who are you again?" Bruce asked.

"Benji. I'm Benji."

"Right. But...who are you?"

Benji deferred to Patricia, who said, "Don't worry about him."

Like that would work.

"Mom, what—"

Something clicked for Randolph. He felt defiant, back within his body and in control of himself once again. "Hold the hell on here. Let me get this straight. You"—he pointed to Benji—"are Benji, but nobody knows who you are or why you're here. You"—he pointed to Patricia—"are Patricia. I know that for a fact. You—"

"Who's Patricia?" Benji said.

Randolph pointed to his wife. "She's Patricia!"

"You mean Cheyenne," Benji countered.

"No, I don't. Who's Cheyenne?"

"I'm confused."

Randolph wanted to ram his head through the wall and scream. What the hell was going on?

"How do you two know each other again?" Bruce said. He was asking about Patricia and Sheila.

Randolph caught Janet sneak behind Bruce and slip out of the room with the baby. She disappeared down the darkened hallway and closed a door—those motherly instincts at work again. He tried to keep it all straight in his head. Benji was Benji—though he still did not know who he was beyond a name or why he was there; Patricia was also Cheyenne, at least to Benji; Sheila was also Shay.

Well, at least he knew who he was.

"Why are you here?" Randolph said to Patricia. "How?"

"Bruce called."

He shot his eyes to his son. "What is she talking about?"

Bruce looked like he wanted to hide under a rock. "Oh, God. I messed up. That was before."

"Before what?"

"I thought you were losing it, Dad. I'm sorry. I was worried. After you told me all that stuff about Mom—"

"What stuff?" Patricia said. Or was it Cheyenne?

"About the money you're taking from me," Randolph said.

"We're still married. It's our money."

"Yeah, well. Not for much longer."

The tension was thick, but nobody moved.

"I need a drink," Bruce said.

"You don't drink," Randolph said.

"Well, I'm going to start."

Randolph stared at his wife with a disdain he did not know he had inside him. For all they had gone through, this was how it was going to end—with all the bitterness and anger between them. It was unfortunate. More than that, it saddened him.

Bruce returned with a glass full of clear liquid. He did not offer anyone else one, nor did he share what it was. He stood far enough away from Randolph so he could not smell it, which was probably for the best.

"This is the last time I'm going to ask," Bruce said. "I want to know who you are"—he pointed to Benji—"and how you two know each other."—he pointed between Patricia and Sheila now—"And if I don't get answers in the next ten seconds, you can all get the hell out of my house and do this shit on your own time."

Randolph was thrilled to hear that. Not only the words but also his son's combative approach; he was the man of the house, and he would protect it. Randolph raised one hell of a man.

"Fine," Patricia said. "You want to know what's going on here? I'll tell you a little story, and then I'll deny I ever said a word of it."

"Let's hear it," Bruce said.

Randolph folded his arms.

This ought to be good.

CHAPTER FORTY-TWO

In the weeks and months following Cheyenne and Shay's meeting, romancing, and unspoken agreement about the future, they began putting their plan into action. Sort of. A weekly rendezvous turned into more frequent late-night visits, which turned into the occasional overnight which was the driving force behind the unwanted emotional intimacy that formed between them.

The partnership was intended to be just that—a business partnership. As they learned, when business and pleasure—intense, passionate, perspective-altering pleasure—mixed, the business became complicated. For Cheyenne especially, it became more about the future and the pursuit of something she did not know she needed or wanted and less about the financial balance they discussed. Shay wanted to keep the relationship strictly business, though not entirely platonic either.

It was complicated.

After months of Cheyenne chasing Shay's emotional affection and Shay thwarting her from doing so, everything changed. It was a Thursday night. Cheyenne slipped on a little black dress and escaped from her prison and showed up at Shay's place with the usual intentions—lust, extreme satisfaction, a likely failed effort at emotionally detaching. While she could not stop herself from pursuing Shay or cut off the physical connection that made the emotional detachment impossible, she was emotionally exhausted. At the end of her rope, almost completely drained of having anything left to give. She needed clarity about the future she envisioned with Shay, but realistically did not see it coming to fruition.

When Shay opened the door and smiled at her like she had not before—something beyond physical yearning—her heart fluttered. What it meant, she could not say, and she tried to maintain her composure and keep herself grounded. But then she saw the table. It was dressed with flowers and a scentless candle and two white plates with silverware on top of a napkin beside each.

"Oh! One minute, I have to get that," Shay said when a beep rang out from the kitchen.

Cheyenne felt warm inside, in all the best ways. She folded her arms and smiled and opened her mind to being pampered by the woman she never thought it would come from. Just when it seemed like all hope was lost, life was full of surprises.

Shay returned with a glass dish pinched between colorful mitts that covered her hands. She set the dish on the cork trivet on the table between the dinner plates and stood back and admired her work in the kitchen.

"What's this?" Cheyenne said, still glowing.

"Dinner," Shay said in the most beautiful, soothing, lovable voice.

Cheyenne sat and draped the napkin across her knees and let Shay serve her, which she did with visual satisfaction. A charming vegetable couscous with a leafy garnish wafted into her nose and activated her happiness signals. But she dare not eat with the knot in her stomach, so she folded her hands on her lap and waited anxiously for what came next.

"What do you think?" Shay said.

"It smells delightful."

Shay smiled. "It's a new recipe. You'll be my guinea pig."

"I didn't know you cooked."

"I don't."

Cheyenne returned the smile.

An uneasy moment passed. Shay forked the concoction into her mouth while Cheyenne picked around the edges of her plate, afraid of the consequences for both of them if she were to force herself to take a bite.

"Why aren't you eating?" Shay asked.

Cheyenne put down her fork and straightened and tried to disregard the vase filled with her favorite flowers—the delicate pink wild rose. "What is all this?"

"Can't I just make a nice meal for my lady?"

"My lady? Shay, this is what I'm talking about with you. You say you don't want to be emotionally involved, yet you do things like this and call me your lady and toy with me."

"I'm not toying with you."

"What would you call it? I don't know how much longer I can take these mixed signals. You know I—"

"I love you."

If Cheyenne was not already sitting, she would have fallen, crashed to the earth in disbelief. There was no way she heard that right. "What did you say?"

Shay smiled. More, she sparkled. "I love you."

"But what about—"

"I've been thinking so much. I've been trying to tell myself the way I'm feeling isn't true, that it's just the newness and excitement of it all. But these feelings I have—how I wake up every day thinking about you, and missing you when I don't see you for more than a day or two, or how I feel when I'm with you compared to not—they're undeniable. I fucking love you, Cheyenne. And I'm not ashamed to admit it."

Tears sprinted down Cheyenne's face. No one had spoken words like that to her in what felt like forever. "I don't know what to say."

"Say you love me too."

"You know I do."

"Say it."

"I love you too, Shay."

Shay's chair slid back and she lurched forward, rushed to the other side of the table. She and Cheyenne intertwined their arms in a tight embrace. Cheyenne squeezed as hard she could, afraid if she did not, Shay may change her mind. Shay's hair was down and covered Cheyenne's face, but she did not care; she wanted to prolong the moment for as long as she could. After a minute, they released and Shay pulled back, and their eyes locked.

"Where do we go from here?" Cheyenne asked.

"I have a way this can all be taken care of cleanly and without a trace."

"I'm listening."

"Hear me out, okay? It's kind of complicated."

The plan was in place. Cheyenne listened to Shay's idea, and while she did not love it—it felt flawed, like if just one thing did not fall into place, everything would blow up in their faces—but it was better than hers. Safer. Could they pull it off? There was only one way to find out. What did they have to lose?

Well, everything.

Shay had befriended a man-boy recently, and it sparked the thought. They met by chance in the parking lot of the bank they shared when he distractedly crashed into her on the sidewalk and she dropped her purse. It did not spill, but he acted as if it did because he dropped to his knees and scooped it up and handed it back before she even reacted. He was deeply sorry, he said. She engaged him in banter, which he reciprocated after an initial reluctance. They met for coffee the next day so he could formally apologize, as he framed it. A slick maneuver, she thought, that deserved the hour of her time to hear him out.

He seemed intelligent but vulnerable, and she thought he could be had. He was nice enough but very inexperienced when it came to love, so he was ripe for being swept off his feet. There was no way around it—the man-boy would get hurt. But collateral damage was part of it sometimes; it was the cost of doing business. It would just take some time to build him up before she could tear him down.

Shay began to spend a lot of time with this man-boy. Admittedly, and perhaps naturally, Cheyenne grew jealous. It was not an emotion she was accustomed to feeling, and despite constant communication with Shay throughout the process, she missed her. Their time together had to be spent apart if any of this was to work. And as she learned, the adage was shrouded in so much truth: distance made the heart grow fonder.

Shay began to spend the night with the man-boy at his place, occasionally hers—it was important to build the perception of a genuine relationship for all parties involved. Shay was just playing a part, though she had to admit, she did enjoy his company. If the circumstances were different, she could have envisioned herself having a genuine friendship with him.

But the circumstances were not different. A friendship was not possible.

When the time came, Cheyenne was to enter the picture. She dolled herself up—threw on the most scandalous blouse she could find and undid an extra button even beyond her Thursday nights at the underground club; bought the skankiest boots she could realistically walk in; squeezed into jeans she had not worn in ages and was somehow able to button them—and went to where Shay said he would be.

She felt like a monster in some ways as she tormented the man-boy with her playful yet borderline inappropriate flirtation. She caught him looking down her blouse more times than she could count and she noticed the bulge in his pants after only a minute or two, so she knew she had him. Thankfully for her, the man-boy was cute—young, but cute. She did not think it was going to be as difficult as she had psyched herself up about. If she was honest with herself, she was looking forward to being with a man again. While being with Shay was spectacular, a man offered her something a woman did not. And it had been a while.

She successfully seduced him and teased him and left him coming back for more, week after week, sometimes more often. She initiated more than she cared to admit, but what could she say? She enjoyed it. And it would not last forever, so she took advantage of it while it lasted. A lot. Shay did not seem to be affected by it—she did spend her Thursday's at the swinger's club too, so she was accustomed to that lifestyle.

That was before.

Now was after.

Shay no longer wanted that life. She told the man-boy she wanted to wait until it felt right to get physical, which was both true and not. She cared about the man-boy but did not want to complicate matters for him more than they already were. Boundaries had to be set. She sensed his vulnerability could be a handicap, and she did not know him well enough to predict how he might react to rejection. Was he the raged jealous type? She did not think so, but she was not interested in finding out either. It was better this way—perceptively close, but still at an arm's length away, for protection.

A month into Cheyenne's new—what was it between them?—relationship with the man-boy, she bluntly came out with it. The proposition. He laughed at first, but then said he would help. There was money in it for him, after all. Lots of money. Two weeks after that, he built a contraption and it was just a matter of getting it into the right hands at the right time. The rest would go up in smoke—literally.

Fast forward two more weeks and the opportunity was now. The man-boy had been paid the first installment as a good faith deposit and the second half was due after it was done. To Cheyenne, the money was pennies. But to the man-boy, it was life-changing. It all felt so easy. Too easy.

Then it happened. The breaking news came across the television screen and she held her breath. But then the live reports started and she knew something had gone wrong. Terribly wrong. The mission was not to hurt anybody else—one piece of collateral damage was enough, and that was only emotional scarring that would heal. Just one victim with physical harm. Just her husband.

And she thought she would faint when she heard his voice—the husband who should have been dead—ring through the house as if he were a ghost haunting her. She laughed at the man-boy's joke—who was on the other end of the phone—despite it not humoring her and quickly flipped off the television. Then she grabbed a butcher's knife from the block and held it close to her chest in case she needed to use it in self-defense. The event had gone wrong, obviously, but did he know? He had not answered or responded to her calls and messages from hours earlier—which were all for show in case there was ever an investigation that tried to accuse her of being involved—so maybe he did. If so, he could have been angry. Really angry. Revengeful angry. She had to be prepared to fight.

It was quickly apparent he did not know a thing.

She rushed over to the man-boy's after and had the angriest, most domineering sex of her life, and waited for him to tell her what he knew. He must have known what happened, and what went so horribly wrong. But he said nothing.

It went on like this for a while—she, pretending nothing was wrong while patiently waiting for him to acknowledge there was; he, not. Eventually he did once she forced the issue, and he confirmed what she knew all along—he was working with someone else, though she did not know who. It was to be expected. How else would the device be planted? He assured her everything was under control, and she believed him since he told her where they could go to track down this person—he had a contact in a call center who gave him call records.

Genius.

All the while, Shay remained at an arm's length from Cheyenne, which was the plan—Cheyenne would reach out when it was done, and they would run off and escape with their newfound wealth and leave the man-boy to take the fall—it was his device, after all; a simple anonymous tip called in to the local police would indicate he was behind it and the rest would take care of itself. He would crack under the pressure of an investigation and take the fall. He may or may not have turned on Cheyenne, but that did not matter—she had carefully covered her tracks. The Cheyenne he knew never existed and would be impossible to track down. Meanwhile, she would not lose two-thirds of the combined nest egg she and her husband shared, or the significant chunk of cash that was untouchable; as the victim's wife, she would get everything.

It was the perfect plan.

Until it was not. Until she saw Shay—the same Shay she had grown passionately in love with; the same Shay who she was planning a new life with once this was over—and she knew the plan had somehow gone haywire.

CHAPTER FORTY-THREE

Benji was aware his mouth was open, but he could not help it. He felt so exposed, so humiliated. Everything had been a lie. It was laughable almost, not possible. The story Cheyenne described was inconceivable.

Or at least that was what he told himself.

It was more plausible than he would initially acknowledge. He was embarrassed—not only that he fell victim to the game but also that his vulnerability was exposed for everyone to judge him. He was enraged.

"Are you fucking kidding me?" he said. His eyes threw flames at the Cheyenne he thought he knew—the one who played him like a fiddle.

"I'm sorry," Cheyenne said. "And I mean that. But it is what it is."

"This is my life we're talking about here. How could you do that to someone?"

She shrugged. "I'm sorry."

"This is bullshit." He walked farther into the room for the first time and sat on the sofa. He felt deflated.

What am I going to do now? I'm fucked.

Then he remembered something. And it could change everything.

He popped up as if on fire with the realization. The energy radiated off him and surrounded him in a halo; he suddenly felt invincible. "Not so fast."

Everyone faced him.

It was Cheyenne who spoke: "What?"

"You'll never get away with it."

"Oh, sure I will."

"Wrong. Remember the guy from the airport? He's coming here, remember?"

"I'll be long gone before he gets here."

"Doesn't matter. He'll find you."

"Who's coming here?" Cheyenne's son said.

"I may not have been totally forthcoming with you about the conversation he and I had," Benji said.

Something on Cheyenne's expression changed. Fear, maybe. Or disbelief. She was not the only one who had protected herself in this.

"That's right," Benji said. "My turn to tell a little story."

Shay was supposed to call him after the event had been carried out. But she did not. He knew right away trouble was brewing. He was not oblivious to the world around him, despite the perception others may have had about him. He knew the stereotype—no college degree, worked at a dead-end job and probably would for the rest of his life, a pothead. The truth was, he was heavily left-brained but lacked a reason to find a traditional, unfulfilling day job—a life so many miserable people insisted they had but hated. But that did not mean he was unintelligent.

He built stuff. Like the explosive device that was supposed to be used for Cheyenne's husband but somehow went horribly wrong. A pipe bomb. To what extent it malfunctioned, there was no way to know. Not without the device back in his possession so he could reverse-engineer it. And that, certainly, was not going to happen.

After he failed to hear from Shay and saw the report about the entire supermarket having gone up in flames, he feared the worst—a mechanical failure that caused the detonation before it was supposed to, one that proved to be devastating. Not just for Shay, but for other innocent people too. That was never part of the plan—nobody else was supposed to get hurt.

Cheyenne had not known who he was working with or what their roles were when it came to executing her husband. He told her the capital he needed to design the contraption—including a hefty markup to account for his services, of course—and she provided it. He made clean, untraceable purchases of the supplies via the dark web—many separate orders, all drop-shipped to various locations throughout the city, always using Bitcoin as currency—and assembled the device in his apartment. When the time came, he handed it off to Shay, who was to transfer it to the husband. Then boom, his truck would go up in flames.

But that was not what happened. And he still did not know why.

When he finally heard from Shay, the relief he felt was indescribable. He had not, in fact, unintentionally killed the woman he loved, which would have torn him up beyond comprehension. He thought that perhaps she panicked and ran off—maybe something happened or someone saw something—so he gave her some leeway. But after too much time passed without answers, he dug and found some, and pursued her like it was his job—both to ensure she was safe, and to find out what went wrong.

Then came the man from the airport—the overly aggressive, combative, intimidating man who took him into the private room—and everything he thought he knew was challenged.

The man took out his phone and showed Benji the grainy security tape he had already hacked into himself, and he pointed at the screen. "That's your girlfriend?"

"That's her."

"I'll be damned," the man said. "Well then, my friend. Benji. I think we may be able to help each other out here."

"Is that so?"

"More than you know."

Benji quietly pondered it, wondered how so. "What are you proposing?"

The man walked toward the table and pulled out a seat, then motioned for Benji to do the same which he did.

"You're going after this girl, aren't you?"

Benji shifted in his seat, which was stiff and cold and not comfortable. "Why do you say that?"

"Why else would you be flying to Nebraska?"

Benji thought about that, said nothing.

"I'm following her too, but for a different reason than you. I was following her, actually. But I lost the track."

"Who are you?"

"Who I am doesn't matter."

Benji stood, started toward the door. "Then no deal."

"Do you always hack into security tapes, Benjamin?"—Benji stopped—"Or build explosive devices?"

Benji turned and faced the man. Sweat filled his pores. "How do you—"

"You're looking at up to twenty years for the hacking alone. Double that for the explosive device. When you account for all the damage—"

"What do you want?"

"Come. Sit. Let's talk."

Benji did because he saw no other path forward that would result in something that favored him; he had no choice now but to at least listen to the man. He crossed his arms and waited.

"You help me find this girl and I'll do what I can to make this all go away," the man said.

"Are you a cop?"

"No. But my contacts go above the police. I could have the county DA on the phone within the hour. You're just an immature kid with an overactive imagination and no prior record who got himself into some trouble this one time. Right? Help clean up the trash downtown, maybe kiss a few babies, plant some trees. A little slap on the wrist, if you will. Not even a misdemeanor."

Benji breathed heavily. Was there a choice? It did not seem so. "What do I have to do?"

"Do you know where she is?"

"What do you want with her?"

"It's nothing that involves you."

Benji did not like the answer, but he got the sense that was all he was going to get from the man. He told him about the phone records.

"Smart move," the man said. "Your resourcefulness is impressive."

Benji nodded.

"Once you find her, you let me know. And we'll never speak again and forget all of this ever happened. Are we clear?"

"How will I contact you?"

"You won't. I'll contact you."

The plan seemed flawed, but who was he to challenge the man on it? "Okay."

The man stood. "Well good. I'm glad we understand each other. Now that we're friends, are you going to tell me who that woman is that you're with?"

"Are you going to tell me who you are?"

"You don't need to know."

"Then nope." Benji stood and walked out, and the man let him.

The next day, Benji received a text message from an unknown number. The person on the other end claimed they knew who he was with and about the money she paid him. And he now had forty-eight hours to find the girl, or the deal was off.

It was a good thing Cheyenne's son called when they were stuck in a hotel room in a strange town with an even stranger gas station attendant and no ideas on how to move forward or leads to track down. The universe worked in mysterious ways.

· · · · ·

Now Cheyenne's mouth was the one that was opened. Except she was smiling.

"You sly dog, you," she said. "I'm almost impressed."

Benji said nothing.

"Tell me, what was your plan?" Cheyenne said. "I have to know."

He looked at Shay, whose head was down. He almost felt bad for her. "I may or may not have recorded our interactions in my apartment."

"You what!"

"Audio and video. All of our conversations...not as private as you thought."

And the trysts—those videos were for him too. Just for later.

"You sick mother—"

"Once your husband was dead and you collected your money, I was going to reappear in your life, threaten to go to the police."

"You were going to blackmail me?"

Benji smiled at her.

"Then what? Ride off into the sunset with her?" She meant Shay.

He kept smiling.

CHAPTER FORTY-FOUR

Patricia shook her head. Randolph knew that look—she was hurt. He was hurt too, as was this man-boy—Benji, his name was. Sheila or Shay or whoever she was, was a serial heartbreaker.

He felt Sheila's presence lurk behind him, smelled the cheap hotel shampoo. He longed to hold her, to comfort her, to look in her eyes and beg her to tell him what he just heard was not true. But he knew it was—all of it. The passion in which his wife and the man-boy spoke about their experiences with Sheila—or Shay, as they knew her—told him it was shrouded in truth. And for that, he felt broken. Because he thought he and Sheila had formed a genuine bond. Love.

Sheila.

"I don't even know what to say," Patricia said.

Neither did anyone else. So they did not. Bruce sipped the clear liquid as his posture slouched. The gulp of his throat was the only sound until Max fussed somewhere down the hallway. Randolph did not know where to go from here.

He thought about what Benji said—about the explosive device he made. That explained what happened at the supermarket, and why Sheila acted so strangely whenever he mentioned the topic. Though he struggled to place how it could have happened.

The scene replayed in his mind as if on a reel. He remembered walking into the supermarket after checking himself in the reflection of the glass, grabbing a hand of bananas, and approaching Sheila's line. He remembered how much his torso shook when he approached her, how tied his tongue felt. How he wondered if he was going to have the courage to strike up a conversation with her. He remembered their exchange—the awkwardness when she initially rejected him, then changed her mind. And how she gave him a sheet of register tape and a pen and told him her number instead of writing it down herself. Then he paid her for the bananas. Then . . .

Wait.

Reverse.

She tore off a sheet of register tape and handed him a pen from her breast pocket and said, "No, keep it." And he would have, had he not been distracted by pulling out his wallet and paying for the bananas. He left the pen near the credit card terminal and walked out. It should have been on his person.

"It was the pen," he said, having come to the realization. Not a question. "The bomb was inside the pen."

It felt as if an elephant had intruded the room. The tension was so heavy it nearly took his breath away while he awaited someone's confirmation.

Sheila burst into tears. "I'm sorry!" she cried out. "I'm so sorry."

Randolph dropped his head and shook it. Despite knowing the answer, knowing did not make it land any easier. Everything between them was a sham. Their entire relationship was a lie.

"I need another drink," Bruce said, and he left the room.

"Was any of it real?" Randolph asked. He felt the tears well up behind his eyes, but he would not give her—any of them, really—the satisfaction of seeing him break down. Everyone in this room wanted him dead.

Sheila grabbed his hand, but he quickly yanked it away. "It was real," she said. "You have to believe me. After we got to know one another, I knew I could never go through with it. What was supposed to happen, that was before."

"Please stop patronizing me. It's embarrassing."

"Randolph, please! Listen. I knew when you came to the hospital that you were different. No one's ever treated me the way you have—

kindly, sweetly, like I have value. You're the best man I've ever met. Why do you think I agreed to go with you? It was the only way I could escape what I'd so stupidly got wrapped up in. I do love you."

He shook his head. "I don't believe you. I'm sorry."

Sheila collapsed to her knees and wailed something sharp and pained from the back of her throat and wept. A combination of regret and guilt and pity for herself, he imagined, for being exposed. She was a fraud in every sense of the word. She was malicious.

"I could never love someone like you," Randolph said. And he meant it. "I don't know how anyone could."

Sheila sprung to her feet as if it were the worst thing anyone had ever said to her, and Randolph was glad. He wanted to hurt her, just like she hurt him. She ran down the hallway and slammed the bathroom door. Randolph heard her weep like a lonely child.

Patricia sat down on the sofa and dropped her face in her hands. Benji stood near the door with his hands in his pockets. All of them ached for the woman they thought they loved. The irony was both disturbing and unfathomable, yet it was their reality. They all loved the same woman—their own version of her—and she did not love any of them back. What a strange world they lived in.

Eventually, Patricia showed her face—streaked with black smudges like an athlete might put under their eyes to block the sun— which was flushed. "I'll sign whatever papers you want. The divorce paperwork, the beneficiary removal, forms to remove me from all the bank accounts. Anything. I want nothing."

"What's in Sweden?" Randolph asked.

Patricia found his eyes. "What?"

"You bought two tickets to Sweden. Why?"

"Shay is from Sweden. We were going to visit her homeland."

He nodded as though he knew that, but he did not. Sheila never told him she was from Sweden. Yet, Patricia knew. This confirmed it: They were not as close as he thought they were. "And Fiji?"

"Somewhere far from here. Somewhere to start over together."

Ouch. It hurt. It all hurt so much. Sheila was a manipulative person, and she had played them all.

He went to the sofa and sat down too, but kept his distance. "Did you know Janet is pregnant?"

She nodded.

He sighed.

They sat together quietly.

"You know that's not enough, right?" he said.

"What isn't?"

"Signing away all your financial rights. You tried to have me killed. And you used my money to do it."

She dropped her head. "I know."

"I'm sorry, Patricia."

She looked back up. "For what?"

"For whatever I ever did to you to make you feel like you had to resort to these dramatics. I'm sorry for not fulfilling you in the way you needed to be fulfilled."

She slid closer and reached out and grabbed his hand and squeezed. They shared a quick moment—a glance at one another for old time's sake, a somber flash of where things had gone wrong between them—and then he pulled his hand away. Despite everything, including her trying to have him killed, he still did not hate her.

"You're going to have to turn yourself in," he said.

Tears fell. But she nodded. "I know. And I will. And I was serious when I said I'll sign whatever you want."

"Thank you."

And that was that. He stood. It felt like closure. At least when it came to his marriage.

Outside, a car door closed. Benji walked toward the window and peeked out, then turned back and announced to the room, "He's here."

"Who's here?" Randolph said.

Benji did not answer. Instead, he opened the door and waited for the guest who walked in.

O'Reilly!

"You!" Randolph said when he saw him. Anger swarmed through him like a nest of irritated killer bees.

"Hello, Randolph. Good to see you again."

"You know this guy?" Benji said to O'Reilly.

O'Reilly grinned at Randolph through a flexed jaw. "We go way back."

"What are you doing here, Gary?" Randolph said.

"So your name's Gary?" Benji said.

O'Reilly glared at him.

"It was you at the airport, wasn't it?" Randolph said. "You're the one who detained this kid, aren't you?"

"Very good," O'Reilly said.

"I know who you are," Randolph said.

"Is that so?"

"Sheila told me all about you. How you two used to be lovers, how you stalked her after she broke it off with you. How dangerous and jealous you are."

O'Reilly laughed. "If we're talking about the same Sheila here—Sheila Backe—then you're mistaken."

"No, no. I don't think so. I know your type."

He laughed again. "Is she here? Where is she?"

Randolph folded his arms. As much as Sheila did not deserve a protector in all this, he was still human; feeding her to the hungry wolf that was her jealous, potentially violent ex-boyfriend was unruly and cruel. He would not do it.

"She's in the bathroom," Benji said. "Down the hall."

Randolph glared at Benji with a level of disgust he could not put into words.

"Thank you, Benjamin."

O'Reilly stormed past Benji, then Randolph, as if he owned the place. Nobody stopped him.

"Who the fuck is this guy?" Bruce said as he staggered from the kitchen with a refilled tumbler. His words slurred just enough to sound abnormal.

Randolph watched from the base of the hallway as O'Reilly went to the first closed door on the right and knocked. Benji stood close to Randolph as if ready to pounce if needed for backup. Then it hit him: There was no sound. The weeping had stopped. Something was wrong.

O'Reilly rapped on the door once and listened, then again and listened. After a third time with no response, he grabbed the handle and turned, and the door pushed open. By now, Randolph knew what they would find on the other side.

O'Reilly stood that way for a few seconds—arm extended, palm around the doorknob, blankness on his face. Then he turned to Randolph and said, "You better come see this."

Randolph hurried there—quickly, but not too quickly—and saw what O'Reilly did, and what he suspected they might. Benji was on his heels like the pest he was. The bathroom window was open and the curtain blew in a funnel from the wall. The toilet seat was closed and the box of tissues that had been on top had fallen to the floor.

Sheila was gone.

CHAPTER FORTY-FIVE

O'Reilly shouted obscenities and ran out of the bathroom, down the hall, and out of the house. In seconds, Randolph saw him through the open window as he scoured the backyard for evidence. He ran wildly around the grass as if chasing an animal and popped in and out of view as he encircled the house. It seemed the rain had mostly let up, the clouds now white. Nobody joined O'Reilly outside. They simply watched.

O'Reilly disappeared into the woods through a manmade trail at the back of the property, and he returned later without Sheila. He got in his truck and drove through the surrounding neighborhoods, so he said, but came up empty-handed. Once he returned for good, Bruce had sobered up and Janet and Max were quiet in the bedroom—napping, perhaps. Randolph and Patricia and Benji sat on the sofa like old friends but did not speak. To Randolph, there seemed to be nothing left to say.

"Did Sammy pass?" Randolph asked at one point to anyone who would listen. Sammy was the dog.

"Yes, Dad, she passed."

That was all there was to say about it.

O'Reilly came in and plopped himself on the sofa and hung his head. "What are the chances I can get a drink?"

"We have water and milk and apple juice," Bruce said.

"Anything stronger?"

"How about Belvedere?"

"You have Belvedere?" Randolph said.

"It was a gift."

"That sounds perfect," O'Reilly said.

Bruce took off to retrieve it.

"I was so close I could smell her," O'Reilly said. "It's like she slipped through my fingers. She's impossible sometimes. She's going to be the death of me."

Randolph looked between Patricia and Benji, but neither seemed interested. Bruce quickly returned with a tumbler with a small amount of clear liquid and gave it to O'Reilly, who thanked him and took it. He held the glass to his nose and scrunched his face, but he threw back a swig anyhow. Randolph practically felt the burn from where he sat.

"So," Randolph said to O'Reilly, "are you going to tell us what you're really doing here?"

O'Reilly winced as he swallowed. It took him a second to find his voice. "Well...what the hell? She's gone anyway."

Randolph waited him out, did not prompt him further.

"Sheila Backe has a blue notice out for her. Are you familiar?"

Randolph was not. He had never heard of such a thing.

"INTERPOL has a notice system regarding international criminal activity. She's a person of interest in an overseas criminal investigation."

Woah.

Randolph had not been expecting that, although nothing surprised him anymore, not when it came to Sheila. Not after all the stories he heard today. He really did not know her at all. He sat up straight. "And you're here to bring her in?"

"I was."

"So you're an INTERPOL agent? She said you were some sort of private investigator."

"Partially true. I am an investigator, but not an agent. There's no such thing. I'm a contractor hired by INTERPOL to, in this case, track down fugitives."

"Why didn't you just arrest her on-the-spot back at the hotel?"

"Can't. I don't have arresting powers. I'm simply a liaison between INTERPOL and local law enforcement. I tried to convince her to come with me to the local station to talk, but she refused."

"What about when you saw her at the hospital? Why didn't you talk to her then? Before all this happened."

"I did. Briefly. But she was out of it, distracted. Maybe it was the explosion at the supermarket that rattled her, hard to say. She was supposed to meet me the next day so we could talk further, but she never showed."

That made sense. It explained her change of heart after Randolph visited her in the hospital—from the initial rejection of the idea of leaving together to the sudden desire to skip town, which came only minutes after O'Reilly left her room.

"And now?"

"Can't stop, won't stop. I have a job to do. I was going to show her the video footage from the supermarket and put the pressure on, hope she'd crack. I'm sure you know about that by now?"

He did. He nodded. O'Reilly's story seemed believable.

"I report into an office in D.C. I've been watching and following her for months, waiting for her to do something that would trigger a red notice."

"What's a red notice?"

"It's the next step up from a blue. If she had a red notice, a warrant would go out for her arrest. I could have called in the local police, wherever she was, and she wouldn't have had a choice but to go with."

Well then. Reality weighed heavily on the room. Sheila was potentially an international criminal being watched by an international crime agency. It was difficult to imagine, but also not when he considered the latest information. Did she seem like an international criminal type? Did anyone? She certainly had the manipulative trait he often heard those kinds of people had. On the contrary, Randolph had driven her across the country without a second thought. She did not seem like the criminal type then— mysterious, sure, but was in all respects a law-abiding citizen as far as he could remember. Did that mean he was abetting a fugitive on the run?

"Am I in trouble?" he asked. "I had no idea."

"Did you do anything wrong?"

"No."

"Then no, you're not in trouble." O'Reilly smirked, almost smiled. Randolph started to like him.

"What did she do? Why are you after her?"

"Maybe nothing."

Randolph stared at him.

"I can't really say. It's an ongoing investigation."

Randolph looked at Benji, who intently listened now, his eyes locked on O'Reilly. The international criminal talk had captured his attention. Not Patricia's though; she was off in some faraway land, completely oblivious.

Randolph turned back to O'Reilly and asked what seemed to be the obvious question: "How do we know you're being honest with us? Sheila told me you two had a personal relationship and you were...dare I say, abusive."

"She said that?"

Did she? She certainly implied it. Implication, in this case, was more than good enough.

"She said that to me too," Benji chimed me. "She told me she had an abusive ex."

O'Reilly looked between them. "And you think that's me?"

Randolph and Benji locked eyes. They were on the same page.

"Wow. Okay," O'Reilly said. "Well, it wasn't me."—he leaned forward and shoved a hand in his back pocket, returned with a folded sheet of paper—"Here." He handed the paper to Randolph, who unfolded it.

It was an official-looking letter on INTERPOL letterhead and a Lyon, France address, and a brief but professionally crafted memo. Sheila Backe was printed in black ink, and it confirmed everything O'Reilly said—a blue notice was issued for her to collect more information about an unnamed crime. There was a signature above the field office address of Washington, D.C., just as O'Reilly said. Randolph showed it to Benji, who handed it back to O'Reilly after he studied it.

"Satisfied?" O'Reilly said.

Randolph nodded. Benji too. O'Reilly folded it using the same creases and slipped it back into his back pocket. Randolph sighed and leaned back. What did any of this mean?

"So," Benji said.

"So," O'Reilly said.

Randolph understood. He looked toward Patricia one last time, but her face pointed at her feet. She was defeated. It was over. "So, where do we go from here?"

CHAPTER FORTY-SIX

A few days later, Randolph was back in Iowa. Another long drive, this one especially lonely. Just him and his thoughts. Was it wrong of him to miss Sheila, despite everything? He did. He could not help but reminisce about the blissful moments they had—all the good ones that led up to a devastating, unforeseen conclusion. He still, despite everything, wondered if at least part of what they had was real.

Patricia and Benji were accompanied by O'Reilly back to Iowa, who flew with them. Randolph did not ask and did not care what was being done with the vehicles they had in Utah. His understanding was that jail was in their futures.

Though the exhaustion suffocated his every thought, he did what he said he would when he arrived back in town—he went straight away to Larry's office, who anxiously awaited his arrival. There was a two-inch-thick stack of papers Randolph was to sign, which he did blindly. His wrist twisted on repeat as if he were a machine while Larry explained what he signed as he signed it. Randolph neither listened nor tried; he just wanted it over.

"We'll talk later," Larry said when the stack was inked. Randolph nodded and left.

He went home, though it felt anything but. If his key did not fit in the door he would have flipped, but not because he would have been surprised; rather, he desperately needed a familiar pillow. He undressed and threw his barely functional body onto the bed and crashed hard against the pillow. He woke up what he thought was a day later, though he was not certain what day that was.

Hunger pangs finally revealed themselves, which was inevitably going to happen. He ravaged the fridge and cabinets in the kitchen, but there was nothing of sustenance that satisfied him. So he had a pizza delivered and ate every slice in the silence of his kitchen, then he sat on the porcelain throne for longer than usual and just relaxed as he waited for nature to call. The door was left open because why not? It was just him now. The only struggle was the numbness in his toes from sitting too long.

After another night of restful sleep, he finally felt like himself again. The malnourishment of late had wreaked havoc on his system and so he spent more time in the bathroom than he would have liked. He made a pot of frozen vegetables for lunch to begin the rebalancing process. A cleanse was in his future.

He showered, finally, with the soaps he was embarrassed to admit he missed—but not the soaps themselves, rather the comforts of them, the familiarity. It felt good to get back to being himself again. He missed the structure. By the third day back home, he was ready to leave the house. His usual supermarket was out of the question—it would be awhile before the wreckage was cleaned up and the store reopened—so he drove across town and hit the Publix, which was a zoo—to be expected, he thought, considering the extra volume of shoppers they were not accustomed to. He needed one of everything, which he bought. Except for bananas—no more bananas. Maybe ever.

He found peace in putting everything away in the kitchen where and how he wanted. All labels faced out and all available space was used efficiently so nothing would need to be moved when he wanted it. As if Big Brother were watching his every move, the phone rang just seconds after he closed the final cabinet door and shoved the plastic bags into the trash. O'Reilly was on the other end.

"She's talking," he said. "Do you want to come down here?"

He did. So he did. He went to the police department.

O'Reilly greeted him with a firm handshake and a friendly pat on the shoulder. They were friends now, apparently. Randolph was not sure when that happened. Larry was present too, and he and O'Reilly chatted among themselves in the corner while Randolph watched through the glass.

Patricia was unrecognizable in her prison orange and no makeup and flats and frizzed hair. Randolph recognized the suited man who sat next to her as her attorney, though the man's name escaped him at the time. The two stiffs on the opposite side of the table had their backs to the glass, but their roles were not difficult to imagine.

Randolph listened without reaction as Patricia rehashed the same story he heard before in Utah, almost word for word. He wondered if it was rehearsed, and what that might mean if it were. But he did not care. There was not much he cared about these days. He noticed the stack of papers in front of her were covered in signatures—at least the top page was—and that was all that mattered. Patricia would get what she deserved.

"Help me understand this," a voice said through the glass. It was not Patricia and it was not the suited man next to her. It must have been one of the stiffs whose backs faced Randolph. "What did you think would happen?"

"The truck would explode and nobody else would get hurt," Patricia said. "And everything would default to me."

Patricia's attorney feverishly wrote on a notepad.

Randolph backed away from the glass. He had heard enough. He understood completely; he should have been dead.

"You okay?" It was O'Reilly.

Randolph nodded. He was.

"You want to keep listening?"

"No. No more."

Now O'Reilly nodded. "Will you come with me? I want to talk to you about something."

He looked toward Larry, who had a phone to one ear and a finger in the other. He was a busy man and there were always fires to extinguish.

"All right," Randolph said because he had nothing to lose. Why not hear what the man had to say? He followed him.

O'Reilly led him to a vacant room like the one Patricia was in, just without the glass. A wall-mounted heater hummed from the corner. An empty Styrofoam cup was overturned on the edge of the table which a handful of chairs surrounded. O'Reilly took one and motioned for Randolph to do the same which he did.

"How are you doing?" O'Reilly said. "Feeling good?"

"I'm okay. Readjusting."

"That's good. Glad to hear it."

Awkwardness.

"You wanted to talk?"

"Indeed. Indeed I did."

"Well?"

"Have you heard from Sheila?"

Sheila.

"No."

"Not at all?"

"Not at all."

O'Reilly nodded. "How do you feel about it all?"

"Mixed emotions. I don't really want to talk about it."

"Okay, I understand. I get that. How would you feel if I offered you the chance to get some closure about everything?"

"Meaning what?"

"The opportunity to get her in a room and ask her all the questions you need answered."

"Do you know where she went?"

"No."

"Then how?"

"We find her. You and me."

Randolph readjusted in the miserably uncomfortable chair he was in. His back was stiff. He did not like the sound of O'Reilly's proposition. "Why?"

"I know this was personal for you, but I still have a job to do. My job goes on with or without you. But it would be easier with you, with someone who knew her. Closure for both of us."

"I'm starting to think I didn't know her at all."

"She wouldn't have run off with someone she didn't trust, I can guarantee you that."

"How would you know?"

"As I said before, I've been following her for a long time. I know her pretty well too."

"If that's the case, why don't you just find her yourself?"

"I don't know her like you do. I know the paper version of her, but not the real her. The person."

"Yeah, well, I think I'd rather just move on."

"There would be a monetary gain on your end. All expenses paid. A hefty finder's fee."

He shook his head. "Wrong guy. Money doesn't motivate me."

O'Reilly interlocked his fingers and rocked in the chair, studied Randolph. "Why don't you think about it? Give your emotions some time to settle."

Randolph stood. "Fine. But I wouldn't expect anything. I think it'll be easier for me if I just move on. I hope you can understand that."

O'Reilly stood too. "I do. I respect your decision. But if you change your mind, you know how to contact me."

"Right."

The men shook hands, and Randolph left.

He ran into Larry in the corridor who was still engaged on the phone. He held up a finger to ask Randolph to wait, which he did. Larry told the phone to hold on, then he pinched his shoulder to his ear and addressed Randolph: "You good?"

"Fine."

"Good. Listen, I'll expedite all this paperwork. Shouldn't be long."

"Thank you."

"This is going to cost you." Larry rubbed his thumb between the other fingers on the same hand.

Randolph tried to smile, but he found it exhausting. He just wanted to go home. Larry stepped away and reengaged his conversation through the phone. Randolph exited the police station, hopped into his truck, and took himself home.

CHAPTER FORTY-SEVEN

Six weeks later. A lot had happened. Larry, despite being cold and impersonal and without anything that resembled empathy, did what he said he would. Randolph's divorce from Patricia was expedited and she was removed from all joint accounts. It surprised Randolph how much of the paperwork could be filled out from afar, with just a witness. He was awarded everything without a fight.

The house was under contract. It would sell for list price after the inspection and bank appraisal all went without a hitch. The couple moving in was young and eager and full of life. Randolph truly wished them nothing but the best. He was happy to pass it along to who seemed like wonderful people. Though what did he know about being a judge of character? He had been wrong before. He would net what felt like an absurd amount of cash from the deal which would be added to the pile he already did not know what to do with.

He planned to reassess his life, realign his values, and determine what was important to him in this new phase. He resigned to the idea that going back to work was both unnecessary and not something that interested him any longer. The firm had stopped calling anyhow and apparently had moved on, so why should he not do the same? He thought he deserved a break. From everything.

Tens of taped, labeled moving boxes filled every room of the house. He had given most of Patricia's belongings to charity. His second garage sale was scheduled for this weekend to purge the rest of his stuff he no longer wanted or cared about. Downsizing and minimizing was the simplicity he desired in his life. He kept most of the books, though, except for the ones he did not enjoy the first time around.

When he needed a break from packing, he phoned Bruce—because that was what they did now; they communicated. At least once weekly since he had been back. Randolph wanted nothing more than to rekindle his relationship with his son and be more involved in Max's life—and soon the new baby too. Bruce and Janet chose to be surprised this time, unlike with Max. Randolph had a hunch it would be another boy. Only time would tell.

"How's the packing going?" Bruce asked.

Randolph heard Max's laughter in the background. "Going fine. I've got the downstairs all set for the most part, upstairs next. Some things are going to have to wait until the very end, though."

"Yeah."

"How're things?"

"Busy. Work's been crazy trying to meet a deadline for a new client. Janet and Max are doing just fine."

Randolph did not know what exactly it was his son did for a living, but that was not because he did not care; he did not understand. It was something with digital communications, he knew that much. He would get a better understanding of it before long, though, so he and his son could have intellectual conversations about it. Anything to reconnect.

"Are you sure you don't need me to come out there and help?" Bruce said.

"No, no. I'm fine. You're busy. I'm going to hire a moving company to do all the heavy lifting anyhow."

"All right. When do you think you'll be out here?"

"Few weeks. I'll have everything shipped and drive myself, take the scenic route, do some sightseeing along the way. Are you sure you don't mind if I leave my pod in your driveway for a bit?"

"Not at all. It's no big deal."

"Thanks, Son."

Randolph was moving to Utah. There was nothing left for him in Iowa anymore. Once the house deal with finalized, that was where he was headed. Bruce agreed to let him crash on his couch for a short time until he found a place to rent. It would not be long, though—Bruce's realtor was on the prowl for a one-bedroom place nearby. It would not be difficult to find with Randolph's substantial budget and minimalist desires.

"How's Mom?"

"Same, I guess. Have you talked to her?"

"No. I don't know what to say to her."

"I get that."

"Yeah."

"Do you want to?"

"Not sure."

"Well, I think you should."

"Really?"

"Sure. If you want to, I mean. What happened between her and me has no bearing on your relationship. But don't let me influence you. Do whatever you think is best."

"Thanks for saying that, Dad. Means a lot."

"Of course."

A female voice chattered in the background. "I've got to run now, Dad. Janet's about to put dinner on the table and Max needs a new diaper."

"Go, go! Please. We'll talk soon, okay?"

"All right then, sounds good."

"Goodbye, Son."

"Goodnight, Dad."

The next day, Randolph called to check in with Herm, just because. Herm still felt bad about what happened, but Randolph tried his best to assure him none of it was his fault. He considered Herm a friend.

"Your money's fine," Herm said.

"I'm sure it is. It's in good hands."

He felt Herm's relief through the phone. He made a mental note to order a pie and have it sent to Herm's house for him and his wife to enjoy. A showing of gratitude, it would be, for all Herm had done to help wrangle up the facts about the missing money.

Later, Larry's bill came in the mail. He opened it and grabbed his checkbook and did not think twice about questioning the amount or the billable hours. For all Larry was not, he contributed so much; Randolph was thankful to have him on his team. He was worth every penny.

He went for a long walk. The days were extended and the temperatures were consistently higher for longer, and he needed to get away from all the dust that had been disturbed and encroached his aura. He left his phone at home, desperate to disconnect from the outside world that did nothing but disappoint him. It reminded him of the version of himself he used to be. The version he liked. The version he was comfortable with.

His legs tired before anything else, and it felt wonderful to break a sweat that was not brought on by anxiousness. Sheila entered his mind only occasionally these days, but it was without angst—he would forget about their fling as if it never happened before long. He would be okay.

The idea that his wife—rather, ex-wife now, which was strange to say after being together for so long—wanted him dead still hurt, though. Worse, she did not just fantasize about his non-existence and imagine what her life might have been like without him in it like a normal person—she paid for it to happen. With his money.

Yikes.

The father of her son, the grandfather to Max, the acquaintance to many—none of that mattered. Not to her. He loved her once, and for many years. He thought she loved him too—no, he knew she did. Things just did not work out. Her reaction to it was theatrical, though, unreasonable. It was proof that you never really know someone.

But maybe that was too simple. Maybe Patricia was disturbed in a way no one else knew. Why else would she have pretended to be someone she was not and pay to have her husband killed? How? There was no way she would have gotten away with it even if Benji and Sheila had succeeded. The evidence of foul play would have been obvious to even the worst investigator. The trail of money made it even easier. And that Benji fellow would have surely ratted her out and provided evidence to prove it.

She must have been so desperate that she ignored those risks. Which had to have meant something. What, though, he could not say. He had not gotten that far in his thought process yet. He needed more time.

Randolph felt sad for her. He genuinely hoped she got the help she needed—there were obviously some demons she had trapped in her psyche that needed massaging. She was troubled.

He made his way back to the house. He hesitated to call it home because it represented anything but. Even with all he had purged and donated, the house still had Patricia's fingerprints all over it. All the paint colors, the thematic schemes with matching curtains, the improvements they made over the years to appease her desires better. The best decision—the only decision—was to move out and move on. The energetic young people would make their own memories, write their own history. Hopefully, their story ended better than Randolph's did.

Cold tap water lubricated his throat as he threw back the glass. Hydration swam through his system—he felt it in his bones. His brow dripped, so he wiped it away with a coarse paper towel and discarded it in the trash. It felt good to be alive. He was thankful for that, if nothing else. He would find himself again.

On the counter, his phone screen illuminated with a missed text, so he checked it. The phone nearly slipped from his fingers when he read it, and it took all he had to keep it from doing that. While dry before, his hands were suddenly damp.

It can't be.

He read and reread the message three, four, five times over. The number was private. His first reaction was to discard it at spam; his second was to respond and wait for a message back. But he did not know what to say, or if he should engage. It could have been a trap. Seven or eight weeks ago he would have pursued it. No question. But not now.

That was before.

Now was after.

That was the old him. The old new him; today's new him was more like the old him. He liked it that way. Instead of taking the bait, he scrolled through his contacts and touched the name of the person who would know what to do. The phone rang.

CHAPTER FORTY-EIGHT

Benji was in jail awaiting trial. While his booking hearing had been weeks ago, there was no follow-up on the calendar anytime soon. Bail was out of his reach—all the money he had been given from Cheyenne that remained had been returned to her husband. Benji had nothing. He was doomed for a life of solitude within the walls of a prison. Though it was still not clear how much time he faced.

The court-appointed attorney he was granted to defend him meant well, but she was green and incompetent. Her advice was to accept a plea deal for a shorter sentence in exchange for full transparency. What she did not know was what that phrase truly meant—full transparency. If he were to reveal the details about everything he had done to get where he was, the deal would be off the table or additional charges would be filed. She had no idea. He lacked trust for the other side to follow through with what they said they would do.

The man from the airport—who he now knew was named Gary O'Reilly, who was not an INTERPOL agent but may as well have been—did not fulfill his end of the bargain. In exchange for help tracking down Shay, Benji was supposed to receive immunity. That, clearly, had not happened. He felt like an idiot; he should have never fallen for it. Though, in fairness, what choice did he have? Gary knew Benji had hacked into the tapes and built a pipe bomb, so it was only a matter of time before he connected the dots.

In short: He was fucked.

Whether the threats from Gary about the sentence he faced—twenty years, he said, maybe forty or more—were real or not, Benji's life was over. If he got out, he would be an old man without any modern skills and no recent life experience. What would he do? Where would he go? The world would pass him by. His life was over.

Would anyone visit him? He was disconnected from his three brothers, who were off living their lives. His father was not in the picture and had not been since he was young. And his mother, well, who knew? She was up to her old tricks, he imagined, spreading her legs and trading her mouth for cocaine. Perhaps she was into harder drugs now, or maybe she was dead. Nobody had contacted him to tell him otherwise, but she had not reached out either. In all respects, Benji was alone.

Even so, Shay could go fuck herself. Cheyenne too. They were liars and manipulators and scoundrels. They used him. Just like they used Cheyenne's husband. Benji felt for the man, imagined the pain he must have been going through. His wife wanted him dead and his new lover was just using him for his money. It was sad, really. If only he could go back to that day at the coffee shop when Cheyenne first came in and not listened to his dick. None of this would have ever happened.

That was before.

Now was after.

It was too late.

Benji slid off the mattress and stood. He paced the box he now called home, free to do nothing but think. His cellmate was bizarre but not dangerous. Public indecency he was in for, so he said. It seemed harsh to be in jail for showing his wiener, but Benji did not ask the details. He was sure there was more to the story than that. Thankfully, the bottom bunk shielded him from as much exposure as possible from his perverted cellie on top. Nothing weird had happened between them.

Though there was always some sort of ruckus during waking hours, the block was relatively quiet today. The two men in the cell next to his constantly debated political issues that neither one knew anything about. It was entertainment, at least, but also insufferable. The intelligence of the men around him was embarrassing. He imagined it was how Andy Dufresne felt all those years in Shawshank—superior to all his peers, entirely out of place. The only difference was, Benji was not innocent.

A guard shouted and the block door buzzed and popped open—the sound was distinguishable, one every inmate stopped what they were doing and paid attention to; was it their lucky day? Without a clock, Benji did not know the time, but it felt early for rounds. He moved closer to the door and listened, hoped to hear the drama of the day—someone's ineptitude to make him smile or laugh. The guard was close now, and he hollered again. This time, the lock on Benji's door disengaged, and he stepped back.

"Griffin!" the guard said. "Come with me."

"Why?"

"Don't talk."

The guard grabbed ahold of Benji's triceps and led him down the short corridor. No handcuffs. Other prisoners shouted, though their voices were inaudible, drowned by Benji's whirlwind thoughts. None of what was happening was normal.

"What's going on?" Benji said.

"Didn't I tell you not to talk?"

He was pushing it. He zipped his lips, let the large man pull him away. The block door buzzed and disengaged, and they walked through. Another door awaited them, then a third. He wanted to ask again what was going on, but he had heard stories about other inmates pressing their luck and overstepping, and about the penalties enforced for doing so; he was not about to be beaten down by this man who wanted nothing more than a reason to do so. Benji kept his lips sealed and his questions to himself.

The guard led him into a conference room and stopped, released Benji's arm. Another man he did not recognize awaited, his suit permanently pressed and his necktie perfect. Not even a single strand of hair was out of place.

"Here you go," the guard said. "He'll take it from here."

"Who is he?"—Benji faced the man—"Who are you?"

The man nodded to the guard, who turned and left and closed the door behind him.

Benji's wrists were free, so he rubbed them. A habit. The man in the suit eyed him with a focus that alarmed Benji. What was going on?

Without speaking, the man handed Benji a folder. Benji looked at it, then the man, then back to the folder. He flipped open the front cover and scanned the document. He thought he knew what it meant, but it seemed too good to be true.

"Is this what I think it is?" he said.

The man nodded.

CHAPTER FORTY-NINE

Randolph shook O'Reilly's hand as he entered the conference room. It was on the fifth floor of an inconspicuous office building without signage. Its typical purpose was unclear.

"Thanks for coming in," O'Reilly said. "And for calling."

"I didn't know who else to tell."

"You made the right decision."

The message from Sheila came the night before. O'Reilly insisted Randolph come in the next day. There he was.

"Tell me again what it said," O'Reilly said.

Randolph pulled out his phone, opened his messages, and read the one from Sheila verbatim: "I know you probably don't want to hear from me right now, but I'm sorry. This is not what I wanted to happen. Can we talk?"

O'Reilly's arms were crossed. "That's it?"

"That's it."

"And you didn't respond?"

"You told me not to."

O'Reilly nodded. "Right."

"Should I?"

"No, not yet. Let's figure it out first."

"How do we know it's even her? The number was private."

"Technically, we don't. But who else could it be?"

"What about Patricia?"

"Do you think your ex-wife is texting you from prison?"

Randolph thought about it quickly. "No, probably not."

Silence fell.

Then: "Should I text back to find out? What's the harm?"

O'Reilly looked puzzled, unsure. "All right, you're right. Do it. See if she responds."

He typed in her name with a question mark and hit send. Then they waited. A minute later, his phone dinged.

"That her?" O'Reilly said.

Randolph read the message and nodded. Then he pushed the screen toward O'Reilly and let him see for himself.

"Yes. That's all it says."

Randolph shrugged.

"Ask her where she is."

So he did.

A minute passed, then five, then ten. No response back.

"What do we do now?" Randolph said when the silent waiting became too much.

"I don't know."

Randolph thought what this meant. Sheila wanted to talk to him. Presumably wanted to clear the air. Why? The countless possibilities ran through his mind. Did she miss him? Did she want to apologize and move on with a clear conscience? Was she trying to manipulate him again? Did she love him?

Did he still love her?

It was all too much. Just when he thought he was ready to move on . . .

Someone knocked on the door which jolted him back to reality. Where was he again?

"Come in," O'Reilly said.

A suited man walked in. He did not introduce himself, nor did he shift his gaze from O'Reilly's direction. "Sir, your guest has arrived."

"Thank you. Bring him in."

Guest? Who could it—

No fucking way.

"What is he doing here?" Randolph said. His hands were balled. He wanted to attack the man-boy and throw fists until he bled. Of all people, of course it had to be him.

"Hello, Benjamin," O'Reilly said.

"What is he doing here, Gary?" Randolph said.

"He's working with us."

"No, he's not."

"He is. I made a deal with him, and I'm a man of my word. And since we're all after the same thing here, why not put our heads together and our differences aside? Plus, he has a unique set of skills that may prove to be valuable for our...situation." —he faced Benji—"I assume you've been debriefed on the ride?"

"If that's what you want to call it, then sure," Benji said.

"And you're in?"

"Anywhere but where I was. So yes, I'm in."

O'Reilly turned back to Randolph. "And you?"

His hands were still balled. He wanted to explode. "How am I supposed to work with this guy? He tried to kill me."

"Nothing personal, man," Benji said.

"And" —he faced Benji—"he fucked my wife."

"It sounds like a lot of people fucked your wife. Even your girlfriend fucked her."

Randolph lunged forward and swung his fist and connected with Benji's jaw. The man-boy fell to the floor as if he were a rag doll. Pain shot through Randolph's knuckles as if he had just hit a brick wall. But it was a rush. It was the first time he had ever hit someone, and he felt alive.

O'Reilly bent down and helped Benji to his feet. "You probably deserved that."

Benji wiped his mouth and inspected his hand for blood, which there was some. "I probably did."

"Feel better now?" O'Reilly said as he faced Randolph. "Get that out of your system?"

Randolph shook with a jolt of adrenaline. His fist ached, but the pain was worth it. And yes, he did feel better. Much better. He nodded.

"Good," O'Reilly said.

Randolph grabbed a box of tissues from the table and passed it to Benji, who took it without hesitation. He yanked a tissue out and dabbed his lip.

"So, gentleman," O'Reilly said. "Shall we?"

"What exactly are we doing?" Benji asked. "I want every detail laid out before I do anything. I refuse to spend another second in that hellhole, but I need some assurances here."

"Of course. Hold that thought."—O'Reilly ducked out for a few seconds and returned with two folders; he handed one to Randolph and one to Benji—"All the details are in here. The terms of our agreement. For you, Benji, a significant finder's fee in exchange for Sheila Backe's safe delivery to me. For Randolph, the same. Plus emotional closure for the both of you."

"And for you?" Benji said.

"For me? I finally get to sit Sheila in a room and interrogate her about a non-related crime. To fulfill my contractual obligations. We all win."

"Do we get to know what she did?" Randolph asked.

"It's not relevant. But I thought you may ask, so it's in your files. But like I said, she's just wanted for questioning at this stage."

"Feels like a lot of effort to just ask her some questions."

"Yes, well, maybe so."

Silence fell while they looked through their folders.

"What now?" Benji said after he slammed his shut.

"You see those boxes?"—O'Reilly pointed at the stack in the corner—"Those are my records on Sheila."

"All of them?"

"All of them. As I said, I've been following her for quite some time."

Benji walked toward them. He removed the lid off the top of the highest box and fingered the folders. Then he replaced the lid and grabbed the box with two hands and carried it to the table. "Where do we start?"

"Before we do that," O'Reilly said. "I've decided I don't like your name, Randolph."

"Excuse me?"

"It's kind of a mouthful, don't you think? Ran. Dolph. I don't like it."

"Well, it's my—"

"I'm going to call you Rand. Starting now. What do you think?"

"I don't think so."

"Yeah, that's what I'm going to call you."

Randolph rolled his eyes. He hated it. He liked the old Randolph—the man and the name.

That was before.

Now was after.

"I don't have a choice, do I?" he said.

"You do not."

Well. It was just a name.

"So, what now?" Benji asked.

"Before we get started, do I need to remind you guys to be careful? How nothing she says can be taken seriously. The stories she told you about the abusive ex-boyfriend are probably untrue, likely just a figment of her overactive imagination to evoke your sympathy. To put it bluntly, she's a liar."

Randolph met Benji's eyes. This was something they could agree on.

"No," they said in unison.

"Good," O'Reilly said. He crossed the room, grabbed a box by the handles, and dropped it on the table. "Let's get started then, shall we?"

THE END

ABOUT THE AUTHOR

Dan Lawton is an award-winning literary suspense, mystery, and thriller author from New Hampshire. Awards include:

The Green House
- Bronze Medalist, Adult E-Book Fiction — 2020 Independent Publisher Book Awards (IPPY Awards)
- Finalist, Fiction — 2020 Next Generation Indie Book Awards
- Finalist, Mystery — 2020 Book Excellence Awards
- Finalist, Literary Fiction — 2020 American Book Awards

Plum Springs
- Winner, Fiction — 2019 New Hampshire Writers' Project Readers' Choice Award

Connect at @danlawtonauthor or at www.danlawtonfiction.com.

AUTHOR'S NOTE

Dear Reader,

Thank you as always for your support and your love of reading. For the first time for me, this novel is the beginning of a three-book series, so be on the lookout for books two and three!

If you'd consider sharing your thoughts about it wherever you discuss books, I'd be grateful. Further, if you want to send me your thoughts directly, I'd love to hear them! I will personally respond to all messages.

You can contact me at
info@danlawtonfiction.com
@danlawtonauthor on Instagram and Twitter,
Facebook.com/danlawtonfiction,
or www.danlawtonfiction.com.

All the best,
Dan Lawton

MORE TITLES BY THIS AUTHOR

The Green House
Plum Springs
Amber Alert
Operation Salazar
Deception

Thank you so much for reading one of **Dan Lawton's** novels.
If you enjoyed the experience, please check out our recommended
title for your next great read!

The Green House by Dan Lawton

"Beautiful, intriguing, and slightly haunting.
I found myself not wanting the book to end."
–Joe Siple, award-winning author of
The Five Wishes of Mr. Murray McBride

View other Black Rose Writing titles at
www.blackrosewriting.com/books and use promo code
PRINT to receive a **20% discount** when purchasing.